ONE
LAST
SHOT

Cover Photography: Paul Henry Serres

Cover Design: Angela Haddon

Produced by Diana Road Books

ONE LAST SHOT

HANNAH SHIELD

Prologue

KEIRA, TWO YEARS AGO

I'D NEVER SEEN Last Refuge look so beautiful. Flower garlands draped over the wooden deck railings and down the tables. Vivid pink and orange painted the sky as the sun dipped behind the mountain range, and fairy lights swayed overhead in the faint summer breeze.

Jessi and Aiden's ceremony had already been picture perfect, and as love songs played over the speaker system and I sipped a glass of something sparkling, my blood fizzed with anticipation.

Then Dean glanced over, catching my eye. He smiled softly. My gaze averted, yet that bubbly feeling inside me bloomed. All cozy and familiar as much as it was hot and sharp with excitement.

This felt like a night when amazing things could happen. Impossible things.

I was *really* gonna have to watch myself tonight. I already in too romantic a mood for my own good, and the wine wasn't helping.

"Hey. Having a good time?"

When I looked up again, Dean was right there in front of me. His expression was warm in that way that made my stomach flip. I could feel the grin spreading across my face, helpless and genuine.

"Hard not to," I said. "Never seen so many people so happy. I'll have to monitor the situation. Could be something contagious going around."

Dean laughed. "There's definitely a lot of alcohol going around." He nodded toward where Stephie and Vivian were laughing with some teenage boys who must've been part of Aiden's family. The Shelborne clan had traveled all the way from California for the wedding. "I assume you're keeping an eye on your little sister?"

"Always. Pretty sure she and Vivian have sneaked a few sips." They were both sixteen. The peak age for rebellion. "But I can't imagine they'll get away with more than that, considering half the guests here are law enforcement and former military."

His dimple appeared as he took a sip from his beer glass. Dean shifted so we stood shoulder-to-shoulder, facing the crowd, but I felt him looking at me from the corner of his eye. "Wouldn't have pegged you as a cop from the way you cleaned up, though. I like the dress."

I smoothed my hands over the soft fabric, suddenly self-conscious. The dress was frilly and girly, pale pink with delicate lace at the sleeves and neckline. Most of the time on duty, I wore my hair pulled back. But tonight my curls framed my face, which had a lot more makeup than usual.

"You'd better not be making fun of me."

"I would never," Dean said softly, in that deep voice of his that moved over my skin like a faint caress, always leaving me wanting more.

He was dressed in nice jeans and a button-down shirt, the

sleeves rolled to his elbows. Simple, clean, handsome. As dressy as I ever saw him get.

"You clean up decent yourself," I said. "You need a haircut though. You look like a glorified ski bum who moonlights as a bartender."

"Ouch. That hits close to home. But unlike *some* people, I prefer to be sincere. You look beautiful." Something flickered in those blue eyes of his, making my breath catch.

"Thank you."

His hand went to the cord he always wore around his throat, rubbing the thin strip of leather between his fingers. Something he did when he was thinking deep thoughts.

Which surely aren't about you, I told myself, *so don't get ideas.*

Dean and I had met a few years ago. I worked for Sheriff Owen Douglas, and Dean was one of Owen's closest buddies from the Marines. Dean and I had never been anything more than friends. Yet he confused me sometimes. How he'd pay me such close attention, his gaze moving over me like he saw something he wanted. Lingering on my lips. Touching my arm or my face affectionately, far more than any other male friend did.

But that was just Dean. He knew how I felt about him, and he'd made clear that he didn't feel the same.

One time last year, I'd worked up my courage and was about to kiss him. Even leaned in, probably with some schmoopy look on my face. Dean had turned away and let me down easy. *I'm way too old for you, Keira.* As if eight years was such a difference when I was twenty-six. Certainly no kid.

Since that mortifying moment, I'd been a lot more careful. Just trying to appreciate our friendship and not dream of more.

Trying.

"So how's the new schedule working out?" I asked. "Still liking the tourist-trap bar in Silver Ridge?"

"It's not that bad. Tips are solid with the summer crowd." He tilted his head toward the buffet line that was forming. "Want to grab some food?"

We talked easily as we moved through the line, filling our plates with barbecue and mac and cheese and beans, all the fixings. Which you'd think would not go well with champagne, but I liked it.

Some combinations were unexpectedly good, and didn't that just make them even better? I thought so, at least.

Like Dean and me. He was a world traveler who'd bounced from seasonal gig to seasonal gig before arriving in Hartley to stay. I was a cop who'd been born here and rarely left the county. We might seem like unlikely friends, given all the ways we were different, but we both loved the outdoors. During the summer, we went hiking together almost every week.

Like a lot of Colorado natives, I'd never learned to ski—too expensive—but last winter Dean had started to teach me. He was obviously a super expert on both skis and a snowboard, but he was always patient, claiming he had as much fun as I did on the bunny slopes.

We found seats at one of the long tables on the deck. The view was spectacular as darkness settled over the mountains and valley. The live band had started playing just inside the dining room, which had all its doors thrown open to the outdoor space. They'd cleared away the tables in the tavern to allow for a dance floor, and we all cheered as Jessi and Aiden had their first dance.

When I looked over at Dean beside me, he was touching his necklace again, frowning slightly.

"You okay?" I whispered to him while everyone was clapping for Jessi and Aiden.

He seemed to snap out of wherever his thoughts had gone. "Yeah, all good. Just..." He glanced over at the dance

4

floor, where other couples had started joining the bride and groom. "Would you like to dance?"

More fizzing in my stomach. I couldn't blame the bubbly anymore since I'd finished my glass a while ago, and I never had more than one drink. In my opinion, a sheriff's deputy was never a hundred percent off duty.

"Sure. Why not?"

As I took his hand and walked toward the dance floor, I told my hopes to settle back down.

Our friend Brynn was dancing with her boyfriend Cole, and she gave me a subtle thumbs up, eyes darting between me and Dean. I returned a quick shake of my head, because this was *not* a thing. He'd made that very clear.

I knew where *hope* always led with this man. Exactly nowhere.

But the alcohol still sang in my bloodstream. Dean's hands settled on my hips as we began to sway to the music. I placed mine on his shoulders. I was intensely aware of every point of contact between us. The warmth of his palms through the thin fabric of my dress. The solid feel of him, close enough that I could smell the crisp, fresh scent of his skin.

I let myself sink into the moment. Let myself stare back at him and look my fill.

What was my favorite thing about Dean? So hard to choose. There was his smile, always gentle at the edges. And those dimples. His dimples flashed when the faint lines around his eyes crinkled, just before he really grinned.

Since I'd met him, there'd been this aura of mystery about him. He could be deceptively quiet at times, like when he touched the leather cord on his neck. He always kept the pendant tucked inside his shirt, but I'd seen it a couple of times.

A rifle round.

Brynn had served as a Marine too, and she had all the bravado and swagger you'd expect to go along with it. Dean didn't. Despite his history, or maybe because of it, he never touched weapons now.

But he didn't seem to have an issue with the fact that I carried a gun for my job. As far as our friendship, I mean. Dean had helped with Protector missions too, though he stayed out of the fray himself.

"Did I tell you about the training I've been doing with Brynn?" I asked. "We're working on my hand-to-hand combat skills. I'm getting a lot better."

A line appeared between Dean's eyebrows. "That's… good. Sounds fun."

My lips pressed tight. "It's not for *fun*. You know that. Trace and Owen have told me no so far, but I'm not giving up." I kept my voice down, even though we were at Last Refuge. There were plenty of people at the reception who had no idea the Last Refuge Protectors existed. "Brynn supports me, and I think River's open to me joining too."

"River rarely thinks about how dangerous something is. He jumps first and thinks later."

"I'm aware of the danger. I'm a cop, Dean. Danger is part of the job description."

"The Protectors are different."

"Which is exactly why I want to be a real part of it." Frustration made prickles of sweat break out over my skin. I didn't want to watch from the sidelines while my friends put themselves at risk.

I respected Dean's choices, but wasn't I entitled to mine?

The song ended, and I went to step away, annoyed at myself for being annoyed at him. I really hated to argue with Dean.

But he grabbed my hand. "Hey, can I talk to you? Somewhere private?"

"About the Protectors? Because I don't want to—"

"No. It's personal."

My heart lurched, coming to life. In one instant, my pulse was beating fast with reckless dreams and aching longing, because what if this was *it*? What if he'd finally changed his mind about me? *Us.*

We walked off the dance floor, going back outside and finding a quiet corner of the deck. Music and lights spilled from the reception. Dean's fingers were tangled around mine as he turned and faced me.

My hopes were flying up into the starry sky.

I wanted him to kiss me. God, I wanted it so badly. I'd imagined what it would be like so many times. The first touch of his lips to mine. How I would put my hand right at the base of his neck to feel how fast his pulse was thrumming. How my thumb would lightly trace over his Adam's apple and the leather cord of his necklace.

How he'd taste when his tongue dipped into my mouth. I'd imagined it so many times without any faith that it would happen, but tonight...

Maybe. *Maybe.*

Please.

"Dean, I—"

He let go of my hand. Gripped the cord at his throat, the bullet still hidden under his shirt. "I wanted you to be the first to know. I'm leaving."

My brain took a moment to adjust. "Leaving? Like, the reception?"

"No, Keira." A soft, humoring smile. His eyes couldn't meet mine. "I'm leaving Colorado. I got an instructor job for the winter at a resort in Canada. Banff. I have a couple buddies who were there last year and—"

"Wait, why? What about the Silver Ridge Ski Resort? I thought you loved it."

"I do. I have loved it, but I don't usually stay in one place too long. That's not my thing. Never has been."

"But you've been here for years…"

"Exactly," he said softly, and that was the instant my heart broke straight down the middle.

Oh, wow. Was I ever stupid. Thinking Dean was finally going to kiss me, like he'd been all tense and weird tonight about *me*, when it was about his new job.

He was leaving.

I wanted to shrivel up and disappear. Maybe I should've been flattered he was telling me first, but he probably just knew how I'd take it. As in, not good.

Like a girl with a crush.

So I lifted my chin and smiled for him. Asked more questions about this Canadian resort and when he was going. Dean was my friend, and I was supposed to be happy for him. He didn't owe me anything.

I listened to him talk about Banff and his plans, nodding in all the right places, keeping that smile fixed on my face even as everything inside me crumbled.

Maybe I was as young as people said after all, hopelessly naive. As if wishing for something could make it true.

As if wanting someone badly enough could make them want you back.

CHAPTER ONE

Keira

"POSITION BETA, I need an update on our status."

I pressed the button on my earpiece. "You got an update two minutes ago, Home Base."

"Exactly," Trace said in my ear. "This mission is critical. I don't think I need to emphasize that, Position Beta."

"These code names are making me yawn," another voice chimed in. "Keira, you should be Barfly One. And Trace, I'm thinking...Papa Bear. Or Helicopter Dad."

"Get off the comm, River," Trace growled. I tried to keep a straight face.

"Is this really a wise use of Protector resources, Trace?" River asked. "Spying on your teenage daughter?"

"Riv, don't make me come over there. Keira, I want my update."

"Copy that, Papa Bear," I said under my breath, smothering a giggle. I checked the view in the mirror behind the bar. "Targets are stationary and secure. No change in status."

"Roger that. Maintain surveillance."

"Wilco."

I was sitting at the end of the bar in a busy roadhouse, nursing a nonalcoholic beer. The interior was all rustic

9

wood paneling, neon beer signs hanging above the bar, and low lighting that caught against the liquor bottles and the smiles of the people around me. Classic rock played from the speakers, just loud enough to compete with conversation.

A typical Hart County Saturday night.

My sister Stephie and her best friend Vivian were sitting at one of the dining tables on a double date. The girls were eighteen now, soon to be high school graduates in just a few months. But they were out tonight with a couple of ranch hands who were over twenty-one, according to the background checks Trace had run on them as soon as he'd gotten their names.

Poor Vivian. Having a former CIA operative for a dad could not be easy.

To be fair, I was protective of my sister. I liked to think that I didn't smother Stephie. But when Trace had proposed this little operation to keep an eye on the girls, I certainly hadn't said no.

The girls had tried to keep the double date a secret, probably because the guys were older. My mom had no clue. But really, did Stephie and Vivian think the rest of us couldn't figure out something was up?

They wanted to stretch their wings, but it was our job to make sure they didn't stretch too far. Break something that couldn't be unbroken.

At eighteen, Stephie was a legal adult, but I just...wasn't ready to let go of my baby sister yet.

"Evening." A man slid onto the stool beside me, giving me a curious smile. I lifted my chin, but otherwise ignored him.

The weight of my concealed weapon was a reassuring presence as I shifted on the stool. The holster sat snug against my ribs, hidden beneath my jacket. Even when I was out of uniform, I was still an officer. It was ingrained in how I thought, how I saw the world.

Of course, that didn't mean I was good enough to be a Protector.

The Last Refuge Protectors were a secret group devoted to defending and protecting people in trouble. Those who needed help but had nowhere else to turn. Whom law enforcement had failed. I saw cases like that way too often, and I'd always wanted to do more.

Trace Novo was their leader, and he was willing to use me for the odd one-off mission. But no matter what I'd done to prove myself in the last few years, I was still just Deputy Marsh. Never one of them.

While I watched the girls through the mirror, I glanced around at the other people at the bar, paying attention to the various scenes and conversations going on. Observing body language, noting who was drinking too much, watching for trouble.

There was one guy in the corner I'd clocked as soon as I'd walked in. He was well dressed in a pair of jeans, a blazer, and a pristine cowboy hat. A gaudy diamond shone from one earlobe, and stubble artfully framed his square jaw.

The rhinestone cowboy had a little cadre of admirers around him. A couple of yes-men who laughed at everything the guy said, and a growing circle of fawning women.

I couldn't say exactly what it was about the guy that set off my alarm bells, but it was something.

By the time my eyes returned to Stephie and Vivian's table, baskets of food had arrived. Their dates were tucking into burgers and fries.

But Vivian and Stephie were sitting there frozen, staring in my direction.

Uh oh.

I pressed the button on my earpiece. "Papa Bear, be

advised. Cover may be compromised," I said, just as foot-steps stomped behind me and an indignant voice spoke.

"Keira, what are you doing here?"

"Yep. Definitely blown," I murmured, before swiveling on my barstool and giving my sister and her best friend an apologetic grin. "Wow, you two are here? Of all the road-houses in the county. Huh. What a coincidence."

Stephie crossed her arms, lipsticked mouth creasing into a frown. "You're the worst liar ever, Kiki."

"Probably not the *worst*."

"You could be out on a date or doing something fun of your own for once. Instead of spying on us."

"But spying on you *is* something fun," I pointed out, because it was kinda true. I did love a clandestine mission, and I rarely got to participate.

"Are you on comms with my dad?" Vivian was eyeing my earpiece. "Tell him I'm fine. And that he's pathological, and I'm going to tell Mom on him."

"Uh, did you hear that, Papa Bear?"

"Roger," Trace said without emotion. "Tell her she'd better be home by curfew."

River Kwon, the Protectors' resident hacker, was snick-ering in the background.

I sighed. Probably time to abort this op.

Actually, it turned out to be a good thing the girls had spotted me. Their dates came over to introduce themselves, and they seemed like nice guys. Clean-cut, polite, work-roughened hands. They confirmed there wouldn't be any alcohol tonight. They were all drinking soda. And they'd defi-nitely have Vivian and Stephie back by curfew, not a minute late.

After the four of them wolfed down their food, they took off, reporting they'd get dessert at an ice cream place on Hartley's Main Street. I'd already given Trace a last update, assuring him I felt confident the girls were okay.

After that, I took out the earpiece and tucked it in my pocket, settling in to finish the rest of my drink.

"Was that your younger sister?"

I turned to glance at the guy sitting on the stool beside me. "What gave it away?" I deadpanned, sipping from my can. Was he making a reference to the brown skin tone Stephie and I shared?

He was probably in his thirties, handsome in a rugged way. A trimmed beard. Calloused hands with just a few traces of dirt under his fingernails. Looked like a working man out to relax for a night. His eyes were a blue so pale they were almost silver, and he had a tiny scar below his right eye.

"Just that you've got the same nose. Same ears."

"*Ears?*"

He laughed. "Sorry. That probably sounds strange. I wasn't staring. Not too much, at least."

The interest in his pale eyes was clear.

He'd left the other seat next to him empty. Maybe he was expecting someone to join him. A buddy or a girlfriend. But a glance at his ring finger showed no wedding ring there.

He wore a ring on his right hand, though. It was large and gold with a flattened blue gemstone in the middle. Like a class ring. There were markings around the gem, but I couldn't read them, and I'd studied the guy enough.

"Can I buy you a drink?" he asked.

I considered it. He was attractive. Seemed nice. *Do something fun for once*, Stephie had said.

But no. No, I wasn't interested.

I moved my eyes to the mirror instead, going back to watching the rest of the room. "Thanks. I shouldn't."

He shrugged and turned away, still smiling. After he finished his drink, he got up and left. So, that was that.

I knew what else my sister would say, if she were the one spying on *me*. Little sisters could give their share of lectures too and believe me, mine did.

It's been two years. You should be over him.

A harsh laugh from one of the tables caught my attention again. It was the wealthy cowboy's table. In the mirror, I watched a server approach him, carrying a tray laden with shot glasses. The man said something to her, his diamond stud glinting, and while she was setting her tray on the table, he put his hand on her butt and squeezed.

Uh, *excuse* me?

I started to get up, instantly furious at the guy's audacity. But the waitress whirled on him, her face flushed. She said something sharp, jabbing her finger at his chest, and he held up his hands in mock surrender, laughing.

"Did you see that?" I asked the bartender.

"Yep. Misty can handle herself. Otherwise I'd go over there." He was wiping down the bar with a rag. "That guy's a jerk," he murmured, dipping his head. "In here a lot, unfortunately. If it were up to me, I'd tell him to stuff it and get lost, but he knows a lot of people. Phelan is his name. Donny Phelan. Some kind of famous podcaster."

"Are you serious?" I asked, settling back onto my seat. "A famous podcaster? He lives around here?"

Hart County wasn't that populous, but it was a big place. Hartley and Silver Ridge were two of the larger towns, and I'd lived in both at various times. I patrolled all over as a deputy for the county. I knew a lot of different corners of this region, but I hadn't been to this roadhouse before. Didn't know all the local characters here either.

Which was probably the reason Stephie and Vivian had chosen this spot for their secret date.

"Phelan moved to a huge property last year," the bartender said, "but from what I hear, he's originally from the Midwest. He makes his money doing some kind of online show, ranting about current events. Got quite a following, I guess. Throws money around like it's nothing." He shook his head. "Doesn't make him any less of a creep."

I filed that information away and sipped my nonalcoholic beer, keeping one eye on Donny Phelan in the mirror.

———

Stephie and Vivian had left a while ago, and I'd planned to take off after I finished my drink. But instead, I stuck around for a soda with lime. *See, Stephie? I'm enjoying my evening.*

Unfortunately, the bar was louder and even more crowded than earlier. The crowd seemed rougher now. Definitely drunker.

But at least the podcaster jerk hadn't groped Misty the server again. Or anyone else that I'd seen.

I was ready to get out of here. I'd had more than enough excitement for one night.

"You need someone to walk you out?" the bartender asked as I dropped some bills to cover my tab and a generous tip.

"I'm all right. But thanks."

He nodded. "Drive safe out there."

"Will do. Have a nice night."

The parking lot was dark, lit only by moonlight and the lights near the restaurant's entrance. My car was parked toward the back, and the gravel crunched under my boots as I walked.

The temperature had dropped, and my breath misted in the cold air. Then I heard raised voices coming from behind the building.

"I said *no.*" It was a woman's voice.

"Come on, don't be like that. I'm just trying to be friendly."

My hand instinctively went to my side where my weapon rested. As I rounded a pickup truck, I saw them. Donny Phelan had Misty backed up against a car, his hand wrapped around her wrist. "Just give me your number. That's all I'm asking."

"Let go of me," she said, trying to pull away. There was a dumpster nearby and a dropped bag of trash, like Misty had been taking it out. And this asshole decided to sneak up on her.

Unbelievable.

"Hey. Sir." I kept my voice calm but firm as I approached. My cop voice, Stephie always called it. "She asked you to let go. You need to back off."

Donny turned, his expression shifting from predatory to irritated. "This doesn't concern you, sweetheart. Why don't you mind your own business?"

"I'm making it my business." I stepped closer. "Let her go. Now."

He tightened his grip on Misty's wrist instead, and that was all I needed.

Moving fast, I grabbed his arm and twisted it with practiced efficiency, applying just enough pressure to make him release her. He yelped, stumbling back.

Misty bolted, running back toward the bar without a word.

"What the hell?" Donny cradled his wrist, his face contorted with anger. "Who the hell do you think you are, little girl? I should call the sheriff on you for assault."

"Please do." I pulled back my jacket just enough to show him the holster at my side. "I happen to work for Sheriff Douglas. Deputy Keira Marsh, at your service. And if I were you, I'd get in my car and go home before I decide to run a field sobriety test on you."

His eyes widened, then narrowed. "You're serious."

"Dead serious."

For a moment, I thought he might argue. His jaw worked, hands clenching into fists. But then he backed toward a sleek Porsche SUV. "This isn't over," he said, pointing at me. "I know people. Important people. You just made a big mistake."

"Get in your car."

He did, slamming the door hard enough to make the frame shudder. The engine roared to life, and he peeled out of the parking lot, gravel spitting from his tires.

I stood there in the darkness, watching his taillights disappear down the road. My heart was pounding, adrenaline singing through my veins.

Despite the noise and voices coming from the bar, the parking lot was now quiet. I strode toward my car and got in, hitting the locks.

Donny Phelan was gone. But as I drove out of the gravel lot, I could've sworn I still felt hostile eyes on me.

CHAPTER TWO

Keira

MY HOUSE WAS quiet as I went inside and turned off my security system. I was ready to get cozy, put something mindless on TV, and hopefully drift off without too much sleeplessness tonight.

Tossing my keys on the table, I stripped off my jacket, then my holster and gun. The handgun went in my lockbox in a kitchen cabinet, where I usually stored my service weapon at home. I had a personal gun locked in a safe in my bedroom too. As a cop, I appreciated always having a weapon close.

Had that been the case since I'd started this job? Honestly, I couldn't remember. But maybe I'd gotten more cautious over the last couple years in particular. Not so optimistic and dreamy-eyed.

Heartache could do that to a girl.

I switched on the lights in the kitchen, then grabbed a pot and set it on the stove. Some warm, spicy chai. That was what I needed.

While I stirred in milk and the spice mix, I checked my phone. Vivian and Stephie were home safe and sound. Steph had even shared a few details about the rest of the date.

STEPHIE

> The guys are really sweet. We might go out
> with them again. Maybe one of them has an
> annoying older brother for you?

I smiled as I sent a message back, telling her goodnight.

After the chai was ready, I added a little bourbon. Then snuggled on my couch and turned the TV on low.

Yet even sitting here curled up with a throw blanket over my lap and my hands around a warm mug of sweet milky tea, I felt an ache for the things I didn't have.

Maybe I should've tried harder to date. I could've accepted the drink from that guy at the bar earlier. Gone home with him... spent the night.

Why didn't I want that? Why did this empty space inside me have the exact shape and feel of the person who didn't want me? Who hadn't even cared enough about my friendship to stay in my life.

It wasn't like Dean and I never had any contact. We were on a group text thread. Just a few weeks ago, Aiden had shared the latest picture of his and Jessi's baby girl, Zoe. Dean and I had each given the picture a heart and said she was precious.

But we didn't talk directly anymore. We used to be close. Maybe not best friends, but tight. Now, he felt like somebody I'd known in high school. Somebody who'd shared a brief part of my history, but who was essentially a stranger now.

Two years should've been enough to get over him. And yet it wasn't. It was just enough for all those feelings I'd had for him to turn bitter. Like a jar sitting on the shelf too long and going rancid.

Damn, I sounded cynical.

I set down the tea and flopped backward on the couch, wishing I'd kissed him just once before he left so I'd know

19

what it was like. Would that be better, the knowing? Or worse?

He was probably an amazing kisser. Giving and careful in bed with a woman, at least at first, and then later he would turn those intense blue eyes on her and pull her so close she could hardly breathe, and then...

"Why?" I asked the quiet room. "Why do I do this to myself? How am I this pathetic?"

My own little sister was going out on dates with cute ranch hands, while I was alone. The only thing that had made my heart race lately was an asshole podcaster harassing a server.

What was wrong with me?

I grabbed my phone, wanting to hurl it across the room even though it hadn't done anything. Because *his* name was in there. His messages. I'd saved every one like they mattered, and they didn't.

I didn't matter to him.

I had to make him stop mattering to me.

Opening my contacts, my finger hovered over the option to block his number. For long seconds, I stared at it. Wondering if this was petty. But then, who the hell cared if it was petty? I was a twenty-eight-year-old woman living my life and doing what I wanted.

Also, I was maybe just a little bit tipsy on bourbon-laced chai.

Snickering to myself, I blocked Dean's number and tossed my phone on the coffee table. Triumph surged through me. Who needed men, anyway?

What I needed was to take a nice, long bath, listen to music, and read one of my favorite books. That would set me right up. Then I could sleep late tomorrow and be ready to go back on duty for my next shift.

I set my mug in the kitchen after downing the last of the

spiked chai, switching off the TV and the lights on my way to my bedroom. There, I pulled off my sweater.

My reflection in the window winked at me. I was undressing, and the curtain was open.

I couldn't see anything outside in the darkness, but I heard a faint sound. Probably a howl from a neighbor's dog or a coyote. My neighbors' houses were close enough to be within sight from the front, but only woods lay behind my home. Something I loved during the day when I could look out and see the trees or take a walk, breathing in nature.

Nobody's out there, I thought to myself.

Marching over, I pulled the curtains closed. No need to put on a show, even if it was just for the bears and mountain lions and nocturnal critters.

I turned on the taps in the bathtub, adjusting the temperature until steam began to rise. While the water filled, I lit a candle on the edge of the tub.

I stripped off the rest of my clothes and stepped into the water, the heat immediately melting the tension in my shoulders. Sinking down until the water reached my chin, I closed my eyes and let out a long breath.

When I reached over and turned off the taps, the sudden quiet was broken only by the gentle lap of bathwater against the sides of the tub.

The old pipes in the wall clanked and settled. Normal sounds. Familiar sounds.

So why did the tiny hairs on the back of my neck stand up?

I opened my eyes fully, staring at the open bathroom door. Beyond it, my bedroom was quiet. Everything was fine. I was being ridiculous, letting paranoia get the better of me.

I closed my eyes again and slid deeper into the water.

There was a loud crash.

I gasped and sat up, water running down my bare skin.

All I heard now was the sound of my own breath and the water sloshing against the tub.

Where the hell had that come from?

It had sounded nearby.

Maybe inside the house.

I got out of the bath, water streaming off me and pooling on the tile. Grabbed a towel and wrapped it around myself. Dashed into my bedroom, my wet feet leaving prints on the carpet. The door to the hall was cracked open, just the way I'd left it earlier, and the hall beyond was dark.

My dresser drawer made a dragging sound as I yanked it open. Tossing the towel aside, I pulled on a tee and sweats, my hands shaking so badly I could barely manage the drawstring.

My gun. I needed my gun. And what about the security system? Shit, had I turned it back on after I got home?

My fingers felt numb as I unlocked the safe where I kept my personal weapon. I checked it quickly, my training taking over even as fear coursed through me.

The metallic slide as I chambered a round made a sharp, definitive sound that seemed to echo in the silent room.

Then I grabbed for my phone where I'd tossed it on the bed, ready to call dispatch. But there was no signal. Next I checked my security app, but it came back with an error message.

I had no cell signal. No internet. Hell. This could not be good.

My breath came fast and shallow. I forced myself to slow down, to think. The smartest thing to do would be to get out of the house. But if there was someone waiting outside, ready to grab me?

No way. I was going to fight.

Padding on the rug to my bedroom door, I listened with my gun ready, finger alongside the trigger guard.

22

I eased the opening in the doorway wider and stepped out. There was a window to my left, closed. An open door across the hall, which led to the small laundry room. Nobody inside. Just the dark shapes of the washer and dryer.

The rest of the hallway stretched before me, leading to the living room.

My vision adjusted slowly to the darkness. Every muscle in my body was taut, ready to spring. I stepped forward carefully, my bare feet silent on the carpet, gun aimed forward as blood rushed in my ears.

I reached the mouth of the hallway. Cold air flowed around my feet, raising goosebumps on my bare legs. Fear washed over me, my brain turning strangely blank, everything slowing.

A figure stood in the kitchen.

The man was wearing a mask. A hideous, demonic face. A nightmare. His arms were down, no weapon visible. But still, the sight of him awakened a terror I'd never experienced.

Another split second passed, slow as an eternity, before the moment broke open and I could move again.

"Police," I shouted, my voice surprisingly steady. "Get down on the ground, hands where I can see them!"

Movement on my periphery. Shit. Shifting, I turned and saw another masked intruder stepping out of the shadows near the coat closet.

A muzzle flash lit up the room like lightning. The gunshot was deafening in the enclosed space, a thunderclap that made my ears ring. At the same instant, fire tore through my left side, just below my ribs.

The impact spun me halfway around. Pain sliced along my side. I fired back. My gun bucked in my hand. I heard a shout as I tried to back away, tried to retreat to the hallway where I'd have cover.

I didn't make it.

The next bullet caught me higher, punching into my chest and driving me backward into a wall. My legs gave out. The gun slipped from my fingers and clattered to the floor.

The world tilted and spun.

I tried to move, tried to reach for my weapon, but my body wouldn't respond. Pain and heat and cold took over my senses.

Then the night closed in around me, and I felt nothing at all.

CHAPTER THREE

Dean

PAUSING at the top of the mogul field, I took in the panoramic view below me.

The Swiss Alps stretched out in every direction, their peaks still crowned with snow. The morning sun caught the ridges and turned them gold, casting long purple shadows across the slopes.

Pine forests climbed the lower elevations, dark green against the white. The air was crisp and thin, sharp in my lungs.

"Tell me that's not the most breathtaking thing you've ever seen," my friend Alina said beside me.

I chuckled and nodded amiably, because she was just making conversation. No point in telling her this was definitely *not* the most breathtaking thing I'd seen, despite the fact that it was incredibly beautiful.

That title belonged to something back in Colorado. Some*one*.

I pushed off, my board hitting the moguls. A sense of calm overtook me. Up here, there was nothing but the mountain, the sky, and the quiet hum of the wind. I could've been anyone, just a traveler with no past and no worries about the future.

When we reached the bottom of the slope, I lifted my goggles and unsnapped one boot from the board. Alina did the same. Her tanned face appeared, surrounded by wisps of pale blonde hair.

"Another run?" I asked.

"We could. Unless…" She smiled in a way that probably worked on most guys. Alina rarely left alone at the end of a night of drinking with our fellow resort instructors.

It was also a smile she'd given *me* plenty of times, to no effect. But it looked like she was giving it one last go.

"Unless you want to call it a day early," she said in faintly accented English. "Do something else for fun before you leave."

Fuck. This was awkward.

It had been a great season here at Verbier. But now that it was late spring and the crowds were waning, it was about time to get moving again. Something I'd done pretty much every season since that longer stint I'd spent in Colorado.

I'd learned my lesson. These days, four months in one place was long enough.

"I can't," I said apologetically. "Though that's a very tempting offer."

Alina shrugged off my rejection. "All winter, I've never seen you with anyone. There's someone else? Maybe back in the States?" She nudged my arm. "Come on. You never talk about yourself."

Someone else.

How could I explain that there was no one waiting for me, not in the way she meant? No one I could ever be with, anyway.

It was easier just to agree. Easier on Alina's ego, which probably didn't need that much help if we were being honest.

26

But also easier on me. I'd never enjoyed confessing my secrets.

"Yes. Someone else."

"Just a drink then?" she offered. "If you wanna talk about it." When I hesitated, she added, "Or another run would be lovely too."

I grinned. "Another run."

As expected, the snow didn't hold out long, and by the late afternoon we found ourselves at the preferred watering hole of the seasonal instructors.

We were an international crew. Alina was a local, while Lars was Swedish. Matteo had come from Italy, and Yuki from Japan.

"So where's everyone headed next?" Lars asked, leaning back in his chair with a beer in hand.

"Got a line on some hotel work in Mykonos for the summer," Matteo said. "Sunny days, wild nights."

"I didn't think your nights could get any wilder," Yuki joked. There were backslaps and playful nudges around the table. They were all grown adults in their twenties and thirties, but acted like teenagers. I wouldn't claim to have all my shit together, but sometimes I felt like the boring older brother. At thirty-six, I was set in my ways.

"What about you, Dean?" Yuki asked. "Where are you heading?"

"Don't know yet."

Lars guffawed. "But aren't you taking off tomorrow morning?"

"I guess I'll decide by then."

Yuki shook her head, smirking. "So mysterious." She tipped back her drink, then thunked it on the table. "I think Dean sprang fully formed into the world one day, jumped onto a snowboard, and never looked back."

I laughed. "That's pretty much it."

"I'd say that works well with the ladies," Lars said, "but you never take advantage there." He nodded toward Alina, who was dancing with some new face.

"Or with guys," Matteo added. "Haven't seen you with any of them either."

I pushed my hair back from my face. It had grown out almost to my shoulders, and I'd tied it back, but it never wanted to stay in place. "Why are you all so curious about me?"

"We might have a betting pool going," Lars admitted.

I took another sip of my whiskey, the ice clinking against the glass. "You need to get out more. Promise I'm not very interesting."

"That's exactly what someone interesting would say," Matteo pointed out. "Especially one who wears a bullet around his neck. Is that some strange American custom we don't know about?"

I was certainly not answering that question. Just smiled instead.

Soon the conversation veered away from me, thankfully, and as the night wore on, some people decided to call it and head home, while others found hookups.

I headed back to the flat I shared with Lars and a couple others. They were still out, so I had the place to myself to pack before my train in the morning.

I preferred to keep my life simple. I could fit most of my possessions in a duffel and a cardboard box or two, plus an oversized bag for my equipment. My Rossignol skis and Burton snowboard were my prized possessions. Top-of-the-line gear that I maintained meticulously, the one indulgence I allowed myself.

Back when I was a Marine, my life had been equally mobile, if far less under my own control. My most prized possession had been something very different.

I touched the pendant hanging from the cord around my neck. A reminder that always calmed me when I thought about those days.

The smell of gunpowder and metal and machine oil...

I gripped the round on the cord tighter, shaking off those thoughts.

That's not my life now, and it will never be again. That's not me.

Peace was a choice I made, every single day. Freedom. Maybe I couldn't ever make up for the things I'd done, but I could find a way to live with myself. And hopefully bring a smile to someone else's day. Give more than I took, even if it meant denying myself anything more.

Where-to next? That was the question. I liked to keep things up in the air, especially for the summers. Just seeing where the wind took me. Where inspiration might lead.

There was always a voice in the back of my mind whispering *Hart County, Colorado*, but I knew that was a bad idea.

My best friend Owen constantly gave me shit about it. *When are you going to get back here? Not like I miss you that much, but you do stir up a nice old-fashioned.*

As I grabbed a book from my shelf, a folded piece of paper fell out. Already knowing what it was, I bent to pick it up. Unfolded it.

I'd printed out this photo at some point during a moment of weakness. In the image, Keira and I were standing with our heads together. Smiling.

I stared at it for a long moment, memories flooding my mind.

After tucking the paper inside the book and packing it away, I took out my phone and opened the photos app. There were other pictures I'd kept and only let myself look at on occasions like this, when I was transitioning from one place to another. When I let myself wonder...what if?

In one, Keira was making a face at the camera on the

summit of a fourteener we'd hiked. Her dark eyes were bright with laughter, genuine and unguarded.

The way she'd looked at me before I'd ruined everything.

But I'd had to ruin it. I'd had no other choice. I'd stayed way too long in Hart County, telling myself it was because of Owen and the other friends I'd made there. Genevieve, Aiden, Jessi. Trace and Scarlett. Cole and Brynn.

When really, the whole time it had been *her*.

An awful, empty ache started in the pit of my stomach and spread outward. Two years, and it hadn't faded. Two years, and I still saw her face when I closed my eyes.

That's enough, I told myself. *No more. No fucking more.*

Ireland, I decided. It was incredible this time of year, based on my previous visits, and I'd probably be able to find enough work to occupy myself. A cash-only job that paid under the table. I'd already perfected my skill at pouring a Guinness.

Now that I'd decided, and the temptation of Hart County was past, I exhaled.

Forcing myself to close the photo app, I noticed a missed call. It was from Owen. Worst possible timing, given where my head was at.

Then I noticed there were *two* missed calls. From hours ago. He must've called when it was the middle of the night there. Dread made me go still.

I hit Owen's name in the call log. Listened to it ring.

"Dean." His voice was tight. There was noise in the background, like he was in a busy place. "Hey."

"Owen, what's up? Everything okay?"

"I'm sorry to call like this."

That just freaked me out more. My pulse kicked up. "Did something happen?"

There was a pause that seemed to last a lifetime. Every instinct I had screamed that something was very wrong.

That everything was about to change.

"It's Keira. She was attacked last night. She's in the hospital."

As he gave me a few more details, my back hit the bedroom wall, my knees going weak. "Who?" I managed to choke out.

That one question pulsed with the vein at my temple.

Fucking *who* had done this?

"We don't know yet," Owen said. "We're going to find out. She's in stable condition. I just wanted to let you know. Figured…" There was a hell of a lot in that silence.

"Yeah," I managed to say. "I gotta go."

My phone dropped to the floor. I grabbed for the cord around my neck. The rifle bullet bit into my palm. I squeezed it so hard the point dug into my skin, giving me something to focus on. But it wasn't enough. Not like it usually was.

The rage built and built until I couldn't take it anymore, and I exploded.

I twisted my body and drove my fist into the wall, hearing a scream of agony that could only have come from myself.

Fuck.

My knuckles were bloody, and there was a hole in the drywall. Some rational part of my mind said I'd have to explain to my roommates. Leave money to cover the repair. I felt shitty about making a mess for them, which was not the kind of thing I liked to do.

But I had to go.

I had to find the first flight that would take me back to Colorado.

CHAPTER FOUR

Keira

"YOU'RE COMFORTABLE, HONEY?" Mom fluffed my pillow, as if an insufficiently fluffy pillow was my main issue at the moment. "How's your pain?"

"I'm just fine, Mom. I'm good." I smiled, trying not to grit my teeth. "No pain." The word came out as more of a wheeze.

My sister leveled a glare at me. She wasn't buying it.

Yeah, I was full of it. But I was weaning off the stronger meds, since I hated feeling loopy, and I was sick of Mom fussing over me. Sick of *everyone* fussing over me.

All this time with nothing to do but heal was already killing me. Sorry, that was just my dark humor talking. But I'd been shot twice, and as I'd learned from the scores of flower arrangements and cards I'd received, injuries like mine bought a girl some sympathy.

The first bullet had hit me in the side, a through-and-through wound that would heal up easy. But the second caught me in my upper chest. The bullet had torn through muscle and shattered my clavicle, missing my lung by less than an inch.

My attackers had meant to kill me. I was so damn lucky

they hadn't shot me in the head to check their work. Thank goodness a nosy neighbor had scared them off. Just a few small differences, and I wouldn't be here.

It was…a lot to think about. I was trying hard *not* to think about it, especially when Mom and Stephie were around.

It was my third day now in the hospital, and they were doing their best to cheer me up. "I brought you something," Mom said, producing a container.

Even through the plastic lid, I could smell the tomato and basil. Spaghetti and meatballs soup, she called it. A tomato soup base with tiny meatballs and noodles. Something she used to make for me whenever I was sick when I was little.

"Thanks, Momma." I accepted the container even though I wasn't hungry. My appetite had vanished somewhere around the time I woke up with tubes coming out of various parts of my body.

"Remember how I used to think the meatballs looked like eyes?" Stephie said, a smile playing at her lips. "Remember?"

"Yeah, I remember. You were pretty cute." I managed a small laugh. "And ridiculous."

"I always said the tomato broth looked like…"

"Stephanie Ann Marsh," our mom said sharply.

Stephie's face crumpled like she was going to cry. "I'm sorry. I didn't mean to."

"It's okay, sissy," I said. "I can handle a joke about blood."

Ugh, it had been like this constantly. Mom and Stephie trying to keep their chins up, stay strong. All the while ready to cry at a moment's notice.

There was no way I could let them know how angry and terrified I really was. If anything, as the days since the attack had passed, those churning emotions had only gotten worse.

There were some parts of the night of the attack that I still couldn't remember. Most of the evening at the road-house was clear. Seeing Stephie and Vivian with their dates.

That guy in a cowboy hat harassing the waitress in the parking lot.

Phelan. That was his name. Right. I'd told Sheriff Douglas about him in my statement. How I felt like someone was watching me even after Phelan took off.

Then being at home. How I'd tried to relax, even though I'd felt deep down that something wasn't right. And then the sounds when I was in the tub… The crash.

The rest was just in flashes.

My gun in my hand. The dark hallway.

A horrible face appearing out of the shadows. And…that was it.

My attackers had used some kind of localized signal jammer to block cell service and internet at my house. A brave neighbor had heard the gunshots and came running, carrying his own shotgun. The suspects fled in a black Ford SUV. No plates.

I'd been in surgery for nearly three hours. My left arm would be in a sling for at least six weeks. Absolutely no lifting anything heavier than a couple pounds. No driving for a month. Physical therapy would start in about a week, once the initial healing began and the swelling went down.

Full recovery could take three to four months, maybe longer depending on how my body responded. It could've been so much worse. I knew that. Everyone kept reminding me how lucky I was.

But three to four months until I could return to duty… The time yawned open in front of me like it might swallow me whole.

I wanted to be at work. I wanted to help find the assholes who'd broken into my home. Of course, that was not going to happen.

I lay back against the pillows, staring at the ceiling. My chest and side ached with every breath.

"Honey, are you sure you're okay?" Mom asked.

How on earth could I be okay? I almost said. But I couldn't. It wasn't fair to her.

"Maybe I could use a little more pain medication after all," I gritted out instead.

Mom scampered off to find the nurse, eager to have something to do.

"You're not okay," Stephie said quietly.

"I have to be." Because if I gave in to everything I was feeling, then I wouldn't be able to hold myself together.

Thankfully, my friend Brynn Somerton turned up a minute later. She swanned into the room, looking put-together as always. Today it was dark jeans, ankle boots, a crisp white button-down. Her long straight hair was up in a sleek ponytail.

"Good morning," Brynn announced. "How's today treating you, Keira? Sucking as much as yesterday?"

"You know it," I said, managing a smile.

"She's acting like she's great, even though she's not," Stephie grumbled from the chair where she was slumped.

Mom returned with a nurse, who offered a dose of NSAIDs for my pain. I was saving the stronger stuff for nighttime.

"Two visitors," the nurse reminded us.

Brynn smiled. "Yes, ma'am. We'll sort that out."

When she'd gotten the news about the shooting, Brynn had been in Mexico at the house she shared with Cole. She'd arrived in Hartley just yesterday, stopping by the hospital to see me for a few minutes, but a ton of other people had wanted to stop and see me too.

I was so glad she was here. I hadn't had the chance to talk to her alone yet, and I needed to.

I needed my friend.

As if she'd read my mind, Brynn worked her magic,

convincing Mom and Stephie to go home and rest for a while. "Thank you," I breathed, relaxing into the pillows when they were gone. "I love them, but it's a lot having them here constantly."

"Of course it is." Brynn carefully sat on the edge of the mattress beside me. "I heard from the nurses you're the most cheerful GSW victim they've ever encountered."

"Trying."

"I admire that. But you were shot, Keira. You're allowed to be awful. Nobody expects you to be sweet right now."

Brynn was a former FBI agent. I'd met her when she and Cole came to Hart County to partner on an undercover Protectors mission. They wound up falling in love.

These days, she and Cole were bounty hunters, spending summers in the States and winters at their beach house on the Pacific coast of Mexico. Brynn and Cole were also members of the Protectors, carrying out missions whenever their particular skills were needed.

Brynn didn't hold much back, especially not after finding love and happiness with Cole.

"You can tell me how you're really feeling," she said.

I groaned, and my eyes burned. "I hate this. I'm so…"

She held my hand, the one not trapped in a sling. "Tell me."

"So *pissed off*. People have been really kind, coming to visit and check on me and bring flowers and food. My neighbors, everyone from Last Refuge, and our church, and from the station. But I just want to…scream. Or cry. Or something. But I can't cry in front of any of them, B. Especially not my family, and never Owen or Trace or River. If I do, I'll prove that I'm…"

A mass had gathered in my throat, choking me. I grabbed for Brynn's hand and squeezed as hard as I could. Which wasn't all that hard considering I was lying helpless in a bed, barely able to move and with my left arm in a sling.

"Weak," I finished, my voice just a whisper.

When those men had tried to kill me, I'd put up little resistance. Yeah, I'd shot one of them. He'd left blood at the scene, and forensic techs were searching for DNA matches. But my attackers had gotten away easily. I hadn't stood a chance.

How could I ever be a Protector if I couldn't even defend myself?

Brynn leaned closer. "We all fall apart, every single one of us. But tough folks like us, like you and me, we choose who to do it in front of. You can fall apart in front of me."

"Thanks."

Gah, I sounded so sad and dejected. I was sick of myself. Sick of everyone and everything.

"Have you cried yet? Even alone?"

I shook my head. That lump was stuck halfway, refusing to budge.

She smoothed the baby hairs along my hairline. "I have a story. So, after my first firefight when I was initially deployed as a Marine, I yacked up every bit of dinner and cried silently into my pillow. First time I'd ever really been shot at, and I was so damn scared. I..."

A knock interrupted Brynn's attempt to make me feel better.

Another visitor. Yay.

Then I glanced over and saw who was in the doorway, and the shock hit me full force.

Oh my God. *What?*

Dean. Dean Reynolds was standing in my doorway.

"Keira," Dean murmured, taking a step into the room. "Hey."

His hair was longer, pulled back with light-brown strands

slipping out around his face. He looked tired, but that didn't take away from his handsomeness. The sharp line of his jaw or the soft plumpness of his lower lip that I used to imagine kissing. His usual smile was missing, but the rest of him was so familiar. A vision straight out of my memories.

"How are you here?" I croaked.

Brynn glanced sharply at me, then at Dean as he walked toward my bed. He held a vase of flowers. Gardenias, my favorite. "I came as soon as I could. Sorry it took me so long."

For a moment, I wasn't in the hospital, immobilized and in pain. I was on that dance floor again. My chest caving in from a different kind of pain.

Two years. Two years, and he'd just walked in like it was normal. Like it was nothing. Like he was still my friend.

"Brought these for you," he said, holding up the vase.

I didn't take the flowers. I mean, I couldn't lift them. *Hello*. There wasn't any spare real estate on the table either. Dean set them on the floor, then clasped his hands in front of him, fidgeting slightly. Maybe waiting for me to say something.

But I couldn't even get my head around the fact that he was here. *Here*, at Hart County General. Where I was lying in a smelly hospital gown. My hair was a horror show, and I had no makeup on.

Wasn't this just flipping *great*?

Two years, and he showed up now?

"There were delays from a storm on the east coast, and sometimes I forget how far Hartley is from, well, every-where." Dean's dimple flashed, and it was a punch to my sternum. "How are you?" he asked.

Brynn crossed her arms over her pristine white shirt. "Dean, maybe this isn't the best time."

I finally found my voice again.

"You seriously think you can just show up here like two years haven't passed? What the *fuck*?"

Dean froze, while Brynn's mouth twitched with a smile.

Yeah, I was pretty surprised at myself too.

"I know it's been a while," Dean said smoothly. He stuck his hands in his jeans pockets, the only hint that this was uncomfortable for him. "I texted that I was on my way, but I had no idea if you'd be able to get the messages. Keira…"

I pulled my blanket higher. "You shouldn't have come."

"What else could I have done after I heard from Owen? What they did to you, how you were hurt, I…" Dean pulled his hand from his pocket and flexed his fingers. His knuckles were bandaged. My first instinct was to ask how he'd gotten hurt. To *care* about him, as if we meant something to each other.

"I had to be here for you," he finished.

"You don't care about me."

"Of course I do."

Fury lit me up with a terrible fire. Like it might burn me alive and leave nothing but smoldering ashes.

Two years' worth of pissed-off feelings, and it was about to burst out of me all over this room. I was tired of being sweet and cheerful and nice. Like Brynn had said, we got to choose who to fall apart in front of.

Apparently, for me, that short list included *him*.

"Well, I don't want you here." My chin shook. Body quaking. I ignored the pain. "I didn't get your messages because I blocked your number."

Dean's eyes widened slightly. That was the only reaction he gave me, and that sucked, because I'd wanted more. I always wanted more, didn't I?

"Okay." He nodded slowly. "Do you want me to leave?"

"Yes," I bit out. "Get out of here. Go. That's what you're good at."

With a blank expression, Dean turned and walked out. Just like that.

Despite everything, I hadn't thought it would be so easy.

Brynn broke the sudden silence. She started to slow-clap. "That. Was. Amazing."

"Was it?"

"You kidding? I should've caught it on film. That would've gone viral."

Laughter tickled my throat. Starting small, then bubbling up. Brynn was laughing too.

Until hot tears spilled onto my cheeks and streamed to my chin.

"Oh, Keira." Brynn rushed over to me.

"I'm okay," I sobbed.

Everything I'd been holding inside rushed to the surface. The shame and the terror and the helplessness. My rage at the men who'd hurt me.

And my broken heart. The heartache I still felt over the man I'd just told to leave me alone, even though all I'd ever wanted was to have him close. To have him want me.

"Why does it hurt this much? I can't take it. I can't."

She gently put her cheek against mine, trying not to jostle me. "I know it hurts. But you're so strong. I promise you can handle it."

I cried and cried, and strong was the last thing that I felt.

CHAPTER FIVE

Dean

BACK WHEN I used to live in Hart County, I rarely came to see Owen at the Sheriff's Office headquarters. All the guns and nightsticks and cameras, that reek of authority… it didn't sit well with me. Not after I'd left my old life behind.

But today, I was here to see Owen in his official role as Sheriff Douglas just as much as I wanted to see my friend.

The officer at the front desk looked up as I strode inside. Somebody young who I didn't recognize. "I'm here to see the sheriff, please," I said.

He took in my messy hair and rumpled clothes. "Sheriff's pretty busy."

"I texted him on my way over. He knows I'm coming."

Owen hadn't been happy. *You're here right now? In Hartley? Thanks for the heads-up, buddy.*

Owen Douglas wasn't the most sarcastic guy, but I'd certainly heard it dripping from those words. I had some explaining to do. But so did he, and I didn't plan to settle for an official "no comment."

The desk officer looked skeptical.

But then Owen stepped out of his office with a frown. "Reynolds, get your butt in here."

"Nice to see you too, Tex," I said as I strode over to him.

He pulled me into a fierce hug. "It is. But you could've taken a moment on your way back to the US of A to send me a damn message."

We went into his office. He jabbed a finger at the chair in front of his desk, and I sat down. Clearly I was in the hot seat.

Owen went around to his own chair, taking off the cowboy hat he always wore. That was partly why his callsign had been Tex in the Marines. He'd loved wearing that battered hat whenever he was dressed in his civvies, and he had the hint of a country drawl to match. His family also owned a cattle ranch, though Colorado was home rather than Texas.

My best friend had been wilder in his Marine days. Fearless. Now that he was sheriff, he was far more cautious.

"I knew you were upset after my call," he said, "but then you went dark on me. Not a word. I had no idea what was going on."

"You had enough to deal with without focusing on me." I hadn't wanted to take up a single minute of Owen's time when he should've been investigating Keira's attack.

He gestured at my bandaged hand. "What happened there?"

"It's not important."

Owen raised a brow. I scratched my forehead.

"Anyway, there were some flight delays and crap like that," I said. "I let Keira know I was on my way, but apparently she didn't get the messages." Because she'd blocked me, but I didn't want to admit that to Owen. "I'm here now."

"Have you seen her?"

I nodded. "This morning. She yelled and threw me out."

It had been harrowing to see her in the hospital, so small and diminished. Keira might not have been very large in size, but she had a personality that took up space. Not because she was loud or boisterous. But because of her constant regard for other people. The light she brought to any room she was in.

Earlier today, when I'd seen her in that hospital bed, her light had been burning a whole lot dimmer.

Then I'd made her feel worse just by showing up.

Owen's eyebrows went sky high. "Keira Marsh, Hart County's Sweetheart? The woman who was shot twice a few days ago, who's immobile in a hospital bed, threw you out?"

"Figuratively speaking. Brynn probably would've done it on Keira's behalf if I hadn't removed myself. Keira seems pretty furious with me."

"Can you blame her?"

"I guess not."

Owen knew, more or less, how I felt about Keira. Though we'd never discussed it outright. He also had a pretty good sense of why I'd moved away from Colorado after staying here so long.

But I wasn't here to talk about that.

"I'd like to hear about the investigation so far. What progress have you made in finding the people who did this?"

Owen tilted his head, assessing me. "First of all, how is that any of your business? Second, I wanna know what you're thinking, showing up this way after two years."

"At least once a week, you text and tell me I should visit."

"But you're not here for me, and I'm not asking because my feelings are hurt, asshole. It's good to see you. I'm asking for Keira. She wasn't the same after you left. If you show up like this when she's already been through it and then take off again, how do you think that's going to go?"

I was glad Owen was looking out for Keira. She'd been one of his most trusted deputies for years now. I would never begrudge him that.

43

Also, fair question.

"I plan to stick around for at least a while." I rubbed a hand over my rough jaw. "I don't want to hurt her again, Tex. Never wanted to hurt her at all."

Owen's mouth twisted. "I've avoided asking this because I love you and trust you. But before you left, you didn't… There wasn't anything between you and Keira, any reason for her to…"

A bolt of heat crackled in my veins.

"If you're asking if I loved her and left her, the answer is no. I never touched her." I'd cared way too much about her to do that. Regardless of what I might've wanted.

Go. That's what you're good at.

She'd never spoken truer words.

"Good." Owen slumped into his chair, sighing. "You know, you look like a damn hippie with that long hair. All you need is a beard, but you could never grow a decent one."

I chuckled, the tension in me unwinding.

We'd been friends for well over a decade now, and because of my nomadic ways, we'd often gone years without seeing each other face to face. But Tex and I always dropped into our easy closeness like this. He was one of the few constants in my life. I was grateful for it.

Even if that could put us in an awkward position now, considering what I was about to say.

"I appreciate you calling to let me know what happened," I said. "I'm here because I want to make sure the people who went after Keira are brought to justice."

"You think I don't intend to do that?" My friend's voice had taken on a harder edge. I was treading on shaky ground here, and we both knew it. "Every citizen of my county, every victim, matters to me," he said. "But Keira's also my family. She's put her life on the line for me, and I'd do the same for her a hundred times over."

"I know you'll make your best efforts. But I had to come see for myself and make sure."

"Because you're suddenly a law enforcement expert?"

"I didn't claim that." My expertise was in...other areas. "It's not meant as an offense to you."

But there was no way I could've stayed across the ocean behind some bar, just living my life, as if Keira was a mere acquaintance.

As if she meant nothing to me.

Owen picked up a pen from his desk and squeezed it. "I assure you, we're looking at every possibility. This investigation is my top priority, and we're devoting every resource. Does that *satisfy* you?"

His tone told me it was time to back off and stop questioning his authority in his office.

Too damn bad.

"It doesn't satisfy me at all. Sounds like empty words. Do you have suspects yet?"

"You need to let me take care of this."

"When Genevieve was on the line—"

He stood up, his desk chair wheeling back against a filing cabinet. "Yes, I would've done anything when the woman I loved was in danger. You were there for me then, and I've never forgotten it. But this is not the same."

"How?"

"Keira isn't being held by some madman right now. She's safe. She's going to recover, and I need to run my investigation as normally as possible. By the book, so that when we find the culprits, the DA can prosecute and get solid convictions."

"And if you fail? If they get away with it?"

"Keira is one of our own. Beloved not just in my department, but with everyone at Last Refuge." He swallowed.

"Trust that I'll bring the Protectors in if more discreet action is necessary."

Aiden Shelborne had founded the Last Refuge Protectors, and Trace Novo was their leader. Owen had been there since the beginning, but his membership was far less official. He was more like a trusted associate. Given his role as sheriff, he had to keep himself apart and purposefully ignorant of some of their activities.

The Protectors had dealt with some very bad men in the past. Men with no remorse. In those cases, they hadn't shown mercy.

But would Owen truly give the Protectors free rein to target the men who'd hurt Keira? Could I even trust the Protectors to do it? They all had families now. Aiden, Trace, and River were married men, and two of them were fathers. So much to lose. Even Brynn and Cole, both of them Protectors, had each other.

My position was different. I had few responsibilities. Nothing holding me back from doing what I might have to do.

"Do you have suspects yet?" I demanded again. "Names?"

"I can't discuss that with you."

"Fine." I stood. "I guess we're finished for now. Before I go, I'll need the key to my storage locker."

Owen gave me a hard look.

Certain items of mine had been in storage for a long time now. Since I'd left government service. When I'd taken off from Hart County, I'd left those items here, mainly because this place was the closest thing to a home that I had.

I'd given Owen the key so he could stop me from doing exactly this.

"What is it you're planning to do?" he asked.

"Whatever I have to."

His eyes narrowed. "Fucking hell. You're serious about this."

"I am."

"Trace asked you to join the Protectors years ago. You have skills they can use. But you said *no*. For good reasons. You were true to yourself, and I've always respected that."

I glanced at the wall. "But what the hell do my reasons matter if she gets hurt, and I don't step up?"

There was a long pause. "This isn't you, Dean. You're not Bullseye anymore, and I know you don't want to be."

Hearing my old callsign made a muscle in my neck twitch. I resisted the urge to reach for my necklace, holding out my hand instead.

"The key. Please. It's my property."

He dropped his volume to a harsh murmur. "You said you closed the door on the man you were. Not that I judged anything you had to do back then, or any choice you made, but... Don't destroy what you've built."

What I'd built? Like that amounted to anything. Seasonal jobs and fleeting friendships. Freedom and peace of mind meant nothing if it meant turning my back on the only people I cared about.

Turning my back on *her*.

"Are you planning to make illegal use of what's in that storage unit?" Owen asked.

"I can't discuss that with you," I said, throwing his own words back at him.

Shaking his head, he opened a desk drawer. Pulled out a small keychain with a single key attached. "For the love of all that's holy, don't be an idiot."

"I'll try."

"Not a very convincing answer."

"Best I can do."

CHAPTER SIX

Dean

MY VISIT to the storage place didn't take long. I drove through the units, following the signs, until I came to the correct number range.

Everything inside the locker was exactly as I'd left it. If far dustier and cobwebbed than any self-respecting Marine would've permitted.

You're not Bullseye anymore.

I stowed two large locked cases in the back of my rental car. I didn't open either of them. Hadn't made up my mind about opening those hardback cases at all, despite Owen's clear concerns.

But I needed to have these items close. Just in case. I was nowhere near fighting shape despite my active lifestyle and hours spent on the slopes or in the gym.

You closed the door on the man you were.

A shudder ran through me, and I fingered the bullet hanging near my throat as I drove out into the country.

Who was I now? The easygoing bartender and laid-back ski instructor?

The answer had to be yes.

The highway twisted back and forth through the canyon,

then curved gently as the landscape opened up and I left Hartley behind.

Turning onto a quiet, two-lane stretch of asphalt, I drove onward, the road passing through a narrow valley with mountains framing either side.

I'd only visited this property once. It was a fifty-acre stretch of ranch land and foothills. The place had been about to enter foreclosure, and I'd bought it on impulse for dirt cheap during my time living in Hart County. Nobody else knew. Not even Owen or Keira.

At the time, I'd thought of this property as an investment. I'd planned to fix it up and start renting it out. I hadn't let myself think about actually living here.

But of course, deep down, I'd wondered what it would be like to put down actual roots. To stay.

If only that were possible.

The exterior was rustic wood and stone. Not unlike the ranch property Aiden and Jessi had transformed into the Last Refuge Inn and Tavern, though that was on a mountainside instead of in a valley.

I unlocked the front door and stepped inside, waving away the dust that I kicked up walking across the wood floors. The living spaces were rough, with a sawhorse left over from some of the work. Drop cloths and a few forgotten tools littered the corners.

In the two years since I'd left, I'd hired a contractor to redo all the plumbing inside the house, which had been in rough shape. Same with the electrical.

I went around the house, checking the main electric box and switching on the water, which was fed by a well. Everything seemed to be in working order, at least the basics.

It wasn't much. No furniture. Barely livable.

But I didn't need much. I had a bedroll in my things. Running water was an upgrade from some of the perches

49

I'd holed up in, back in the day. This was enough to get started.

I had a hell of a lot to do.

First on my list would be connecting with River Kwon. I figured I might need River's hacking skills, and of all the Protectors, River was the least likely to care about playing outside legal lines. Even if River's wife was the lieutenant governor.

And then, I had to find a way to get Keira to talk to me again.

I told myself it was because I needed her eyewitness account about her attackers. But also, I just wanted to see her.

When she was so close in distance, there was no possibility of me staying away.

That had always been the issue, hadn't it? When Keira was right there in front of me, she tempted me to believe a different ending was possible.

————

By two in the morning, I was still awake.

I rarely slept more than a few hours at a time. Tonight was no different, and jet lag hadn't helped. I'd passed out early in the evening, and now I was up. Eager to make some kind of progress on my mission.

I moved through the rooms on instinct, listening to the quiet. Like a wraith in my own house. The place was silent around me, settling into itself with the occasional creak of old wood.

Moonlight filtered through the bare windows, casting pale rectangles across the floor.

I slipped through the cellar door and down the rickety wooden stairs in my bare feet. Switched on the exposed bulb using the pull chain. There was a dirt floor at the bottom and several sets of shelves for storage, most of them empty except for the cobwebs I didn't bother to clear.

I took out one of the cases I'd stowed here earlier. Well, I supposed it was yesterday now.

This case was long and narrow. I unlocked it. The hinge squeaked, and I peered inside.

Light caught against dark metal.

Technically, this rifle was still US government property. But at the end, I'd been a ghost. The things I'd done had no official government sanction and would've been disavowed. After that final mission, my superiors had hardly been concerned about checking my rifle back into inventory.

I traced my fingers over the metal. The unrelenting cold seeped into my skin, yet even now, it felt like coming home. Like seeing an old friend again.

I hated that feeling.

Owen had it wrong. Deep down, I was still Bullseye. A killer. I could never wash away my sins enough to deserve Keira's love.

The best I could offer her was vengeance.

CHAPTER SEVEN

"I WISH I had better news for you," Owen said through the phone.

I pulled a blanket over my lap, wedging myself between the couch cushions. "There's nothing else we can do? You're sure?"

"Afraid so. Phelan has invoked his right to an attorney and refused to answer any questions, so we can't interrogate him again. Unless something new turns up to connect him to the shooting, we can't consider him a suspect."

I was quiet.

"Keira? You there?"

"Yeah. I'm still here."

Barely.

It had been almost three weeks since I'd returned home from the hospital. When I'd first been released, I'd stayed at Mom's house over in Silver Ridge. I was so grateful to Mom for taking time off work to help me, and Stephie had stayed up with me night after night when I couldn't sleep. I'd still been on plenty of pain meds, constantly exhausted. A stream of well-meaning friends and neighbors had stopped by, sometimes by the hour, to visit or bring food.

The couple of times I'd gone to the station, the other deputies clapped and cheered like I was a *hero*.

I didn't feel like a hero. I was a victim. A cop only in name, at least for the time being.

After the sheriff's department had given the okay and special cleaners came, I was able to return to my own home over Mom's objections. This was *my* house, dammit, and I wouldn't let anyone scare me away.

Even if I saw demonic faces every time I closed my eyes.

So far, our only person of interest in the shooting was Donny Phelan, the podcaster with the diamond earring and cowboy hat. During my confrontation with him in the road-house parking lot that night, I'd told him my name. He could've decided to get back at me in the worst way possible.

But Donny Phelan had an alibi for the time of the shooting. He'd been at his property with half a dozen witnesses. He could've sent someone else after me, but with Phelan refusing to say another word, we had nothing to go on.

"We've been looking into other leads," Owen said. "Arrests you've made in the past. Confrontations with other citizens. Any reason for someone to bear a grudge. We'll find something. You know how quickly a case can turn around, Keira."

"Right. I know." I picked at the lint on the blanket.

"If you remember anything that could help us, anything else about that night, call me."

"I will."

The electronic lock on my front door whirred as Brynn let herself in, carrying takeout bags. She waved, and I waved back.

"Thanks, Sheriff," I said into the phone. "Talk to you later." Setting my phone on the coffee table, I heaved a sigh.

Brynn set the takeout bags on the kitchen counter. "That was Owen? He had an update for you?" she asked hopefully.

"Yes, but nothing good." I made my way over from the living room. I could get around well enough, though my left arm would still be in a sling for another month as my collarbone healed.

"Phelan is untouchable, it seems," I said. "We have no way to prove he was involved."

"If he was."

"Right. If he was. But it's been three weeks, and there are no other suspects. No leads."

"These things take time."

"Yes, Agent Somerton," I snarked. "I'm aware."

Smirking, Brynn set a takeout container in front of me when I reached the dining table. "I brought enchiladas."

"I take back my grumpiness. You're the best." I grabbed a plastic fork and dug in, while Brynn slid into the chair across from me.

"I live with Cole Bailey, practically the king of grumps. You'd have to get a whole lot more ornery to bother me."

With a smile, I took a bite of my lunch, which was smothered in pork green chili. Brynn really was an amazing friend. She listened to me complain and joked around and didn't look sad when she saw me wince in pain.

Driving was a no-go for me, so Brynn had been acting as my chauffeur whenever Mom couldn't do it. Twice a week, Brynn took me to Hart County General for my physical therapy appointments. The therapist had me doing range-of-motion exercises that made me want to cry, but I pushed through.

I also couldn't lift anything, even with the arm that wasn't in a sling, or reach overhead or behind my back. Certainly no carrying groceries or laundry baskets.

Once a week, I also met with a psychologist. Before I could go back on duty after I healed, she'd have to clear me as mentally fit.

No problem at all, right?

"Need to run any errands?" Brynn stuck her fork into her enchilada.

"Nowhere to go today," I said dully.

"Want to start a movie marathon this afternoon? The Fast and Furious franchise?" Brynn was an action-movie girl, like me, and we were all about the classics.

"I've already watched every thriller movie starring Jason Statham over the last week." One of my late-night standbys, since my sleep patterns had been a mess.

"We can skip the ones Statham was in."

"But I can't watch the Fast movies without the full experience of the narrative arc. That's just wrong."

She snickered. "You're being very difficult."

"I know. Thanks for putting up with me."

"Please. Like that's a hardship."

I poked at the last of my enchiladas. Something else had been on my mind almost constantly lately, and it wasn't old action flicks.

"Um, B?" I asked. "Have you heard if Dean is still in town?"

Just saying his name aloud made my heart skip. I'd been replaying everything I said to him at the hospital. His lack of reaction. But he'd come all the way back to Hart County for me, and my foolish heart really wanted that to mean something.

Brynn set down her fork. Grabbed a paper napkin to dab her mouth. I knew what buying time looked like.

"I think so. People have been talking about him making appearances on Hartley's Main Street. Apparently, he bought a used pickup from someone a couple weeks ago. Which suggests he plans to stay here awhile. There are rumblings he's staying someplace outside of town."

My head shot up. "So, not a hotel? Is he with Owen and Gen?"

"Not as far as I know. River mentioned he's been in touch with Dean, and that it has something to do with you. But that's about it."

I didn't know what to feel about any of this. Dean was still in Hart County three weeks after I'd told him to get out of my hospital room. He'd been talking to River about me.

I tried to find the rage that had overwhelmed me in the hospital. But it was quiet. My anger at Dean had been quiet for days, replaced with confusion and uncertainty.

I'd kept the gardenias, though. Just because they were my favorite, obviously. Not because I'd forgiven him. The vase still sat on my nightstand in my bedroom with the stems bent over and wilted.

I still felt a mess of conflicting emotions about what had happened. Both Dean and the attack. But the flood of anguish that had made me break down in front of Brynn was distant enough that I could get through the day. The rage and sorrow were under glass. Still there, easy to see, but separate from me.

"Is he still blocked in your phone?" Brynn asked.

"Yes." So I had no idea if Dean had tried to contact me again. I wasn't sure I wanted to know.

Ugh, that was a lie. Of course I wanted to know. That was why I was asking about him. At the same time, I wasn't ready to welcome him back.

But I was also obsessing about where he was and what he was doing. Why did I still care so much?

The corner of Brynn's mouth lifted. "I thought that was badass, by the way. You blocking him."

"You don't think I was being childish?" Dean had never done anything awful to me. Just failed to write back to a couple of texts, and then silence had stretched between us, days turning to months and then years. But I could've called or texted again if I'd wanted to. Right?

"Hell no." Brynn pushed away her plate. "He deserved it. If Dean wants back in your life, he has to learn to treat you better. You can't give an inch on that. Make the man sweat."

I felt a smile on my lips matching hers. "I wonder what Cole would say about it."

"Cole can have an opinion when I tell him he's allowed. But don't tell him I said that."

We both laughed, which turned the ever-present ache in my chest and shoulder to a sharp jab. But it was worth it.

I helped round up the takeout containers and throw them away. After Brynn put in a load of laundry for me, we returned to the couch to queue up the first installment of the Fast and Furious franchise. But before hitting play, Brynn turned to me.

"Have you thought more about having a personal security presence here, now that you're alone at night again?"

I squirmed on the couch. "I already said no when Owen and Trace offered before. I don't want a babysitter."

"I get that," Brynn said. "But the people who attacked you could come back. You know this."

I did know it. I'd had this conversation several times already, including with her. It was clear to everyone that those masked men had come here for me specifically. They hadn't robbed the house, and everything about the attack had seemed intentional. Professional, even. Not random.

Most likely, the masks had been meant to hide their identities in case a camera somehow recorded them or a neighbor saw them. But they'd known those demonic faces would terrify me too, so that my final moments were spent in terror.

They'd tried to kill me and didn't succeed. Which meant they might try again.

I grabbed a throw pillow and held it against my stomach. "Owen's been sending deputies on new patrol routes that happen to go down my street." As if that wouldn't be obvious to me. Even when my fellow deputies were using their own cars, I knew every single one of them. Same with the people from other nearby departments who'd been helping out. "You've been staying late almost every night, too. I know it's not just to hang out and have girl time."

She smiled. "Hey, I love me some girl time. I don't get nearly enough of it when I'm home with Cole."

Right, living in that beach house was so rough. "I also think River's done something to my security system. Hacked into it. Wouldn't be surprised if there are cameras watching us right now."

River had come over to overhaul my security setup, supposedly to make it harder for someone to jam the signal again. But he was devious.

Brynn was shaking her head. "I doubt even River would go that far."

"I don't." I tossed the throw pillow onto the floor. "I've got plenty of people looking out for me, whether I want them to or not. That's what I'm saying. But if those assholes come back for more, I'm going to be ready."

"Even though you can't fire a gun?"

"Who says I can't? My right hand works. You think if it's life or death, I'll be worrying about my broken collarbone?"

"I guess that's a fair point." Brynn didn't look happy to hear it, but she didn't sugarcoat things, and neither did I.

My personal handgun was locked up in evidence because I'd fired it in the attack, but I still had my service weapon. I would not give those assholes the chance to hurt me again.

But what about Dean? Not like I was comparing him to

the men who'd broken into my house. Not at all. But he *had* hurt me. Broken my heart.

I didn't know which thing I dreaded more. The thought of him leaving Colorado without another word.

Or the thought that he'd show up at my door.

CHAPTER EIGHT
Keira

BRYNN STARTED up The Fast and the Furious, while I propped myself with pillows on the couch. I fell asleep sometime during the second movie and woke up groggy from my nap, finding a note on the coffee table.

Went to run a few errands and stop by Last Refuge. Text if you need anything. -B

I set the note aside, again feeling grateful that Brynn was being such an incredible friend, and also guilty that I needed to be taken care of. I was going to have to buy Brynn something really special as a thank-you gift.

Brynn wouldn't be able to stay here forever. Cole was still in Mexico, working on some case or other. Brynn was only here for me. I knew she missed her man like crazy. How long until I would have to say goodbye to her?

Frustration burned in my chest. I liked being out on patrol. Hiking up mountains. Helping people. Not just sitting on my couch feeling sorry for myself.

There was a knock on my door, jarring me out of those thoughts.

Immediately my pulse raced. My body jolted with alarm, sending a sharp twinge of pain through my shoulder and chest.

Mom, Stephie, and Brynn all used the electronic code to just walk right in. A knock meant someone else. A neighbor, dropping by to check on me?

Or...

I looked toward the front door as if it might explode inward at any moment, those masked figures materializing in my living room again.

"Get it together," I told myself. "If your attackers come back, they aren't going to knock." Unless it was some kind of trick, of course.

That thought was *not* helping.

Sneaking over to a window, I pulled back the curtain. My heart thumped even harder.

Shit.

Dean stood on my front porch.

Okay. This was fine. I'd been wanting to know what he was up to, and here he was. I wasn't ready to see him again yet. But at the same time, I wasn't going to hide from him like a coward.

I could handle this, right?

Moving slowly to steady my sling, I made my way to the door, my free hand adjusting the scarf covering my hair. I was in yoga pants and an oversized sweatshirt, no makeup. At least I'd showered this morning.

My fingers fumbled with the deadbolt. I took my time, gathering my thoughts, trying to decide what I would say.

But as soon as the door opened and I saw him, face to face, everything sensible disappeared from my head.

"Hello," he said.

"Hi."

Yep. That was my brilliant comeback. *Hi*.

He looked *good*. Why did he have to look so good?

Dean's hair was loose today, all those light-brown strands framing his face and brushing his shoulders. He was dressed casually in loose jeans and a plain gray henley, almost like he wanted to blend into the background. As if that were possible for a man like him.

And he was holding a huge picnic basket. Which was odd, but somehow endearing.

"I hope it's okay I stopped by. Brought you something."

My hip leaned against the doorframe. "What is it?"

He smiled slightly. "Can I come in and show you?"

"Why should I let you?"

"Because I miss you. And I'm sorry."

Not fair. Not fair at all.

I exhaled. His words had knocked the breath out of me. I wished I wasn't still so affected by him, but some things were involuntary.

Maybe I was too soft. But he'd said he was sorry, so didn't I owe it to him to let him explain?

I opened the door wider and stepped aside to let him in.

He crossed the threshold, set the basket down, and paused in the entryway, looking around. "Nice place. I was surprised when I heard you'd moved back to Hartley. I thought you liked Silver Ridge."

"You thought I would stay in exactly the same place after you left?" I asked testily.

"Not what I meant."

"It's better being closer to headquarters. And to Last Refuge." I sounded so defensive.

"Makes sense," he said simply, and for some reason, that annoyed me. Why was he so easygoing sometimes, and impossibly infuriating at others?

"You've changed. Why wouldn't I?"

"Have I changed?" he asked, blue eyes drilling into me.

"Well, there's the hair. For starters."

"Too long?"

"No, I..." My throat felt too dry when I swallowed. "I guess it's all right."

His dimple appeared, and that was way too much for me.

Goosebumps spread over my skin, prickling with sensitivity. I had to get out of this narrow entryway because there wasn't enough space for the both of us here. He was too warm, and he smelled good, and my memories of him were colliding with my present in too many ways.

"Might as well come all the way in." I shut the door. Dean untied his boots. He'd remembered I didn't like shoes tracking dirt inside.

His socks were green with tiny skis on them, and I wondered if they'd been a gift. If some girlfriend had bought them for him.

Ugh, not my business.

I walked into the living room and sat on the couch. Dean carried that ridiculous basket with him, setting it at his feet when he took the chair across from me. He clasped his hands together, elbows on his knees.

"How are you feeling?" he asked.

I remembered what I'd meant to say to him earlier, when I'd opened the door. I was going to demand, *What are you really doing here?*

But when I opened my mouth now, that wasn't what came out. "You missed me? Really?"

"I did. I really did." His eyes were as soft as his voice. Dean never had a problem sounding sincere. Really, I couldn't claim he'd ever lied to me or made me any false promises.

63

"Missed what about me?" I asked, because I was trying to be tough.

"So many things. Our hikes together. Your smile." Both dimples flashed this time. "I miss our friendship. I messed up. I know that. But I'd like to make up for it."

I will stay strong, I repeated to myself. *My heart is made of stone.*

I nodded at the basket. "That thing is the size of a small continent."

He laughed. "Yeah, I drove out to this gift shop in Pine Creek. The woman there upsold me big time. But I told her I had some groveling to do."

He got up, carrying that basket, and went to one knee beside me. Flipping the lid open, he started taking items from inside. "You're stuck at home, so I figured you could use a care package."

There were a couple new pairs of fuzzy socks, one with cats on them, the other with little coffee cups. Cellophane bags of nut clusters from Scarlett's Sweet Shop. A lavender-scented candle and jars of local honey and jam.

A soft throw blanket in my favorite shade of blue. Same blue as his eyes.

"You must've cleaned out the store."

"Trust me, there was plenty left. You should've seen the place. She tried to sell me one of those wooden signs with an inspirational quote painted on it, but I figured you'd kick me out for sure."

An involuntary smile tried to tug at my lips.

"I stopped at the bookstore too." Dean held up a stack of novels with bright covers. "The woman at the shop said these are all brand-new action adventures and really good. I was hoping you hadn't read them yet."

Ugh. I kept trying to keep my emotions distant, even though I was touched by everything he'd picked out. And he kept kneeling there, like that position was symbolic or something.

The stone wall around my heart was already crumbling.

"Thank you," I said finally. "You can get up now."

"You're not going to kick me out again?"

"Bribery works on me, I guess. Also, I've been pretty bored, so you can stay a little while. Until Brynn gets back."

"Gives us time to talk then," he said, rising and taking the chair again.

I had to get myself back on track, because I was about to melt into a pile of goo. I was supposed to be hardened and cynical now, not the same girl I'd been two years ago who got her heart broke.

I called up the pain of him leaving. The ache of realizing that he'd basically ghosted me.

There. That was what I needed. Some righteous anger. But it was more of a fizzle than a bang.

"What happened to your knuckles?" I asked.

His brow knit. "My knuckles?"

"You had them bandaged before."

Dean opened his mouth. Closed it again. He looked down at his hand, flexing his fingers. "I didn't realize you noticed."

The bandage was gone now, just a few red marks left behind on his skin. But yeah. I'd noticed. "I might be just a sheriff's deputy, but I know what it looks like when someone has split knuckles from punching something."

"When Owen called me with the news about what happened to you, I punched my bedroom wall."

I stared at him. "Where?"

"Where what?"

"Where was your bedroom?"

"It was in Switzerland."

A sound huffed out of me. *Switzerland*? "That's where you live now?"

65

"That's where I spent the winter. I was about to move on now that it's spring. Hadn't totally decided where I was going. And then I heard. I was... I'm not sure I've *ever* been that angry. Keira, when I heard what they'd done, I lost it."

"But two years ago you left this country, then acted like you lost my phone number and my email address."

"When have you ever sent me an email, in all the time we've known each other?"

"Not the point!" My voice was rising, and I could feel tears building behind my eyes.

There was the anger I'd been searching for, but it didn't feel good. Not one bit.

"You could've kept in touch. I thought we were close. That our friendship was important to you. Then you just disappear like I meant nothing to you? And don't you dare say those group chats made any difference. They just reminded me you were willing to keep in touch with some people, but not me."

He sighed. "You're not letting me off easy, huh?"

"You're the one who said you're sorry. I don't even know what exactly you're sorry for."

"No, you're right. I've been a really shitty friend." He'd had his gaze on his hands, but now he lifted his eyes to mine, piercing me right in the heart. "I do care about you, Keira. It wasn't about you. It was about me."

"Which is the worst, tired-out excuse known to man."

"Would you believe me if I told you I was punishing myself more than I meant to hurt you? I never wanted to hurt you."

"But you did." I was trying and failing to keep my voice steady. "If you didn't have enough reason to stay in Hart County, fine, but..."

"I left so I wouldn't hurt you even worse."

CHAPTER NINE

Dean

"WHY IN THE world would it have hurt me for us to stay friends?" Keira asked.

Because I wanted more than just your friendship.

I did not say that aloud.

Her pretty brown eyes blinked at me, waiting for an answer. I'd always been a sucker for those eyes. Long lashes, with a tiny mole beside the left one.

Once, I probably could've drawn a map to the freckles on her skin. I'd studied the curve of her lips and the slope of her nose.

I'd imagined kissing each one of those freckles that dotted her shoulders, following them down her spine to the dip of her lower back. Then around and up between her breasts. I'd wondered what shade of rose her nipples were, and how they'd respond if I sucked each one gently into my mouth.

Fuck.

I forced myself to look away, standing up to take a stroll around her living room instead. Pure avoidance. I was great at that.

"You know I was a Marine," I said.

"Yes," she replied softly.

"Once a Marine, always a Marine. That's what they say. But it's not so straightforward for me."

"Okay."

I tried to gather my thoughts, even though they tried to run away from me. It wasn't a simple thing for me to talk about this, especially not with her. Because it was going to change how she saw me.

If Keira knew the real me, would she value my friendship as highly as she seemed to? I'd always wondered. But I owed her the truth.

Still, I gave myself a couple more minutes, using them to take in the sight of her again. She looked so much healthier than she had in the hospital three weeks ago. The smooth sheen had returned to her skin. Her dark eyes were fierce.

The scent of gardenias reached my nose. Like the flowers I'd brought her at the hospital, her favorite, but this was just Keira herself. Shampoo or something. She'd always worn that scent.

She had a pretty scarf wrapped around her hair too. When I first stepped inside, I'd had to resist the urge to reach out and touch the fabric, to adjust how it sat a little askew.

Touching Keira was a privilege I'd lost, even if I'd never been able to touch her the way I wanted.

I hated to see that sling on her arm and the delicate way she carried herself. She had to still be in pain. She looked fragile enough that I could imagine scooping her up and cradling her in my lap.

I stopped and leaned against the wall, still keeping my eyes on her. Reminding myself why I had to do this, had to give her the truth about who I really was.

The short version, anyway. Condensed down to as few sentences as possible.

"I've also told you I was a sniper."

"You mentioned it, sure. But not much else. You never told me much about your past."

I could hear the frustration in her words, the hurt that I'd kept myself distant even during our friendship. She was about to find out why.

"Pretty early after I'd joined up, my superiors recognized a natural talent in me and pulled me out for special training. They nicknamed me Bullseye. Over time, I started carrying out covert missions that were classified at the highest levels." I took out my necklace, feeling the heat of the metal bullet against my palm. "Ghost ops."

"Wow. There's probably a lot more to that story."

More than I ever intended to confess. "I shouldn't be telling you any of this. But it's all true. If my superiors wanted someone dead, I didn't ask questions. I made it happen using any means necessary."

Until that last mission. The one I refused to complete.

My chest tightened as memories surfaced. The weight of the rifle. The stillness before each shot. The way everything narrowed down to a single moment, a single breath.

I closed my fist around the rifle round, my stomach churning.

"Okay." Keira exhaled a long breath. "Okay. I get it."

"When I left that life, I had to leave those parts of me behind too. I swore I'd never allow myself to be that person again."

She nodded slowly. "I figured it was something like that. The reason you won't touch guns anymore. It's hard to think of you as some kind of assassin. You're one of the least violent people I've ever met."

That's my penance, I thought.

I swallowed, and my throat was dry. "I've killed a lot of people, Keira."

"So? You were doing your job. I've killed people too. Well,

only one. Technically. It was in the line of duty, and I was just doing what I had to. I would've killed those men who tried to kill *me* if I'd had the chance." She huffed a laugh without humor. "Honestly, I still would if I could find them."

I stood up again, unable to sit still. "Don't be so sure of that. It's not easy to take a life, especially when you actually have time to think about it. When you have a choice."

When I turned back to look at her, her features had darkened into a scowl. Even worse, her eyes were glossy with indignant tears. "Of course. Because I'm so different from you. You must think I'm pathetic."

"What? No. Of course I don't think that."

Her hand, the one that wasn't in the sling, clenched into a fist and released again, her entire body rigid with tension. "You're exactly like Trace and Owen and the rest of them. I'm just a small-town deputy who'll never be part of your exclusive ex-military club. The Protectors."

"They're my friends, but I've never been a part of that group. Never wanted to be."

"But they wanted *you*, even though you carry spiders outside instead of killing them and can barely even look at a weapon. I've brought at least half a dozen people to Last Refuge who needed protection, but that doesn't matter. I've trained with Brynn and I've taken martial arts classes and put in countless hours at the range, but it's never good enough."

She was trembling. I went to sit next to her and took her hand, trying to get her to relax that fist, but she resisted.

"Leave me alone, Dean."

"I don't think I should." I touched her cheek, brushing away a tear with my thumb.

The contact sent a jolt through me. Two years. Two years since I'd been close enough to touch her, and the longing hit me like a physical ache. Her skin was soft and warm, and I wanted to cup her face in both hands, tell her everything I'd been holding back.

But I couldn't. I had no right.

"Some people are capable of doing terrible things to other human beings," I said quietly. I let my fingers trace along her jawline, the gentlest touch I could manage, before brushing my thumb across her cheekbone. "That's not you, and I'd never want that to be you."

My hand moved to tuck a tiny strand of hair behind her scarf, lingering there.

"I don't want you to have to make that choice," I finished.

She turned her face away, and I dropped my hand, the loss of contact immediately leaving me cold.

"Why are you really back in Hart County?" Keira demanded. "To drop off a care package before you take off again? Just because you feel sorry for me over getting shot?"

"I don't feel sorry for you. I'd never pity you."

She laughed derisively. "Then why? You said you missed me, but I don't believe that's it."

I wanted to tell her. Lay it all out, everything I'd been carrying for years.

That I'd left because staying was torture. That I couldn't stand being near her and pretending friendship was enough when every cell in my body screamed for more. To kiss her and taste her and find out how it felt to call her mine.

I'd thought distance would make it easier, but it had only hollowed me out.

Telling her would be selfish. It would burden her with knowledge she didn't ask for, and she had enough to deal with. So I swallowed the truth and gave her what I could.

"I came because I'm going to find the men who hurt you."

Keira turned back to me, eyes widening. "And then what?"

"I'm going to kill them."

She choked on a cough, pressing a hand to her throat. Stared. "You're serious?" she whispered.

Same thing Owen had asked me, though I certainly hadn't spelled out my intentions to him.

I nodded.

Keira glanced around her living room, taking a few seconds to recover. "And I assume you'll leave again, after this revenge mission of yours is finished? Assuming you don't get arrested or killed in the process."

I nodded again. There was no other option.

Keira scoffed. "The man who won't hurt a spider or swat a fly. You gave up your old life, but you figured it was time for an encore of your assassin days. As a favor to me that I *never asked for*. You know how insane that sounds?"

That was just now occurring to me. "Yeah, I suppose I do."

"There's no point to this conversation. It's ridiculous. I'm tired and aching, so I'm going to lie down, and when I wake up, I want you gone."

With that, she stood up and walked away from me, disappearing down the hall.

CHAPTER TEN

TWO YEARS AGO, I'd left Keira behind of my own accord. Three weeks ago, I'd left her hospital room when she threw me out.

Today? Once again, she'd told me to go. But this time, I couldn't.

I decided to stay.

It would give her the chance to yell at me some more, right? I had the feeling she needed an outlet for some pent-up feelings, and I was happy to bear the brunt. I owed Keira that much, and I was under no illusions about my failings.

I'd been wrong to cut off contact with her. I could see that now. I'd screwed things up every which way. And I'd told her I was sorry for that, but I had to show her I meant it.

My first thought was the chai Keira had always loved so much. I could make a pot of chai on the stove for her. But I'd probably just screw it up. Instead, I decided to help out by emptying the dishwasher, which had just finished its cycle.

That wasn't prying too much into Keira's privacy, right?

How much had changed about her in the last couple years? Of course I hadn't expected her to stay the same. But at the same time, I had an image of her in my mind, something I'd been carrying around with me to every new job, every new place, and it was hard to think that wasn't her anymore.

Could I get to know the woman she was now? Would she let me?

While I was pulling plates from the dishwasher rack and setting them on the counter, the front door opened, and Brynn walked in. We both stopped in surprise, staring at each other.

"Dean. You look better than when we saw you at the hospital. You looked like complete shit then." Brynn carried a couple bags of groceries over and set them on the counter.

"Candid as always, Brynn. I missed that."

"I'm just saying, there's been an improvement. Keep doing what you're doing. Whatever it is."

I couldn't help but smile.

"What *have* you been up to since you came back to Hart County?" Brynn asked. "If I seem nosy, that's because I am."

"I've been catching up on some training."

She'd started unloading the groceries. "I'm intrigued."

I didn't elaborate. Instead, I pitched in to help put things away, grabbing a box of pasta from the counter. "How are you and Cole doing?"

"Cole's as ornery as ever, and I love him for it."

I opened a few cabinets, found a spot for the pasta, and slid it in. I used to know where everything went in Keira's kitchen at her old house, back when we spent so much time together. This was different, unfamiliar, but I was a quick study.

Brynn handed me a can of soup, watching me with an assessing look. "I wasn't all that surprised to see you back in town," she said.

I glanced at her. "No?"

"Nope." She pulled out a bag of coffee. "There's something unresolved between you and Keira. I'm hoping this will be an opportunity for you both to sort that out."

"I thought you'd be more protective and tell me not to hurt her."

"Oh, don't get me wrong. I'm extremely protective of my friends." Brynn put a jar of pasta sauce on a shelf. "I couldn't stand River the first time I met him because I knew he'd hurt my best friend Charlie in the past. Turned out I was completely wrong about him. He's solid. Now, Charlie's his wife and very happy." She met my eyes. "And unlike River when I first met him, I actually think you're a good guy already, Dean. I consider you a friend."

Something loosened in my chest. "That means a lot."

"You're a fellow Marine too. That common ground counts for plenty." She handed me another can, and I put it away with the others.

Brynn's gaze drifted to the dining table, where I'd set the basket. "Did you bring that?"

"Yeah."

"It's massive." She walked over and poked through it, letting out a low whistle. "Damn. You're knee-deep in groveling mode, aren't you?"

"I suppose it's obvious."

"You're none too subtle, Marine. But I approve."

I rubbed the back of my neck. "How's Keira really handling everything? The stress of all this?"

Brynn leaned against the counter, considering. "She's doing the best she can. Which is a hell of a lot. I'm lucky to call her a friend, and I'd be happy to have her guarding my six. Sometimes we're forged through fire, you know?"

And sometimes the fire destroys everything we hold dear, I thought ruefully. But I just nodded.

"It's also convenient that you swore off violence," Brynn added, her tone light but her eyes serious.

"You know about that?"

"Sure. Keira told me."

"Why's that convenient?"

"Because you won't be able to defend yourself too well if you hurt her again and I have to whoop your ass."

I chuckled. "Duly noted."

Before I could respond further, Keira emerged from her bedroom. If anything, she looked more tired than before. If she'd taken a nap, it hadn't been restful.

Keira fixed me with a glare. "You're still here. I told you to leave."

I glanced guiltily at Brynn, who raised her eyebrows.

"You did," I agreed.

"But you stayed."

"Yep. In case you changed your mind and were willing to talk more."

"Also, he emptied the dishwasher," Brynn chimed in. "Just saying."

I thanked her silently.

Keira nodded at Brynn, the two of them exchanging some silent message with their eyes.

Then Keira turned to me. "I had time to think about what you said earlier, and I have some things I want to discuss."

"Okay. That's good. I—"

"Let's go outside." Keira's expression was impossible to read. A contrast to how well I used to know her, when her features gave away so much of her heart. She was closed off now, and I really hoped I wasn't to blame.

Fuck, who was I kidding? I was probably to blame.

While Brynn stayed in the kitchen, Keira and I went through the side door and out into the woodsy area behind her house. I noticed the shiny new lock and repairs to the doorframe, fresh wood replacing what had been ruined during the break-in. The sight of it made my jaw tighten.

There was still snow in the shade between the trees, stubborn patches clinging to the shadows. The beginnings of leaves dotted the aspen branches, that fresh spring green that looked almost unreal.

Keira lost her balance, stumbling on a patch of uneven ground. I swooped in to steady her, my arms going carefully around her, one hand at her waist, the other supporting her good arm.

She fit against me like that night two years ago on the dance floor, like no time had passed at all. I could feel her breath, the warmth of her body, and for a moment I forgot everything else. Forgot why I'd left, forgot the distance I was supposed to maintain. All I knew was that she was here, solid and real in my arms, and I never wanted to let go.

But I had to.

Reluctantly, I loosened my grip, making sure she was steady before stepping back. "You okay?" I asked. "Are you in pain?"

"It's fine." She took a breath, and I watched her carefully, staying close in case she needed me again.

We continued walking slowly, the sunshine warm on our faces, the air smelling of pine and thawing earth.

Finally, she spoke again.

"You told me you came here to find the men who hurt me. To *kill* them. Did you really mean that?"

"Yes. I realize how it sounds, but unless Owen arrests them and has an airtight case, I'll do what I have to."

"Even though nobody asked you. *I* didn't ask you."

"The thing is, Keira, I'm not sure I can live with myself if I don't do something. There's still a chance they could come for you again."

"I know that," she snapped.

"But even if they don't, I can't allow those men to go free after what they did to you. I *won't* allow it."

77

My last few words had come out harsh and guttural. The wind picked up, rustling through the branches above us. The shadows between the trees seemed darker now. The air felt charged, waiting.

Her chest rose and fell. I wasn't sure, but I could've sworn her dark brown eyes had dilated.

Keira came closer to me, holding my gaze. "Then I want in. I'll help you. Whatever you're doing. Investigating. Tracking them down. Punishing them."

"Keira…"

"Don't you dare tell me no. This is my fight. Either you do this with me, or you don't do it at all."

This woman was so much fiercer than the Keira Marsh I'd known two years ago. Could I possibly agree to this? It could put Keira in further danger. If Owen found out, which he probably would, he wouldn't be happy. But he already wasn't happy with me.

The intensity in her eyes said she wasn't backing down. She knew what she was getting into.

"Okay. We'll work together to track down your attackers."

As for the rest…we'd worry about that later.

She blinked at me like she hadn't expected that response, but quickly recovered. "Thank you."

"Will you unblock me in your phone? I might need to message you."

She rolled her eyes. "Did it already this afternoon. But there's also another thing."

"Since you're making demands?"

"They're not demands when I have every right to make them. This is my fight, like I said."

Our fight, I thought silently. When those men had gone after her, they'd made it my fight. I hadn't expected to feel that way. But the moment I'd heard, I'd known it, to the depths of my soul. Even if I had no right to take that responsibility, it was still mine.

"Go ahead, then. What else?"

"You have to swear you won't break your vow. You *will not* kill them. I mean it. If you go back on your promise about not using violence, it won't be because of me."

Well, damn. This would be an issue.

I shifted my weight. A twig snapped under my boot. "If you're in danger again, I'm not just going to stand by."

"Self-defense and defense of others are different, right? The law treats those differently. Loopholes."

I snorted softly. "Loopholes?"

"Close enough." Hell, the little smile on her lips was worth breaking a million vows for. It disappeared too soon. "Please, Dean. Promise that if you break your vow, it won't be on me. I can't take that on my conscience."

And that was completely fair. Whenever I broke that vow, I would make sure she didn't take the blame.

"Done. We have a deal. Now, I need to know every detail you can give me about the night of the attack. Whenever you're up for it," I added, thinking of how tired she looked.

But she nodded. "It's already been over three weeks. I want to nail those sons of bitches, and I can't wait to get started."

CHAPTER ELEVEN

Keira

"SO THIS DONNY PHELAN is our primary suspect." Dean glanced up at me from the paper he'd been studying. "What's your level of certainty?"

We were sitting at my dining table with the contents of a file strewn across the tabletop. A tablet screen showed more photos and information about Phelan.

"Not high," I said. "But this is what we've got."

We'd spent the rest of yesterday and this morning going through everything I remembered about the night of the shooting, including my confrontation with Donny Phelan at the roadhouse. Maybe that had just been a coincidence, but cops rarely believed in coincidences. Usually, when something happened at a certain place and time, there was a reason for it. Motives mattered.

River, our friendly neighborhood hacker, had provided us with both the police report and some preliminary background on Phelan. River had agreed to keep our project to himself and under the radar of the rest of the Protectors, including Sheriff Owen Douglas.

The sheriff was still keeping me at arm's length from the official investigation, which of course I understood. He had to be careful to keep things clean. Honestly, I wouldn't have been surprised if Owen knew River had access to confidential department records. Owen might've even given him that access. But it was all about deniability.

By now, Dean and I had read through the sheriff's report and the transcripts of the interviews with the witnesses at the roadhouse that night: Misty, the server. The bartender. Even Stephie and Vivian, who'd given statements too. There was no security camera footage from the roadhouse, though the dashboard cam on my personal vehicle had recorded my arrival and departure.

Aside from that, we had little to go on. Phelan had an alibi, and unless he talked to the police and gave something away, the official investigation had to look elsewhere for leads.

As for the DNA evidence from the shooter I'd managed to wound, the technicians hadn't found any matches in the national databases. Another dead end unless the sheriff had a suspect to compare samples.

But maybe Dean and I could somehow knock something loose. Unofficially.

As we looked through the papers and scrolled through the info on the tablet, I kept casting glances at Dean. It was impossible not to. Having him this close after so much time apart was distracting.

My chest ached with longing I couldn't quite suppress. I'd tried staying angry at him. Lord knew I'd tried. But my anger was slippery, and underneath it, something softer kept rising to the surface.

Was it just a physical reaction to this man? Something about his pheromones made me weak when he got near.

Brynn had been here when Dean arrived this morning. He'd brought coffee and breakfast for all three of us. To-go containers from Jessi's Diner with omelets and home fries, danishes and fruit. An entire spread.

After breakfast, Brynn had pulled me aside and asked if I was really okay with having Dean around again. I'd explained that we were going to do some investigating of our own into Donny Phelan, though I'd left out the whole *revenge* thing.

Brynn wouldn't necessarily have a problem with vigilante justice. But I hadn't wanted her to worry about me.

"I can handle Dean," I'd said.

"I know you can. Just wanted to make sure you know it too. And that you know that I know."

"I'm confused, B."

She'd laughed. "Me too. You're fine with my leaving you alone with him? Thought I'd get in some gym time today. Trace offered to spar with me. I look forward to handing him his ass."

"Yeah, go. Have fun. I'm good."

Then after Brynn left, Dean and I spent hours going over the files on Phelan. I was wearing the fuzzy socks Dean had given me, and last night, I'd slept with the new throw blanket over me and the lavender candle on my nightstand.

Yesterday, after I'd told Dean to leave, he'd defied me and stayed. I was trying not to read too much into that. Even though all the things he'd said yesterday kept running laps around my head.

I missed you. I care about you.

I'm going to find the men who hurt you.

I'd be damned if I let him treat me like some helpless damsel in distress. But I'd be lying if I said his words didn't affect me.

None of that mattered. Once we were finished with this, whatever *this* really was, he would leave. I was determined not to fall under his spell again. No pining for him, no daydreams. Absolutely none.

I had a zero-tolerance policy for romantic feelings toward this man.

"Alright," Dean said. "Let's go over what we have so far on Phelan. Even on paper, I can't stand this guy."

I huffed a laugh. "Trust me, he's worse in person."

Donny Phelan was thirty-two years old. A self-made media tycoon who'd first gotten attention through posting rage bait on social media. He'd quickly amassed a following of hundreds of thousands, who now tuned in every week for his online show, which he also reposted as a podcast. He ranted about current events and put forth his opinions about how to fix the world. Mainly, it was all about blaming women.

His show was called *The Real Man Formula*.

Phelan had moved here to Hart County in the last year, buying up a massive property, as the roadhouse bartender had told me. Phelan made money from his show via advertising, but the real money was in merch and all the extras he'd started selling. Like personal coaching, supplements, books on his Real Man Formula for finding your inner masculine strength, and online seminars on the same subject.

We'd even listened to a couple episodes of the show. It had sounded like he stuck a variety of sound bites in a blender, mixed them up, and spewed them back out, claiming to have all the secrets *they don't want you to know*. It had a lot to do with the dangers of women working, talking, having independent thought.

A real catch, this guy.

Dean shifted through the papers, looking contemplative. "So, Phelan imagines himself as a Real Man. Whatever that's supposed to mean. But we need to understand how much is marketing and hype, and how much he really believes. What makes him tick. Who he's connected to."

"Right," I said. "The average podcaster doesn't have

trained killers on standby to call up in case he wants to teach an off-duty cop a lesson."

From everything we'd learned, Phelan wasn't the type of guy to forget about being humiliated, especially by a woman. Yes, sending masked gunmen to kill me was an extreme reaction. But I'd heard of worse.

Dean rubbed his jaw. "I need to talk to him. Face to face. As sheriff, Owen can't question Phelan if he's invoked his right to an attorney, but I'm a private citizen. I can ask him any questions I want."

"You mean, *we* need to talk to him."

Dean stared across the table at me. "You're a cop. That means you're barred by the same rules as Owen."

"I don't feel like a cop right now. I'll be acting as a civilian, just like you. We can't force him to talk to us, but if he's willing?" I pointed at the background on Phelan on the tablet screen. "The man is all about saving face. Looking important and authoritative. If I come to him, he won't be able to resist finding out what I have to say. If only so he can tell me I'm wrong."

"Maybe. But you're still healing. If he lays a hand on you…"

"That's not his style. The worst he might do is say nasty things to me. So what? The important thing is, I doubt he'll refuse to talk to us if I'm there. It's one thing to hide behind his lawyer when it comes to the sheriff. But hiding from the little girl who made him look foolish in that parking lot?"

Dean's fist squeezed a pen so hard it creaked.

And then the thin metal snapped, making me jump. He muttered a curse, wiping ink on a spare piece of paper.

"But you have to stay calm," I pointed out.

"I'm always calm."

"I thought you were. When we first met, you had this whole Zen aura going on. All quiet and thoughtful, listening behind the bar to other people's problems. Now, I'm not so sure." He'd always been mysterious to me. But just how much of himself had Dean hidden under the surface?

"I'm a highly controlled person, Keira. I may not be a sniper anymore, but those skills are ingrained."

"Right. Highly controlled. Says the guy who punched a wall and just destroyed an innocent writing instrument."

"It seems I'm sensitive when the subject is your safety."

I raised my eyebrows.

I'd been thinking constantly about what else Dean had confessed yesterday. That he'd been a government assassin. I just couldn't imagine him killing someone. The man I'd gotten to know when he lived in Hart County was so different from that image.

"All right," he said. "I guarantee I will stay calm when we're having our casual, unofficial chat with Donny Phelan."

"Or I could do this by myself. You can be my driver and wait in the car."

"No way in hell," he growled. Not his usual, laid-back voice at all. But the sound of it sent vibrations of pure want along my spine and down between my thighs.

Shit. Dean had always been sexy to me when he was gentle and sweet. Pure catnip. But vengeful Dean?

Dangerous. In every sense of the word.

———

I wanted to drive out that very afternoon. But Dean urged caution. He wanted me to get past my next physical therapy appointment and make sure I was healing well.

We also took the time to do a bit of recon, getting a better sense of the online activities of Mr. Real Man Formula. Filling in more details.

Phelan was one of those people who kept his followers

apprised of his daily activities, which made it pretty easy to predict when he would be home. He always recorded his show on Wednesdays and spent Tuesdays on prep work.

Which meant he'd probably have the time to see us on a Tuesday as well, if we could convince him. We figured surprise was better than trying to make an appointment and giving the guy a chance to claim a scheduling conflict.

On one Tuesday afternoon, Dean pulled up in front of my house in a beat-up truck. I climbed inside. The interior smelled faintly of old leather and motor oil, and the bench seat was patched with duct tape in two places.

"Hey," he said. "I brought drinks in case you need an afternoon pick-me-up. Coffee for me, chai for you." He nodded at the two cups in the center console.

"Thanks. Extra caffeine is probably good." Though I'd already been up early to style my curls. I would be spending all day with Dean. Could you blame a girl for wanting to look good?

Since we'd started working together, this was my first time venturing outside my house with him, and somehow, it felt momentous. Not just because we were going to see Donny Phelan.

"Brynn told me you bought a truck," I said. "People have been talking about you in town. Nobody knows exactly where you're staying or what you've been up to."

I'd also decided not to ask him those questions myself. Because I *wasn't supposed to care*. Yet here I was, bringing it up.

"People do like to talk in small towns," he remarked. Giving nothing away.

Fine. Whatever. After this was over, Dean was going to leave again. That was what I had to keep reminding myself.

The Phelan property was almost an hour's drive away. We took a winding mountain road north, climbing through stands of pine and aspen until the trees thinned and the view opened up. Late spring had painted the landscape in vivid greens. Snowy peaks rose in the distance.

Then we descended into an open, sweeping vista. Rolling hills stretched as far as I could see, divided by split-rail fences and studded with grazing cattle. It was breathtaking. Views like this were the reason I'd never wanted to leave Hart County. Dean was the opposite. Always in search of something newer and better, it seemed.

Today he was quiet, his hands squeezing the steering wheel and making it squeak. Those white knuckles gave away the tension he was feeling.

Funny enough, I wasn't even that nervous about seeing Phelan again.

Maybe it was because I was finally doing something, and that felt good. Or maybe it was just knowing that Dean was going to be there beside me. No matter how frustrated I got with him, I did like being around him. And I certainly needed his help with this makeshift investigation.

"So," I said. "We still haven't settled on our approach."

"I know." The muscle in his jaw twitched. "I really think you should let me take the lead. We go in, and I politely explain to Phelan that we'd like his help. I'll ask if he noticed anything suspicious at the roadhouse that night. Give him cover for engaging with us and playing along, so that he can act like the hero."

"Then we're just inviting him to lie."

"We have to expect he'll lie regardless. But the liar always gives something away. Some hint of the truth. That's what we need. We need certainty that he actually did this. If it *wasn't* him, there's no point in us wasting our time."

The house appeared in the distance. It sat on a rise, commanding a view of the entire valley, with a circular driveway and a huge garage off to one side.

"You and I both have the same strategy," I argued. "We

want to get him to show his hand. But I think making him angry will be the fastest and most effective approach. You just don't want him to say mean things to me."

"Of course I don't. You made me promise to stay calm. If he's mean to you, it'll be much harder."

"And who exactly are you supposed to be, anyway? In this scenario where we show up and you're all buddy-buddy with him at first."

"Your friend. Exactly what I *am*."

My chaperone, more like, I thought.

"Are we friends again?" I asked. "Have I given my consent to that?"

Dean chuckled. "I'll keep working on earning back your friendship."

I kept my eyes on the view outside the window. "We can compromise."

"Frenemies?"

I snorted a laugh. "No. I mean about the approach to Phelan. We'll start your way. Playing nice, asking for his help. But if that doesn't work, I'll try *my* way. Provoking him. And you will be the calm, reasonable Dean you usually are."

Because there was no way Phelan would actually lay a finger on me today. He didn't seem like the type to get his hands dirty, certainly not in front of an audience.

Dean smiled, and there was a new edge to it. Something harder and far more intimidating. A brief glimpse beneath his surface.

"Alright. The good cop/bad cop routine. Sounds like a plan."

CHAPTER TWELVE

Dean

WE REACHED the end of the driveway, and I slowed as we approached the circular paved area in front of the house. A covered parking lot stretched along one side, and I pulled my beat-up truck in next to a row of pickups and SUVs.

We had a plan. But I wondered if Keira knew the old military adage: No plan survives contact with the enemy. If she didn't, I wasn't going to bring it up.

I would be ready for anything. My top priority was Keira. Second, getting inside Donny Phelan's head. On methods, I was flexible.

As we got out, Keira's gaze lingered on the vehicles. She stopped beside a black Ford Explorer, her expression hardening.

"That one," she said quietly. "Matches the description of the getaway car the shooters used. It's spotless. Like it was recently detailed."

I studied it, then shook my head. "Would've been pretty stupid to just park it here, don't you think?"

"True." She exhaled slowly. "Then again, Owen hasn't been able to get a search warrant, so maybe Phelan really *is* that overconfident."

Which meant I had to be on my guard to ensure Keira's safety here. I kept my eyes on the vehicles as we walked toward the house, cataloging details.

Beyond the parking area sat a massive garage, large enough to hold a boat or RV the size of a city bus. All the garage doors were closed, revealing nothing of what lay inside. Yet these vehicles were parked outdoors.

The front entrance of the house loomed before us, all wrought iron and dark wood. Oversized lanterns flanked a door that looked like it belonged on a medieval fortress.

I was surprised nobody had stopped us yet. With this guy's media empire and massive ego, I'd almost expected security checkpoints and guards with clipboards.

I pressed the doorbell and heard it echo inside. Keira glanced up, tilting her head. "Camera." She nodded toward a small black dome mounted above the door.

I gave a slight nod back. We were already being watched.

A moment later, a female voice crackled through an intercom speaker. "Can I help you?"

"We're here to see Mr. Phelan," I said.

"I don't believe you have an appointment."

"It's a casual visit."

Keira stepped forward, her voice taking on a lighter tone. "I met Mr. Phelan about a month ago. He might remember me. I'm Keira Marsh. Um, Deputy Marsh, but I'm on leave. We'd be very grateful if he would give us a few minutes of his time."

I hid a smirk, hoping the camera hadn't picked up her eye-roll.

A few seconds later, the front door opened. A middle-aged woman in a crisp skirt suit appeared in the doorway.

"You can come in." Her expression was professionally blank, her posture rigid. "I'm Mr. Phelan's assistant, Natasha."

"I'm Keira. And this is Dean."

Natasha stepped aside to let us in. The interior of the house opened up into a dramatic vaulted entrance that made me tilt my head back to take it all in. Chandeliers made of antlers hung from the ceiling, not unlike the ski resort lodge in Silver Ridge.

Natasha led us into a sitting room. Deep burgundy leather couches sat arranged around a coffee table made from what looked like a single slab of wood, polished to a mirror shine.

"Mr. Phelan will be with you shortly," Natasha said, then disappeared.

Keira and I looked at one another. Communicating silently. There were no cameras in sight here, but it was wise to be careful.

Fancy place, Keira's eyes seemed to say. *No expense spared. What a showoff.*

Be careful, I tried to convey back. *Don't underestimate him.*

She smiled.

Less than a minute later, Donny Phelan made his entrance. He strode into the room in a light blue cowboy hat, a diamond stud winking from his ear. His jeans looked fresh from a high-end boutique, paired with a thin t-shirt with the word *Armani* subtly embossed across the chest. If you could call that subtle.

"Mr. Phelan. Thank you for seeing us." Keira's tone was polite, even apologetic. I was impressed with her acting skills. "Wasn't sure if you would remember me, but—"

"Deputy Marsh. Of course I remember you."

I studied him as he approached, wondering if this was the man who'd ordered the attack on Keira.

"I heard about what happened to you. Just terrible." Phelan looked at her arm in its sling, and then his gaze continued to slide over her in a way that had me tensing. "But I suppose you make a lot of enemies as a police officer.

91

It's a risky job." He paused, his smile sharpening. "A lot for a young woman like you to handle."

Keira blinked and glanced away. She was being careful, like she was supposed to, but now anger flared hot in *my* chest.

Fuck this guy for saying shit like that to her.

"We're sorry to interrupt your day and come unannounced," I said.

Phelan focused on me. "And you are? I didn't catch your name."

"Dean Reynolds." I stepped forward, holding out my hand. Then, on impulse, I added, "I'm a fan of your show."

Phelan's entire demeanor changed, his chest puffing up. "You don't say. Always a pleasure to meet a fan."

We shook hands, and I forced myself to grin, hoping my face wasn't revealing too much. Such as, the way I wanted to plant my fist right in the center of his smug expression.

Stick with the plan.

"We were hoping for your help," I said. "I understand you were at the same bar and restaurant as Keira on the night she was injured. We were hoping you might've seen something, anything, that could point us toward a lead."

Phelan tilted his head. "Sounds like the sheriff hasn't made any progress."

Keira shifted beside me. "You *did* refuse to answer Sheriff Douglas's questions."

Phelan narrowed his eyes at her. "On the advice of my lawyers. That's all."

"Then I'm sure you wouldn't mind talking to us," she countered. "Unofficially."

I put a hand on her arm. "Keira and I are here as civilians. Just fellow residents of Hart County, asking for your assistance."

"Dean, what's your connection to Miss Marsh, exactly?"

His gaze bounced between us. "Are you here for moral support? She and I had some strong words the night in question, so I wouldn't blame her for being nervous about coming here alone and begging for my assistance." He smirked.

Keira made a low sound in her throat. "Begging? I'd be happy to show you—"

"I'm her boyfriend," I interrupted.

Keira started coughing.

I slid my arm fully around her shoulders. "You okay, babe?"

"Oh yeah," she wheezed. "Just great. *Babe.*" Her glare told me I was going to pay for this later.

But too bad. I wanted to leave Phelan with no doubt about my loyalties, even if I was pretending to kiss up to him.

As far as he was concerned, Keira was *mine.*

"So your boyfriend's a fan," Phelan said to Keira, sounding more amused than suspicious. "What a coincidence."

"Sure is."

"I suppose you didn't know who I was when we first met." Phelan held up his hands in mock modesty. "But we all make mistakes. Let's sit down. Natasha!" He raised his voice. "Get our guests something to drink. Anyone hungry? My chef baked up some buttermilk biscuits for lunch. There are leftovers."

"That sounds downright homey," Keira said sweetly, "but I'll pass. What about you, *babe?*"

Her eyes warned me that if I took one of those biscuits, she might make me choke on it.

"Just some iced tea," I said.

We sat on one of the ornate couches. The leather creaked under our weight. Phelan perched across from us in a high-backed chair, settling into it like he was sitting on a throne.

Natasha reappeared with a crystal pitcher of iced tea and poured three glasses with exaggerated care.

"Seems like you're creating a real empire," I said. "Hart County's lucky to have you."

Keira snorted, then covered it by taking a gulp of tea.

Phelan either didn't notice or chose to ignore her. "Thank you. I needed space, and this property has it. The house is coming along. The original structure had good bones, but it needed vision, you know? I'm having tennis courts built outside." He gestured vaguely toward the windows. "And I'm expanding the wine cellar. You have to think big if you want to achieve big things."

I nodded along. "That's what you always say on your show."

"Exactly right." He leaned back, warming to his topic. "I'm helping my followers reclaim their power. It's about taking back what's rightfully ours from the domineering women who want to control us. And you know what? I really love helping people. That's why I do this. The money's great, don't get me wrong, but it's about the mission."

Keira started coughing again, her shoulders shaking.

"You *sure* you're okay?" I asked, patting her back.

She nodded, eyes watering. "Actually, I need to use the bathroom. If you don't mind, Mr. Phelan."

Oh hell, what was she up to?

He waved a hand. "Natasha will show you where it is."

I caught her eye as she followed Natasha out of the room. But Keira's expression was neutral.

Once they were gone, Phelan leaned forward slightly. "I wish I could do something to help Deputy Marsh with her situation. But I didn't see anything suspicious that night at the bar."

"You're sure?"

"Completely." He paused, his expression turning knowing. "She's got a fiery temper, doesn't she? Quite a mouth on her. Probably pisses people off wherever she goes."

"She does have a mind of her own."

"It can be a problem. Women like that need strong men to keep them in line."

I shrugged, forcing a rough grin. "I've been working on it. Trying to keep her safe." That much was true.

I stood and strolled around the living room, examining the expensive objects scattered on various tables and shelves.

Phelan leaned back in his seat, relaxing. "Maybe your Keira shouldn't have poked her nose into business that wasn't hers. But that's a lesson she needed to learn."

I stopped, turning my head slowly to look at him. My body had gone rigid.

"A lesson, huh? But those men who invaded her home and hurt her, they had nothing to do with you, right?"

Phelan laughed. "My goodness, not at all. Of course not. I didn't—I just meant my conversation with her that night. I warned her to be more careful."

"For her safety?"

"Exactly. A woman like her shouldn't be a cop. She's small and fragile. Too pretty for her own good. She shouldn't have been out by herself at all. She should've had you with her. No offense."

It pissed me off that I *almost* agreed with him, at least in part. If only I'd been there that night. But not remotely for the reasons he was suggesting. Keira was a great cop, and I would never hold her back, even if we sometimes disagreed. She knew how to do her job.

The thugs who invaded her home took her by surprise. That could happen to anyone. Man or woman, cop or civilian.

But I smiled and nodded. "Right. Like you talk about on your show. Men need to be in charge of what's theirs. Never show weakness."

"Exactly." He beamed at me like I was his star pupil. "Now, how about you? What industry are you in, Dean?"

I stuck my hands in my pockets, keeping my posture casual. "I'm a ski and snowboard instructor in the winters. Off-season, I'm a bartender."

"But I suspect you're eager to get more out of life. Take more for yourself than just working by the hour for someone else."

"You read my mind."

"If you're looking for a new opportunity, I need salespeople."

I stroked my jaw, feigning curiosity. This could be an opportunity to learn more about the guy. Get close to him. If I could stand engaging with him long enough to stay undercover.

"Yeah? I might be interested."

"Natasha can give you an application." Phelan sat forward. "But here's some free advice. The key is taking a stand at home first. Make sure Keira knows her place." He paused, his gaze turning appraising. "Not that I fault you for being hoodwinked by a girl like Keira Marsh. That sexy little body? Her face? It would be hard for any man to resist."

Yeah, no. Fuck this guy, and fuck his job opportunities. I wouldn't make it working undercover for this fool.

Fury ignited in my chest, hot and immediate, and I barely managed to keep it from showing on my face. My hands stayed in my pockets as I stepped closer to him casually, like I was just shifting my weight.

I'd told Keira she shouldn't provoke him. But she wasn't here right now, and I had no problem doing it myself.

My plan had been to stay calm, but hey. *Plans changed*.

"But you've got to keep her in hand," Phelan continued, oblivious. "Show her who's boss at home. Who's king of the castle, the big cock in the henhouse. You catch my drift?"

96

He laughed. I nodded, grinning.

And that's when I lunged.

The first two fingers of my right hand jammed hard into his nostrils and squeezed, while my other hand clamped over his mouth to cover his scream. His eyes went wide as saucers, and his cowboy hat tumbled off his head and down behind the chair. His hair was limp underneath.

"I think I've heard enough," I said quietly. "Now, it's time for you to listen. You were talking about the importance of learning lessons. I've got one for you."

Phelan started to struggle. I controlled him by squeezing my fingers tighter inside his nose. Tears streamed down his face. I leaned closer, keeping one ear out for Natasha and Keira, but there was no sound from the hall.

"You see, I wasn't always a ski instructor. I used to kill people for a living. I was very, very good at it. My skills are slightly rusty, but I'm training up again, Donny. Just for you. Because you really are an inspiration."

His face was turning red. His breath wheezed through his nostrils as he inhaled around my squeezing fingers.

Was I already breaking my vow? Some would call this violence. And it felt way too good. Making him suffer a little after how he'd treated Keira.

"I know you threatened Deputy Marsh the same night she was shot. I know all about it, Donny. How you were harassing a server. Making a nuisance of yourself. How you told Keira she'd made a big mistake, because you *know people. Important people.*'"

Phelan shook his head frantically, his eyes bugging out even wider.

I leaned in close so I could murmur in his ear. Just to be sure I got my point across. After all, the key was taking a stand. Right? Making sure this asshole knew his place.

"If I find out you sent those men to hurt her, I'll destroy

you. I will end you. I'll go Jack and the Beanstalk on your ass and grind your bones down to bake them into bread. Same thing if you ever bother her again. Am I getting through to you, Donny? Do you catch my drift?"

I lifted my hand from his mouth just enough for him to rasp, "Yes!"

"Do you feel like a Real Man now? Like a king in his castle?"

Donny shook his head slightly, leaking more tears from the pain in his nose.

"Good. I'm glad you're catching on. The thing is, real men, *good* men, take care of their families and friends. They're not selfish. They choose forgiveness over cruelty. But guess what, Donny?"

I leaned in one last time.

"I'm not a good man. I'll break you apart, piece by piece, until there's *nothing fucking left.*"

CHAPTER THIRTEEN

Keira

I WALKED down the hallway with Natasha just ahead of me. A thick rug muffled our footsteps, swallowing every sound in the oversized corridor.

Ugh, I'd been suffocating in that room listening to Phelan speak. Thank goodness I was out of there.

I was far more curious about his assistant.

"So, do you like working for Mr. Phelan?" I asked Natasha, keeping my tone conversational.

"It's an excellent position." She walked with brisk, efficient footsteps, zero inflection in her voice.

"Are you from Hart County?" I tried again.

No answer.

I walked a little faster to pull up beside her. "Are you a fan of The Real Man Formula? I'm curious about your perspective. Since you're a woman and all."

"I'm focused on the logistics of Mr. Phelan's business. He has other people who consult with him on content."

Okay, then. She wasn't going to give me any dirt on her employer. Not that I'd really expected it.

There had to be something else I could learn about Phelan in this house. The place was gigantic.

A branch appeared in the hallway to our left, and I started to follow it, curious about what lay down that direction. I thought I heard voices, low and muffled, but couldn't make out any words.

Natasha's hand landed on my shoulder. "Not that way," she said sharply.

Oh, sure. That wasn't suspicious at all.

She steered me onward. A few seconds later, we stopped at a door halfway down the main corridor. "Here's the restroom. Go ahead."

I tried to look embarrassed. Not that hard, actually. I had enough practice with discomfort in awkward situations. "Actually, do you have any tampons? I think my period just started." I paused, then couldn't help adding, "If Mr. Phelan even allows things like feminine products in his Real Man mansion."

I smiled sweetly.

She looked unamused, but dipped her chin with a nod. "I have some in my purse, but it's in my office."

"Great." I pointed a thumb at the bathroom door. "I'll get started. Might take me a while. You know how it is." My face scrunched up.

She gave me a pinched look, but turned on her heels and strode back the way we'd come, her footsteps quick and purposeful.

Well. That hadn't been so hard.

I went into the bathroom and closed the door, just in case she was going to look back and check. Then I stood perfectly still and listened.

After about ten seconds, long enough for her to turn the corner, I opened the door and peeked out again. No sign of her.

I hurried down the hall, this time taking the turn that Natasha had pulled me away from. I wanted to know what else Mr. Phelan was up to here, because it didn't seem like we were going to get anything useful out of him through polite conversation.

It had been almost impossible to sit there and not start ranting about the obnoxious things the man was saying. *It's a risky job. A lot for a young woman like you to handle.*

Trust me, buddy, I was a lot to handle too. Just try me.

My mom had been scared to death when I became a cop. But not because she doubted me. She'd always supported me. Mom had stayed home when I was growing up, and she was the heart and soul of our family. For years, she'd struggled to have another child, which was why Stephie was so much younger than me. Then Dad had passed away, and it was just the three of us. Mom went back to work while always teaching us we could do anything we set our minds to. We could have any life we wanted.

Mom rarely raised her voice, and she probably couldn't bench press a bag of groceries. Much less a heavy bar at the gym. But I was sure my mom had more strength of character than a fool like Donny Phelan could ever comprehend.

Whatever. Dean could stay there and play nice with the man and hope to pick up a few measly crumbs of information.

Meanwhile, I was going to look around and actually try to find something we could use. And if Dean didn't like that? Well, he just had to deal with it.

One domineering woman here, folks, present and accounted for.

I passed an open doorway and saw a person moving cardboard boxes around. The guy glanced up, but I kept moving, not giving him time to ask questions.

It had been a few minutes now, and Natasha would be heading back any moment.

I picked up my pace, hoping to find something, *anything*, before my window of time closed.

Maybe the men in the demonic masks had worked for Phelan. Maybe they were here *right now*. That thought sent a shudder of fear through me. But I kept going.

Then I heard voices again, like I'd noticed earlier when I was with Natasha. My footsteps slowed as I neared the next doorway. The door was partly open, and I could see a man sitting in a chair inside, his large hand resting on a table. He wasn't looking my way.

"Ryan is pissed that the shipment's delayed," the man said.

The guy had a sharp nose and a heavy, muscular build. I'd never seen him before.

"Yeah, but what else is new," someone replied from deeper in the room. "Not like it's our fault. He's the one who—"

"Keep your mouth shut," snapped the man I could see. "It's our job to make sure things get back on track. No excuses."

I noticed the large ring he was wearing as he tapped his thick fingers against the desktop. Like a class ring, with a large, flat blue stone in the middle. Something about it nagged at me.

I'd seen a ring like that before somewhere.

Taking my phone out, I carefully took a few pictures, zooming in on the guy's hand and the distinctive ring.

"What are you doing over here?"

I jumped and spun around. Natasha was standing right behind me.

I quickly turned off my phone screen and stuck it in my pocket. "Sorry. I finished up in the bathroom. Didn't actually need a tampon. False alarm. I was heading back to that sitting room we were in, and I guess I got lost."

Natasha didn't look like she believed me for a second.

Then there were heavy steps behind me, and the man wearing the ring was suddenly there, scowling at me. "What the hell is this?"

"She's no one," Natasha said quickly. "We were just heading back to Mr. Phelan." She hustled me as quickly as possible down the hall.

When I looked over my shoulder, the sharp-nosed guy was staring at me.

"I don't know what you think you're up to," Natasha murmured quietly, her voice tight with warning, "but you need to stop. Mind your own business."

Yeah, people kept telling me that. I wasn't very good at it.

"Does that man work for Mr. Phelan? What kind of shipment was he talking about?"

Natasha stopped. But her expression wasn't blank anymore.

The woman looked *frightened*.

"Mr. Phelan will be wanting to get back to work," she said, her voice barely above a whisper. "I think it's about time that you leave."

———

As we neared the sitting room where we'd been talking before, Dean was already waiting outside in the hallway. There was no sign of Donny Phelan anywhere.

Dean's face was flushed. "We're finished," he said evenly, his jaw set. "Let's go."

"But—"

"No arguments, Keira."

Natasha didn't say another word, just walked us to the front door and closed it firmly behind us as we left.

When we were sitting in Dean's old truck, I turned my

glare on him. "I didn't get to say my piece to Phelan. I was going to tell him exactly what I thought about him."

Dean started up the engine. "I already did it for you. Trust me, he got the message."

"What does that mean?"

"Means he knows what will happen if he doesn't leave you alone."

"*What*? What did you do?"

"I failed to remain calm."

My jaw dropped.

Then I started to giggle.

"You think that's funny?" Dean asked.

"Maybe I'm delirious." Which only made me laugh more. So much that my chest and shoulder ached, but that still didn't stop me. I was just relieved.

And more than a little pleased that Phelan had experienced some payback after all.

"What exactly did you do to him?" I asked.

"Nothing that would leave much of a mark. I'm sure it hurt like hell, but I think we reached an understanding. He nearly peed his pants." Dean was smiling, glancing over at me as he drove us down the long driveway away from the house. "What were you doing when you claimed to be going to the bathroom?"

"Me?" I asked innocently. "I just needed to tinkle. And check my mascara in the mirror."

He side-eyed me.

"Okay, I was doing some recon. Since it didn't seem like we were getting anything useful out of Phelan."

"You could've gotten hurt, Keira."

"But I didn't. And I learned something." I told him about the brief conversation I'd overheard. "The guy mentioned someone named Ryan. Like this Ryan is in charge. Maybe the late shipment is just supplements or coaching workbooks, but I don't think so. There's something weird going on there."

Dean tapped his fingers against the steering wheel. "Could be. Did they see you? These men you heard talking?"

"Well, yes. But I noticed an odd ring one guy was wearing. I took a picture of it. I'm sure I've seen something like it before." I held up my phone, showing him the picture on my screen. Dean glanced quickly at it.

"You've seen it before? Where?"

"That's what I'm trying to remember. It was recent." The memory itched at the back of my mind, so close I could almost grasp it. "It could've been—"

As I was thinking, my eyes wandered over to the right-side mirror on Dean's truck.

Huh. Another vehicle was on the highway a good distance behind us. It hadn't been there before, but now it seemed to be keeping our exact speed.

It was black and boxy. Like the SUVs that had been parked outside Phelan's home.

"Dean. I could be wrong, but we might have a tail."

He cursed, checking the rearview. "Maybe they're just making sure we leave the area." With his eyes on the rearview mirror, Dean accelerated. The SUV matched our speed.

Then started to gain on us.

"Shit. It's possible we pissed them off more than we realized. I'll get rid of them. Hold on. This might get bumpy."

"Okay." I did my best to brace myself as we raced out of the valley, and the road started to curve.

The SUV kept gaining on us, closing the distance with alarming speed.

Just a few minutes ago, poking that hornet's nest had seemed like a good idea.

The highway climbed, the road narrowing as it wound

through towering pines. Around the next curve, a cliffside appeared to the right of the guardrails, and the ground below dropped away into a ravine that seemed to go down forever.

"They're getting closer," I said, gripping the door handle.

Dean's knuckles were white on the steering wheel. "I see them."

The dark SUV surged, its engine roaring. It pulled up alongside us, and that's when I saw him.

The driver was wearing a demonic mask.

"Dean," I breathed, my voice tight with fear. "That's him. That's one of them."

"Hold on."

The SUV swerved toward us, trying to force us off the road and over the guardrails. Dean's truck tires screamed as we skidded closer to the edge of the ravine. Gravel sprayed out from under our wheels.

"Too close," I gasped.

Dean yanked us back onto the pavement just as the SUV came at us again. This time Dean was ready. He accelerated hard, pulling ahead just enough to avoid the impact.

The road curved sharply to the left, hugging the mountainside. Dean took it fast, the truck leaning as we careened around the bend. The SUV followed, staying right on our tail.

"There's a straightaway coming up," Dean said, his eyes scanning the road ahead. "When we hit it, I'm going to brake hard. Be ready."

The curve opened up into a straight stretch of highway, bordered on both sides by thick forest. Dean floored it, and for a moment we pulled ahead. The engine whined in protest, but the old truck had more in it than I'd thought.

The SUV accelerated too, gaining ground.

I braced myself. Then Dean slammed on the brakes and twisted the wheel.

I lurched forward against my seatbelt, my healing collarbone screaming in pain. The SUV shot past us. For a split second, I saw the masked face turn toward us.

Then the driver over-corrected. Swerved. The SUV left the road, and its right front bumper smashed into a tree with a sickening crunch of metal and breaking glass.

Smoke began rising from the crumpled hood.

"Should we—" I started.

"No," Dean said firmly. "We're getting out of here."

He accelerated, and we raced ahead, leaving the wreck behind us.

CHAPTER FOURTEEN

Dean

I KEPT DRIVING until I was sure no one else was following us, then pulled off where I had several miles of view.

Keira was still breathing hard in the passenger seat, her right hand gripping the dashboard while her left was cradled against her in its sling. Her expression was dazed.

I pushed my hair back from my face and unbuckled my seatbelt. "You okay?"

"Yeah." She took a deep breath, clearly trying to steady herself. "Yeah, I'm okay. That was some driving."

"Lots of practice on icy mountain roads. Are you sure you're not hurt? You didn't hit your head? Let me see your eyes."

She narrowed her dark brown eyes at me. "Dean, I'm fine."

Everything inside me had gone quiet while I was trying to keep us alive and get us out of there, but now emotion started to creep back. Anger that blurred my vision. Fear that something could've happened to her.

I had to touch her.

I reached out, smoothing my hand down her cheek. As if I

were making sure I hadn't truly lost her this time. And to my surprise, Keira reached back. She grabbed my arm and tucked her face against my shoulder. She was shaking.

My lips pressed to her hairline, and I inhaled the scent of gardenias.

Longing made my stomach swoop.

"The mask on the driver?" I asked, barely keeping my voice steady. "Was it definitely the same?"

"Yes," she whispered.

"We should probably call this in to the sheriff's department. Second time they've tried to go after you. They could've killed you."

She lifted her head. "Killed *us*. But we already know these people are careful. Owen's investigation hasn't gone anywhere, and it seems like Phelan is basically untouchable. By the time the sheriff gets a car to that crash site, the driver and any trace of evidence will be gone. No. We're doing this ourselves. We wanted to provoke a reaction, and we did."

"But are you still up for this?" I asked.

She scoffed. "Of course I am. Are you? Or are you going to drop me off at home and make the decision for both of us? Take off and leave me behind again?"

I didn't like the thought of continuing to put her in danger. But we'd both known the risks.

"No."

Slowly, I forced myself to sit back and stop touching her. Stop breathing her in.

I certainly wasn't going to leave her unprotected. It was my fault she even thought I was capable of that.

"I'm not taking you home at all."

"Where are we going?"

"Someplace we can regroup and figure out how to respond. Where they won't find us. Just for tonight."

"For tonight?"

"That's what I was thinking."

"A hotel?" Keira glanced at me from the corner of her eye.

Sharing a hotel room with her... That really wasn't an image I needed in my head.

"No, it's somewhere else."

I buckled my seatbelt again and put the car in gear.

We pulled up to the ranch house about forty-five minutes later. The sun was sinking, painting the sky in shades of amber and red. Long shadows stretched across the grass from the mountains in the distance. She'd been quiet on the drive. Pensive.

Keira finally asked, "Where are we?"

Fuck me. Now I had to explain.

"A property I own."

"A...wait, what?"

"A property."

"Yeah, I know what *property* means. But that's a house." She pointed. "That's yours?"

I nodded.

"You own a house," she said evenly.

"Yes, Keira."

"This is *your house*. Here in Hart County."

"Now we're starting to sound like an old-timey comedy routine. Who's on first..."

She glared, showing my joke was not appreciated. Or funny.

"It was purchased under an LLC," I said, "so my personal name isn't on it. It's safe."

"I'm not focused on the safety part. It's..." She shook her head. "This is where you've been staying since you arrived in Colorado?"

"It is."

With a huff, she pushed the truck door open and got out.

My head dropped back against the seat. So far, this was not going well.

I brushed loose strands of hair from my face. The last thing I'd expected this morning was to be bringing Keira to this place. Since returning to Colorado, I'd already revealed secrets about myself that I'd never imagined confessing to her.

Yet somehow, showing her this house meant...*more*. And she was already pissed about it. That was clear. But I knew we'd be safe here, which was what counted.

Grow a pair, Reynolds, I told myself. *Get out there and face her*.

How was this scarier than fleeing for our lives while some maniac tried to force us to crash into a ravine?

Taking a deep breath, I jumped out and closed the door of the truck. When I caught up with her, she was glancing around hesitantly at the porch.

"The wooden trim needs paint," I said, "and I haven't gotten around to fixing all the porch steps. It's on the list."

Keira just kept staring, ignoring my lame attempt at focusing on the details of the place instead of, you know, the fact that it existed.

"I had no idea you owned anything that couldn't fit in a couple of suitcases, and it turns out you own an entire house. And the land it's sitting on, I guess."

"Fifty acres."

Her eyes widened. "Fifty? Wow. You didn't hold back, huh?"

"The price was good."

"Are you sure? You're not going to tell me next that you're a billionaire or something?"

"Afraid not."

"Who even *are* you?"

I sighed. "I'm me, Keira. Same guy I've always been.

You're just seeing the messy parts I didn't used to let you see."

She blinked a few times.

Then she waved her right hand. "Well, go ahead and show me around your top-secret hideaway, Mr. Assassin."

I chuckled. "You don't want to sit down for a while? We were just in a car chase. That would rattle anyone, and you're already injured."

"Show me the damn house, Dean," she said through gritted teeth. "Or I'll show it to myself."

———

The house was two stories, not counting the cellar storage area. One bedroom on the ground floor, two more on the second.

I hadn't touched the upper-floor bedrooms yet, so it didn't take us long to walk through. Keira peered into the rooms from the hallway. The bathroom up here was functional but nothing pretty.

Downstairs, tools and tarps were lying around, paint cans stacked in corners. It had some nice details though, if you looked past the mess. High ceilings with old crown molding. Wide windows that would let in good light once I replaced the cracked panes. Hardwood floors that would be beautiful once I finished sanding and staining them.

If I managed to get around to it.

Paying someone else to do all the work would be expensive, and while I had plenty of money saved up, I'd always been indecisive when it came to this property. Deciding what the hell to do with it. Trying to understand why I'd bought it in the first place.

I wondered what Keira thought of it. What she saw.

"I've got internet. I can give you the wi-fi password, since cell coverage is shit. Did you want to let your mom and Brynn know where you are?"

"Not now, Dean," she muttered. "I want to see the rest."

The kitchen was next. The electrical and gas were running, and I had appliances now. Along with some dishes and cooking stuff, which I'd picked up from a thrift store on Hartley's Main Street.

I also pointed out the downstairs bathroom, mentioning I had a first aid kit and pain meds if she needed them after being jostled around.

The sun was nearly down now, and the interior of the house was fading into dimness. I switched on a couple lights.

"That's everything?" she asked quietly.

"There's, uh, a third bedroom. It's down this way."

When I reached the end of the hall, I went inside to switch on a lamp. Then stepped out again and let Keira go inside.

I leaned against the doorframe. Waiting. Fucking holding my breath.

This room was nothing like the rest of the house. It was finished and ready to live in. The lamp cast a warm yellow glow over the blue-painted walls and the simple, modern curtains. The bed was a queen, dressed in white sheets and a navy comforter. Two mismatched nightstands flanked it.

A worn leather chair sat in the corner by the window, and an armoire of plain dark wood stood against the far wall since the house was old and there was no original closet in here.

It wasn't fancy. The only real decoration was an art print I'd picked up already framed. But the place looked nice. At least, I thought so.

I hoped she thought so too.

Keira stopped by the window, which had the curtains pulled closed. She stayed there with her back to me, even though there was nothing to look at. Was she hiding her face from me?

I stuck my hands in my pockets. "What do you think?"

She didn't turn around. "Hardly matters what I think."

"Sure it does. Matters to me."

"Yet you didn't even bother to tell me about it," she said hoarsely. "The only reason you brought me here is somebody tried to kill us today."

This was true. Completely true.

Maybe I'd had a vague idea of bringing her here at some point, but not yet. The state of it right now made me feel exposed, like parts of me were laid bare that I wasn't ready for.

So much had happened today, and *this* was still the thing that was throwing me. Really?

Keira turned around. "How long have you owned it?"

"Bought it about three years ago. While I was living here before."

"I don't get it, Dean. But I guess I shouldn't be surprised. There's so much about you I still don't know. Makes me wonder who you really are."

"Sometimes I wonder that too."

"And that's supposed to make me feel better?" Keira shook her head. "When you left, you said you'd stayed too long. That you're not the type of person who sticks around. But you bought a *house*? How the hell does that make sense?"

I scratched my head. If only I could explain it, even to myself. "It was supposed to be an investment. I didn't think I'd actually live here."

"Oh," she murmured. "Then maybe it does make sense." Her smile appeared, but it didn't reach her normally expressive brown eyes. Those were flat. Distant. "I'm sure it'll make a lovely home for someone someday. Once you're finished and you rent it out. We're lucky it's available as a safe house for now. Highly convenient."

"But you *do* like it?"

"Just told you I did."

"I'm glad," I said softly.

"But I'm still kinda pissed you didn't tell me about it."

"You being pissed off at me seems to be a common occurrence these days."

"Yeah. Because I finally realized how damn annoying you are. I'm getting to know the real you." She brushed past me as she left the room.

CHAPTER FIFTEEN

Dean

"SORRY IT'S NOT MUCH," I said as I put a plate in front of her. I'd thrown together some sandwiches for dinner, just from the meager supplies in the fridge.

"Looks good to me."

"Want to eat on the deck? There's a picnic table."

Keira cast a pointed glance around. "Seeing as you have nowhere to sit in here, that makes the deck an ideal option."

Her sarcasm had been out in full force, not giving me a break for a single minute, but if anything, that reassured me. She wouldn't be snarking so much if she were traumatized after the car chase.

I'd take an angry Keira over a sad, silent one.

We sat side by side on the picnic bench, looking out at the starry night sky instead of at each other. It was chilly, but not too bad. I wasn't worried about our security here either. Great thing about fifty acres. You could put motion-activated cameras in the key directions and set them up with phone notifications.

While I'd been making dinner, Keira had called her mom, Stephie, and Brynn to let them all know she wouldn't be home tonight, in case they'd planned to stop by her place.

She'd assured them everything was fine. *Just needed a change of scenery.*

That was one way to put it.

She'd kept the call with Brynn nice and short, clearly avoiding Brynn's questions about what the heck was really going on. Brynn had no idea what we'd been up to today, but she had keen instincts and knew something was up. Keira and I would need to get our stories together.

I just wished I knew how Keira was really handling things. What she was thinking. Aside from the *pissed off at Dean* part. That, I had down.

Suddenly, she gasped.

I leaped up to standing, my plate clattering and the last few potato chips flying to the ground. My hand was on her before I knew what I was doing.

"What is it?" I asked. "You okay?"

"Uh." She blinked up at me. "Remembered something. Didn't mean to startle you."

My hand slid around to the back of her neck. With her soft skin under my palm, it made me think of how I'd held her after the car chase. How she'd leaned into me. I knew she hadn't forgiven me for the ways I'd screwed up before, but in that moment in my truck, with her head on my shoulder, I'd wanted to pretend.

I carefully lifted my hand away from her. Sat back down, straddling the bench to face her. "Sorry. Did I hurt you?"

"I'm not that delicate." Her tone said she was annoyed at me, once again.

"You remembered something?"

"The ring the man was wearing today. I remembered where I'd seen it before. It was the night of the shooting. The same roadhouse where I argued with Donny Phelan."

"Someone else was wearing a ring like that?"

"Yes. There was a man sitting next to me at the bar that night. Beard, pale blue eyes. He offered to buy me a drink."

"Did you say *yes*?" The question came out far more accusatory than I'd intended.

She tilted her head. "If I did, what's it to you?"

As if I had the slightest right to be jealous. We hadn't even talked about whether or not she was seeing anyone.

But if she had a boyfriend, and the guy hadn't been hanging around her house, getting in my face when I suddenly showed up back in her life, then what the hell was wrong with him?

I cleared my throat. "Nothing at all. Just trying to get a clear picture of what happened."

She frowned at me another few seconds. "I did not accept a drink from the man. I didn't think anything was off about him, though. He seemed…fine. Wish I'd asked for his name." Her eyes moved to the darkness beyond the house, as if she was remembering. "How could it be a coincidence, though? Seeing someone else with that same ring today at Phelan's house. Then someone in a demon mask chasing us and trying to run us off the road."

"I agree. It has to be connected."

"We have to find out how."

I was relieved she'd said *we*. She wasn't kicking me off this investigation. "We will," I said. "We make a good team."

"Don't try to butter me up, Reynolds."

"What? I mean it." I shrugged. "It would help if your arm wasn't in a sling, and you could lift more than two pounds. But you have other talents. You've got a real set of balls, Deputy Marsh. Strolling around Donny Phelan's house like you owned the place."

"You were mad when I left for the bathroom. I saw the look on your face."

"Maybe. But I was wrong. Because of you, we have a new lead."

She lifted her chin. "Thank you for acknowledging that."

"My pleasure."

We took the dishes back inside, and I rinsed them off. Keira lingered on the single rickety stool at the kitchen island, checking her phone.

When I finished, she set her device down. "We should probably talk about how this is going to go tonight," she said.

My brain leaped straight to dirty places. "I'm sorry?"

Keira's eyes couldn't quite meet mine. "The *one-bed* situation, Dean. There's no couch. Nowhere else to sleep."

"Oh. *Oh.* Right. No, the bed's yours. I should've mentioned that already."

"I'm not kicking you out of your room and making you sleep on the ground."

Was she saying she'd share the bed with me?

My cock twitched just from thinking about it. I was such an asshole.

"I don't sleep in there anyway. I have a bedroll in one of the upstairs rooms. That's all I need."

"You sleep on the floor when there's a bed all set up?" she asked incredulously. "Why else would you finish the bedroom?"

"You said it yourself. There's a lot about me that doesn't make sense."

She sighed, shaking her head. "And I should just start taking your word for things."

I walked her down the hall, pausing before we reached the bedroom door. The lamp was still on from earlier, and in the tight confines of the hallway, Keira's floral scent was intoxicating.

She was right here. In my house. Still couldn't get over that.

"Feel free to shower," I said. "Use whatever of mine that you want. I'm sorry you don't have your own stuff here."

"I'll make do. Just don't expect me to look pretty."

"Like you're ever anything else."

"I wasn't fishing for a compliment."

"I wasn't trying to flatter you. It's just the truth. You're beautiful."

She glanced away.

"I mean it." My hand lifted, fingers caressing her chin and making her look at me.

Fuck, what was I doing?

I was pushing too far, given the awkward *one-bed* conversation we'd just had. But I couldn't help it. We'd been spending a lot of time together, I was all kinds of riled up from our narrow escape, and for the first time in maybe *ever*, we were about to sleep under the same roof.

Then, to my shock, Keira rose on her tiptoes and pressed her lips to my cheek.

Nerve endings ignited all over my body. When she pulled back, there was less than an inch between us. A single step, and I could fit our bodies together like we'd been on that dance floor two years ago. When I'd told her I was leaving, even though my heart had been telling me with every beat, *Stay.*

"Thanks for letting me crash here tonight," she said. "And for the fancy driving earlier. You saved us."

"Any time. Goodnight, Keira."

"Night."

Keira went into the bathroom, so I took the opportunity to grab some clothes for her. In case she wanted to change.

After rushing upstairs and taking several long minutes to

decide what to grab for her, I jogged back down. She was still in the bathroom.

I set the small stack of clothes on the dresser, glancing around one last time at the bedroom. A room I hadn't slept in once, yet it had been the first part of this house I'd finished.

Why? Fuck if I knew.

But now Keira was here, and she had a nice place to sleep. And maybe that was answer enough to the mysteries inside my brain. It was for her. Everything I did, no matter how contradictory.

It was *all* for her.

While Keira finished up in the bathroom, I tidied up the kitchen. I heard her emerge. Then the click of the bedroom door latch closing.

Go upstairs, I told myself.

But I didn't.

Instead, I quietly padded over to the hallway again. Stared at the closed bedroom door. Like a damn creeper. One question was suddenly wearing a groove inside my mind.

I was pretty sure she'd wanted me two years ago. Did she still?

Make that two questions: if she did want me, could I allow anything to happen between us?

I stood there and put my palm flat on the smooth wood surface, wanting so fucking bad to be inside that room with her.

What if I told her how much she really meant to me? How much it drove me crazy to think of her with anyone else. Would she let me kiss her? Would she kiss me back?

I imagined walking inside. Lifting her gently into my arms. Lowering her to the bed and slowly undressing her, being careful of her injuries.

Way too fast, my fantasy turned filthy instead of sweet. I

imagined Keira telling me she needed me, and then I'd strip down, freeing my cock. My tongue would work its way down her body, inch by inch, until I got a taste of all her hidden places. I'd thrust myself inside her, going slow. What I'd wanted for so long.

Shit, we would be so good. And so unforgivably wrong at the same time.

She was never supposed to be yours.

Finally, I forced myself to back up and turned away.

CHAPTER SIXTEEN

Keira

WHEN I WOKE in the morning and blinked at the ceiling, there was no moment of confusion. I knew exactly where I was. Remembered everything, every minute of yesterday.

Holding on for dear life while that SUV tried to force us off the road. The way Dean held me afterward, breathing me in, his touch lingering on my skin.

Yes, I'd noticed.

Then how he drove me out here to the house he somehow owns. Even though he'd told me he's the wandering type, never staying in one place too long.

Now that Dean was back in Hart County, I understood him even less than before.

I sat up against the soft pillows, feeling the layers of cozy blankets pool around my waist. My gaze landed on the framed poster on the wall across from me.

Gardenias.

I mean, really? An art print featuring my favorite flower? Hanging in this bedroom that he never slept in?

What was this man's deal?

I had no clue if all this meant something or nothing at all. Like the way he kept insisting he cared about me, would actually *kill* the people who'd hurt me, and yet he still kept me at a distance.

The man was exasperating.

And I wanted him so, so badly. Wanted to wake up beside him, with his arms wrapping me up instead of these blankets. Wanted his body pressed against me, making me light up and feel alive after we could've died yesterday.

But none of that was ever going to happen.

"And that's enough wallowing for one morning," I said to the room.

Now, it was time for a little spying. I had to get some benefit out of staying here, right? What else did Dean expect, leaving me on my own down here while he squirreled away upstairs?

I was eager for any small clues to him that I could get. Clearly it was some kind of sickness on my part.

I got out of bed and poked around the rest of the room. Last night, I'd been exhausted and went right to sleep, secure in the knowledge that Dean was close by. But now, I had the time and energy to check things out. And he couldn't stop me.

I opened up the armoire, finding it nearly empty. Dean wasn't keeping his clothes in here, which I supposed made sense if this wasn't his room. In all the time I'd known him, he had tended to live out of his suitcases, even after he'd been living in an apartment for a year. An obvious clue about that nomadic tendency of his, which I had chosen to ignore.

And yet, he'd also apparently bought this house.

Whatever. Trying to understand Dean Reynolds was a fruitless exercise.

On the dresser, he'd left a small stack of clothes. He must've put them here last night when I was in the bathroom. I was in my underwear right now, since I hadn't bothered thinking about pajamas.

I put on a long-sleeved shirt along with a pair of basket-ball shorts that hung low on my hips. Then fit my sling back over my head and around my left arm. Thank goodness I would be able to ditch it in another couple of weeks, if the doctor agreed I was still making good progress. Hopefully all that rattling around in the truck yesterday when we were fleeing for our lives wouldn't be an issue.

Probably best not to mention our dramatic getaway to my physical therapist or doctor.

The bedroom was disappointingly devoid of anything else interesting. Dean had created a tasteful yet anonymous guest room despite not expecting any guests. Or having a bed of his own to sleep in.

After a quick visit to the bathroom, where I brushed my teeth and pulled my curls back into a poof, I ventured into the kitchen. The sound of running water whooshed overhead, which must've been coming from the bathroom upstairs.

Dean was showering.

I thought of him naked up there, water running over his muscles, that shaggy hair hanging into his face as his hands glided over his body...

Coffee. That was what I needed. A jolt of caffeine to hope-fully break through that stream of images of Dean getting all soaped up in the shower.

The kitchen was pretty well stocked, as I'd seen yesterday. The coffeemaker was a standard brand, same one I had at home. Within a few minutes I had it gurgling.

The water was still going upstairs. And I did not need to be thinking about what *else* he might be doing in the shower.

I headed into the open living space. A wall had been torn down between two rooms here, and everything was still unfinished and mid-construction. Nothing much of interest.

But in a closet, I hit pay dirt.

Two cardboard boxes were stashed here. Finally, something of Dean's that I could shamelessly poke through like the nosy cop that I was.

The first box held paperwork. Tax-return type stuff, not what I'd been after. Even I wasn't *that* shameless about invading his privacy. I set the box aside.

But the second box held books. Fair game.

I sifted through the titles on top. Mysteries, thrillers, classics. There was a well-thumbed paperback of *Catch 22*. Something I'd always meant to read. Maybe Dean would let me borrow it.

Then, while I was flipping through a sci-fi epic, a folded piece of paper fell out.

I picked up the folded paper from the floor. Opened it.

And my heart squeezed.

It was a photo of *us*. Me and Dean, smiling together on some random afternoon in Owen's backyard. No, actually I remembered this day. We'd gone to a barbecue there. Just a casual get-together, full of friends from the station and Last Refuge.

In the photo, Dean was leaning into me. I was touching his arm. We looked like a couple. We'd been so close then, and I'd been dreaming of more.

I'd somehow convinced myself Dean would stay in Hart County forever. Be in my life forever.

My eyes stung, and nausea rose in my throat.

The creases in the paper were all worn, like he'd folded and unfolded it countless times. Who even printed out photos anymore, then kept them inside a book like this?

It was so stupid. *I* was stupid for ever believing Dean could be mine.

And the fact that he had this, stashed away in this weird secret house of his, was just one strike too far. I wanted an explanation for all of this. *All* of it. I was tired of his mysteriously vague non-answers.

Maybe I'd been sweet, naive Keira two years ago. But I wasn't anymore. I was tough, and I didn't put up with shit.

"You're going to tell me what the hell all this is about," I muttered as I marched toward the stairs.

On the upstairs landing, I didn't slow. Just kept striding from one doorway to the next. The bathroom was vacant, the mirror all fogged up with steam.

He wasn't in the first bedroom I reached. Which left the second, the room at the very end of the hall.

The door was partway open, so I barreled in, shoving the door wider. "Dean, I want to know why—"

The sentence dried on my tongue as I got an eyeful of him standing there.

Several things became evident at once.

Dean had just gotten out of the shower. In fact, his towel was still falling to the floor with a soft sound. Beads of water slid from his hair down his shoulders and along the slope of his spine.

Also, he was completely naked. Two firm butt cheeks were right there, searing into my brain matter.

His face was *not* the only spot on his body that had dimples.

If I'd been more dignified, I might've calmly backed up and averted my eyes. Instead, I screamed. Which made Dean jolt and start turning around to face me, in all his naked glory, and *holy shit that was Dean's cock*.

My hand clapped over my eyes. "Oh, fuck me. Fuck. I am so sorry."

I didn't usually curse this much. But I also didn't tend to walk in when a man was undressed.

Buck naked. I'd seen everything.

There was a shuffling sound. "Towel's back on. I should've closed the door, but I didn't think you'd—"

"No, I really shouldn't have—"

"It's okay, Keira." There was amusement in his voice. While my heart was sprinting and my skin was on fire. "What did you need?"

"It's nothing. I'll just, um, downstairs—" I started backing up. Stumbled.

Then a thick arm closed around my waist, and my eyes popped open. Dean was right there, heat and steam radiating from him.

"You might want to uncover your eyes before you attempt the staircase."

"Right. Good idea. You can…" I swallowed. "I'll go now."

But he didn't take his arm from my waist. Instead, a bead of water slid from his temple to his lip, and he licked it. I glanced down and saw his pink nipples, which I'd somehow missed staring at before. Probably because my eyes had been lower, on places now covered by his towel.

Gah.

And then, as I forced my gaze higher again, I saw the blue fire smoldering in his irises. Waves of something languid and heady rolled through my veins.

"I should go," I breathed.

He nodded. It was still a full five seconds before he let go of me and stepped back. "Yeah," he said, voice husky and low.

I turned around and made my retreat, only realizing when I was back in the kitchen that I'd dropped the photo somewhere upstairs. Along with my dignity.

Dean's body was thick in all the right places. Not much hair on his chest or stomach, but what was there accentuated his athletic frame. I'd seen him shirtless before, years ago, but the full effect of his body was different. Dark curls had framed his soft, cut cock.

What would it look like when he was hard? How would the weight of it feel in my hand?

I was about to combust.

About five minutes later, Dean came down wearing jeans and a T-shirt. His damp hair was tied back.

I'd mostly calmed down and stopped visualizing his naked body. *Mostly*. I pushed a mug of coffee toward him, avoiding his eyes. "I'm really, *really* sorry about barging in on you."

"I'm not that modest. Not a big deal."

Yet when I glanced up at him, that sharp, hot look he'd given me earlier hadn't faded much. He pulled the photo of us from his pocket. "You found this? That's what you wanted to ask me about?"

"I changed my mind. I don't need to know." Some questions were better not having the answers to.

"Keira—"

"Can you drive me back to Hartley? I really need to get home. Sleeping here last night was just a precaution. Right? The coast is clear now."

He studied me. "I'll take you home. We can check your house, make sure there's no reason for concern. Could someone stay with you tonight? Brynn? I'll feel better if I know you're not alone."

"Probably." I could give her a call later, but I wasn't excited about the thought of keeping so much from her.

But I'd figure that out later. Staying under the same roof with this man any longer was going to do me in.

CHAPTER SEVENTEEN

Keira

"I FEEL like I should explain to you about the photo," Dean said.

I adjusted the strap of my sling. Sunlight strobed between trees as we drove down the highway. "It's not necessary."

"You seemed to think it was necessary earlier. Enough to come upstairs and confront me."

"I wasn't *confronting* you."

"The way you were stomping sounded confrontational."

"So you heard me coming?" I glared from the corner of my eye. "Why'd you drop your towel, then?"

"I was already mid-drop!"

"It's not that lengthy a process! You could've aborted the drop. Or, how about not turning around."

"You screamed. You startled me. You're the one who barged into *my* space."

"You said it wasn't that big a deal!"

He shrugged one shoulder. "I'd like to think it's *somewhat* big," he muttered.

I blinked. "Did you just make a reference to your dick?"

There was a moment of silence in the truck as we kept driving toward town.

Then I started snickering. Dean's dimple appeared. It was a lot like yesterday, when we'd both started laughing after leaving Phelan's place. At least there were no SUVs chasing us down this time.

"I used to love that about us," Dean said, after we'd gotten our giggles out. "How easy it was to laugh together about the dumbest things."

My smile faded. "It was nice."

"Seems like we've still got it."

"Guess so. Even if nothing else is the same."

Another silence, but this one didn't lead to laughter. It was full of awkward, sad tension.

"Keira, I had that photo because I missed you. I told you that before. I have photos of you on my phone too. I look at them more than I should admit."

I sighed. "Right. Let's not rehash everything."

"I just get the impression you don't believe me. I've told you how much I care about you. How much our friendship meant to me. I left for other reasons, and I've shared those with you too."

"Yes, I *know*," I said testily. "You left so you wouldn't hurt me. And because of your history. We've been over it, so let's drop it."

"You're very special to me."

I squeezed my eyes closed. "Dean, *stop*. Please. I am begging you."

Neither of us said anything for the rest of the drive. We still had to figure out the next step of our plan regarding Donny Phelan, but I couldn't handle it right now. I needed some space and time to think. Distance from *Dean*.

I had to figure out some way to stop these old feelings from choking me every time I looked at him.

Dean took the road leading to my neighborhood. One of

my neighbors was out walking her dog, and I waved as we passed.

Finally, my house was in sight. I couldn't wait to take a bath using all my products, change into sweats, and take a nap.

But as he pulled up my driveway, Dean muttered a curse.

"What is it?" I asked.

"You've got a broken window."

"What? *Where?*"

"Down there. Past the side door. Furthest window on the right, corner pane of glass."

"You can see that?"

He pointed at his eyes. "I've got 20/8 vision. They called me Bullseye for a reason."

I shook my head. So obnoxious.

But dammit, he was right. A pane of glass in my bedroom window was smashed. My security system was on, and it hadn't alerted me. But I didn't have a broken-glass detector on every single window. There was no indication anyone had actually opened a door or window and gone inside.

So, who had done this? Why?

A couple guesses came to mind.

Dread coated my insides as I unlocked the side door and went in, using my code to disable the alarm. Before I could get far, Dean gently put a hand on my hip. "Wait. I'll check things out first."

"No way. Don't act like I'm some scared kid. You're the civilian now. *You* wait."

He held up his hands. "Alright, sorry. We'll go together."

"Fine. Together."

Everything was exactly as I'd left it yesterday, when Dean and I had been sitting at my kitchen table strategizing about our visit to Donny Phelan. Felt like years ago.

In my bedroom, a rock lay on the carpet surrounded by

shards of broken glass. Dean pushed at it with his shoe. There was a piece of paper wrapped around it with a rubber band.

Before he could stop me, I scooped it up and yanked the paper free.

It was a glossy page torn from a high school yearbook. A photo in the layout showed me in my deputy uniform, smiling with an arm around my sister. I'd been on her campus that day for community outreach.

Stephie's face had been circled in red marker.

Oh my God.

"Stephie," I choked out, fumbling to take out my phone. "I have to call her."

My hand was shaking so bad I needed Dean's help to dial. Stupid sling. His fingers brushed my neck as he held the phone up for me, and I took it. He stood beside me as the line rang.

When I heard Stephie's voice on the phone, saying she and my mom were home and everything was fine, my knees nearly went weak.

"What's the matter?" Stephie asked. "You said you were staying with Dean last night. Did something happen with him?"

He was standing at my shoulder, probably able to hear every word.

"Just a second." I held the phone away from me. "I'll go outside," I said to Dean.

He nodded. "I'll double check the rest of the house."

Out on the driveway, I sagged against the hood of Dean's truck. "I...had a nightmare last night. I was worried about you. But everything's okay," I reassured her, though it was nowhere close to the truth. I glanced at the house. "Dean and I are fine."

"Did you guys hook up?"

"Did we *what*? Absolutely not. We're not—*no*."

"Why not? Dude, why else would you stay the night with him except to get under him?"

Good lord. An image quickly flashed through my mind of Dean naked and wet. I pushed that away. *Not* where I wanted my thoughts going when I was talking to my baby sister.

"First of all, do we need to have the sex talk again? Sex is a big deal."

Stephie groaned. "Don't be boring. I'm eighteen, Kiki."

"Second, Dean is not the reason I called. Sheriff Douglas hasn't caught the people who attacked me. They're still out there. Be careful, okay? Be vigilant. You and Mom need to keep an eye out for anything weird. Anyone suspicious hanging around."

"*Why*? Did something else happen?"

"No. Just be careful. Can you do that for me?"

She agreed. We said our goodbyes, and I ended the call feeling worse than before. If anything happened to Mom or Stephie, I wouldn't be okay.

Should I have told her about the broken window and the page from the yearbook? But I didn't want to scare her even more.

Stephie's best friend Vivian had been through some terrible things before Trace and Scarlett adopted her. Stephie knew some of those details, and years ago, I'd been there when my sister woke up sobbing from a nightmare about evil men grabbing her.

I wouldn't let anything happen to Stephie, and that included living in fear.

Dean came back outside. "Hey. How's your sister?"

"Full of attitude, as usual."

He smiled. "That's good."

"It is." I jammed my phone in my pocket. "See anything else inside?"

"No. Rest of the house is clear." It seemed like he had more to say, but he gave me a meaningful stare and nodded at his truck.

We got in. Immediately, he turned up the radio and touched his mouth as he spoke to obscure the words. "It's possible they're watching us right now."

"Hold on, *what?*"

I glanced around at my driveway, the trees, my neighbors' houses. It was bizarre to consider we were under surveillance, but considering everything that had already happened?

Dean reached over and put his hand on my thigh like he was trying to calm me down. "Relax. I don't have anything specific, but the thought occurred to me while I was inside. They might've positioned someone nearby to see how we react to the broken window. The implicit threat."

"Do you think they're following us too?"

"I'm sure they'll try. I doubt they know the location of my property, so I'll have to make sure I don't lead them there."

I'd thought at first this was all about some vendetta Phelan had against me for embarrassing him. But it had to be more. Really, we had no *clue* what was going on.

"Whoever this is, they're sending us a message," Dean said.

"And I got it, loud and clear. If we don't stop, they'll go after Stephie and my mom." I took a stuttering breath, fear seizing my lungs again.

"We won't let that happen."

"Because you're going to tell me to give up? Stop pursuing this?"

"That's one option. You could forget about Phelan and let me deal with this."

Which would probably be the smartest choice. Just try to

get back to my life. Heal from my injuries and go back on duty in another couple of months.

But how could I face myself knowing I'd let those bastards terrify me into submission? Let them win?

Could I allow Dean to fight the entire war for me, while I hid away to keep myself and my family safe? No. It wasn't right to put the burden all on him, even if he seemed determined to take it.

And honestly, the more these people tried to silence me, terrify me, the more I wanted *blood*.

"We're supposed to be in this together," I said. "Just last night, you were talking about how we're a good team. I was the one who saw the guy wearing that ring and made the connection to the night I was shot. It's my lead. Now you're trying to force me out."

"Actually, I'm not."

"Then what? I would love to hear more ideas. I'm not the former assassin with eagle-eye vision and ghost ops experience. I'm just a sheriff's deputy."

"Don't talk down about yourself. You strolled into enemy territory just yesterday, while injured, and refused to be intimidated. You're amazing."

"Options, Dean. That's what I need." I stared out the windshield while touching my lips to hide the movements. Just in case someone really was watching. "I have to put a protection detail on my mom and sister."

"Definitely."

I would talk to Brynn this afternoon, and she could set it up. "But aside from that, how do I keep my family safe and also stay in this?"

"We make the bad guys *think* you gave up. That we both did. Make them believe their scare tactics worked. While we go underground."

"Ideas on how to do that?"

"You move in with me."

Ugh. Really? "Move in? For how long?"

"As long as it takes."

My pulse raced. Just this morning, the thought of spending another hour in that house with him seemed intolerable. Now I was supposed to live there?

With that tempting naked body of his?

"Wouldn't that be more suspicious?" I asked. "We both showed up to question Donny Phelan. If we're together all the time, they'll think we're still investigating."

"Not if we give them another explanation for you being with me. We already told Phelan yesterday that we're dating."

"But we're *not*."

"So, we just have to make them believe it."

"You cannot be suggesting what I think you're suggesting."

He turned toward me, his blue eyes full of intensity and unreadable things. His broad shoulders leaned closer. His body moving into my space.

And then, he kissed me.

CHAPTER EIGHTEEN

I WAS SO GOING to hell for this.

My lips brushed against Keira's the way I'd imagined so many times. She made a tiny sound, a whimper, tilting her head. Which just made me press closer. My hand cupped her cheek as the bow of her upper lip fit perfectly against my lower one.

I knew exactly what I was doing. Knew she couldn't shove me away, in case someone was watching.

Fuck, her mouth was every bit as perfect as I'd imagined. I knew I should stop, but my tongue flicked out for a forbidden fraction of a second to taste her.

Then, reluctantly, I pulled back, and her eyelashes fluttered.

"What was *that*?" she hissed.

"Our excuse for you moving in with me. I'm worried about your safety, so I'm insisting, as your boyfriend, that you live with me."

"You have got to be kidding me. *No*."

"You wanted ideas. Options. This is what I've got."

"Well, it's stupid," she spit out. "Think about it. We'd have to tell *everyone* we're together. That we're…" She gestured between us. "Romantically involved."

I tapped my fingers on the driver's side door. Did I know what I was doing? Not really. But I'd do anything to protect Keira. Help her.

I'd had an ulterior motive for that kiss, though, and I wasn't proud of it.

I'd already jerked off once thinking about her last night, then a second time in the shower. Then earlier, after she'd walked in on me naked and stared at my cock, my dick was longing for a lot more attention.

But I was not bringing her back to my place for *that*, stolen kisses aside.

"We can work on the details. At the very least, you need to pack some things. You can't stay here. These assholes have come to your house *twice* to hurt or scare you and haven't been caught. What's stopping them from a third? Or more?"

"I know," she whispered.

I hadn't wanted her to come back here at all, but after she'd gotten so flustered, I hadn't wanted to argue.

What I *really* wanted was...not something I could have. The best I could hope for was a stolen kiss.

"You agree?" I asked.

Instead of answering, Keira pushed out of the truck and went back inside her house. I followed, unwilling to leave her there alone.

It was an instinctual need. This feeling that I should be close to her. A weakness for sure, but what was the harm if I was also keeping her safe?

Could've sworn she was easier to resist in the past. This version of Keira? A little older but a lot wiser and fiercer?

Fuck, she was my kryptonite.

I found her in her bedroom, throwing clothes and items into a bag. So she was packing.

"Can I help?" I asked.

"No thanks, *babe*." She glared. "I've got it."

"Be gentle with yourself." I went to rest my hands on her hips. "You're still healing."

Her glare was pure murder. But as I touched her, the look in her eyes shifted, and suddenly it was so full of anguish it made me question everything.

"I'll, uh, leave you to it." I decided to pack up the food in her fridge and cabinets so it wouldn't spoil and go to waste. But I paused there in her kitchen, hoping all this wasn't a mistake. I'd never made the best decisions when it came to her.

Keira packed up a couple suitcases, and I carried it all outside. After the bed of my truck was full, we got back in and I started the engine.

"How do you want to handle the broken window?" I asked.

She took her phone out. "I'll text a handyman. I don't want to tell Owen there was another break-in. I doubt they left any evidence behind, and besides, if Owen finds out about *this*, then we'll have to tell him about going to see Donny Phelan."

"He'll likely find out anyway. If Phelan sends his lawyers to complain."

She threw a hand up in exasperation. "Then tell Owen whatever you like! Or don't. Seems like you always do whatever you want, Dean."

"Trust me, that is not true."

She frowned at her lap.

"Text the handyman. If Owen comes asking questions, we can decide together how to deal with him."

"Fine. I'll contact Brynn too about the protection detail."

"What're you going to tell her?" I asked.

"Just that I'm worried about my mom and sister. As for everything else... I don't know." Keira slumped against her seat, sighing, as I pulled onto the road and headed back toward my place.

I took a circuitous route, making sure there was nobody following us. By the time we pulled up in front of my house, Keira hadn't said a single word more to me.

But no problem. The last couple days had been a lot. She needed some time to process and decompress.

And *I* needed to stop lusting after her.

Sunlight slanted down between clouds and blue sky, lighting up some spots in brilliant yellow while leaving others in shadow. I reached for my door handle. And that was when Keira spoke, though she was still looking out her window instead of at me.

"Dean, I can't pretend to be in a relationship with you."

I pushed loose strands of hair out of my face. "Why not? You wanted to go undercover in the past, right? With Brynn. And I think you've done other undercover work as a cop. Haven't you? It's not that different."

"It's completely different."

"Why? It's a mission. An assignment."

"That's all I am to you now? I used to be your friend, someone *special*, but now I'm an assignment. A box to check off, so you can soothe your guilt."

Oh, hell. She was hitting me where it hurt.

"Of course you're more to me than that. I didn't come back to Hart County for an assignment, Keira. I came for *you*. I've told you I care about you. I always did."

"But not the same way I cared about you. Don't deny it. You *knew* how I felt about you." She wiped at her face.

Oh, damn. She was crying. And *I* was the cause.

I cracked my knuckles, the truth so close to tripping off my tongue. How I really felt. Both then *and* now. Because nothing for me had changed. Not a fucking thing.

"I knew," I agreed.

Yes, I'd known years ago that she had a crush on me. I'd told her I was too old for her, just to shut the idea down. But it had been a lot more complicated than that.

"And you didn't want me," she said in a monotone.

"That's where you're wrong."

Keira jolted like she was coming back to life. "I'm not wrong! You didn't want to hurt me, so you left town. So I could get over you or something like that. Right? Because you didn't want me the way I wanted you."

I squinted at her. "That's what you think?"

"That's what I know!"

Don't say it, I thought. But I couldn't hold this back. Not anymore.

"Keira, I wish I could've had everything with you. Every single thing. If I could've stayed forever for *anyone*, it would've been you."

Her head swiveled, those big brown eyes searching mine. I didn't know what she saw there.

A second passed. Two.

Then she said, "Kiss me again."

Turmoil erupted inside me. What I *wanted* warring with what was right.

"I shouldn't do that," I murmured.

"How are we supposed to fool everyone else if we can't even fool ourselves?"

What had I been thinking, suggesting this? Kissing her in the first place?

I'd never been very smart, apparently.

Leaning forward, I met her halfway. Our lips touched, and it was like a chemical reaction, breaking the bonds of my resistance. Keira's hand found the back of my neck, fingers tugging the rest of my hair free from its knot.

Her lips parted. Inviting me in. My tongue stroked hers,

sending sparks along my limbs and down into my needy cock.

I kissed her deeper. Really tasting her this time. Sucking at her bottom lip, then licking into her mouth for more. Electricity danced along my nerve endings, leaving fire in its wake.

Nngh. It was even better than the last kiss. Better than any kiss I'd ever experienced before.

Keira pulled back first. Breathing hard, eyes glassy. She licked her lips. Touched them with wonder. "I was always curious what that would be like. Kissing you."

"Same here."

"Too bad we can't make a habit of it."

I hummed in agreement, though my dick wanted to leap out of my pants and tackle her. My arm draped over my lap to hide the evidence.

Keira patted her hair and rubbed her face. Blinked at herself a few times in the side mirror. Almost like she was putting on some kind of mental armor. I didn't like that she had to guard herself from me, but then again, it meant she was smart.

We couldn't let this go any further. I couldn't.

Don't be an idiot.

"Okay," she said. "We'll do this your way. Pretend to be together, and act like we're giving up on investigating Donny Phelan and whoever else attacked us. That way, when we find out who they really are and how to get to them, they won't be expecting it."

"Good. Yes. That's the plan." Shaking off the desire that had clouded my brain, I reached for the door handle again.

But she wasn't done.

"I still can't understand you, though," Keira said in a small voice. "You're sure you can't stay? You can't even *try*?"

I slumped back into my seat. She was tearing my heart out.

"I did try. The years I spent in Colorado...more than anything, that was because of you. But I'm not made for it. I'm sorry."

She had no idea how sorry I was.

Keira deserved so much better than me.

"Don't be sorry. I'll be fine." Her plush lips curved, but her dark eyes betrayed how much my words had hurt. Exactly what I'd never wanted to do, *hurt her*, and here I was, doing it again.

"You will be fine," I said, needing to believe it.

"So, after this is over, we'll say goodbye. And that's okay. You'll leave again, and you'll rent out your property. No hard feelings. It'll be a clean break, like before, except I'll know it's coming this time. And that will be that."

I nodded too, just once.

"There's something else I want," she added.

My breath stopped. My heart was aching, wondering what she was about to ask. And if I could stand giving it to her. "And that is?"

"I want you to teach me to shoot."

Huh. Not what I'd expected.

"You know how to shoot."

"I mean, shoot like you do. Like a sniper. I've trained with Brynn on hand-to-hand combat, and now I want to train with you on sniper rifles. And assassin stuff."

"Assassin stuff?"

"You know what I mean."

"Still gunning for a spot with the Protectors, after all this time?"

"Yes. And you can't stop me, so you might as well help me."

At least I knew she'd be on the right side of things with

the Protectors, instead of wading into the murky gray waters I'd been living in during my ghost op days.

"I thought you didn't want me using weapons. Because of my vow."

"Teaching me is another loophole."

"You've thought of everything. But your arm is still in a sling."

"Two more weeks. Then I'm free of the sling."

"It'll be almost a couple more *months* until you're healed. You can't fire a weapon until then. Even longer before you can fire a rifle."

"So you can teach me other things in the meantime. We'll also be investigating Phelan and his friends and figuring out exactly what they're hiding. Are you rushing this mission, Reynolds? We don't know how long it will take to nail the bad guys and bring them to justice. I've got time. Do you?"

I stared through the windshield. "I've got time. That's never been a question. I'm all yours until this is finished."

Shit, why had I phrased it that way? *I'm all yours.* If only. But Keira didn't comment on that.

"Then we're agreed," she said.

"You weren't going to stop arguing until I gave in, anyway."

She smiled more genuinely this time. "Nope."

CHAPTER NINETEEN

Dean

I CARRIED in all of Keira's boxes and suitcases. She shooed me out of her bedroom, telling me she didn't need help unpacking.

And that was fine by me. Despite this fake relationship thing we were diving into, that bedroom would be hers alone. Her private domain. It was far better for me to remain an exile in the upstairs rooms.

So that was where I went, taking a seat on my bedroll and pressing Owen's contact on my phone screen.

"Dean," my best friend said warily. Couldn't blame him after the last conversation we'd had a few weeks ago in his office. "Staying out of trouble?"

I thought of the scuffle I'd had with Donny Phelan yesterday. The car chase. The implied threat against Keira's family. Not to mention Keira walking in on me naked, and then the forbidden make-out session that nearly fogged up my truck windows.

Uh, perhaps more than a little trouble. Sorry, Sheriff.

"Mostly. I've been keeping busy. What's new with you, Tex?"

We chatted awhile, and Owen didn't say a single word

about Donny Phelan. Which was good. It meant the podcaster hadn't sent his lawyers to complain about me and press charges. Phelan was keeping this quiet.

But did that mean he was backing off, and someone *else* was trying to intimidate us? Seemed likely. We needed a lot more info. We needed River's hacker skills again.

"How's Keira doing?" Owen asked. "I know you've been spending time with her."

"I have. And she's well. She's healing."

"That last talk you and I had. You were very upset, understandably, about the attack on her. My department's investigation hasn't been as fruitful so far as I'd like. I was worried for a while that you might go after Donny Phelan. I assume Keira's told you about her argument with him the night of the shooting. But I'm glad you're keeping your head cool. "

There. That was *definite* confirmation that he didn't know what I'd really been up to.

But it was also my cue to lay more groundwork. Lying to my friend wasn't something I was proud of, but it had to be done. Keira's and my investigation had to stay secret, including from Owen. If, or rather *when*, Phelan and his thugs disappeared, I didn't want any suspicion to land on Keira.

"Well, there's actually something I wanted to tell you. About Keira and me. We talked, worked some things out, and...we're together now. I guess almost losing her was the push I needed to see what I was missing."

I held my breath, waiting for his response.

"You finally admitted how you feel about her? Fuck, Dean. That's incredible. I'm so damn happy for you."

I flinched, surprised at the pang of guilt that jabbed my insides. Because part of me wished what I'd said was the truth.

"So you're staying in Hart County," he said with a relieved laugh.

"Yep." *For now*, I added silently.

"Are you looking for a new job?"

"Not yet. I've got money saved up. She and I can take a few months to ourselves. And I've got a quiet place now, some land where Keira can recover. I'll show you sometime. But later."

"It's no rush. Keira can have all the time she needs before she's back on duty. If she wants, she can take desk shifts soon, but it's up to her."

"Hey, Tex." I leaned back against the wall, staring at the old water stains on the ceiling. "You think I deserve her?"

"I know you do. But that's not a one-time thing. It's about treating her right every single day. I'm sure you will."

"I plan to. I'll do right by her." And that *wasn't* a lie.

I'd follow through on my agreement with Keira. I'd teach her how to shoot like a sniper. To some extent, the talent necessary to become elite couldn't be taught, but she was already an excellent markswoman. There was plenty I could show her to make her a better cop. A better Protector, whenever Trace let her join.

But when I made good on my threat against Donny Phelan—or against anyone I discovered had tried to harm Keira—then that burden would fall solely on me. Their deaths would be on my hands alone.

I would leave Keira out of it. I had to.

I *would* do right by her.

CHAPTER TWENTY

Keira

"MAYBE WE SHOULD JUST MEET up at my mom's house instead," I muttered. "Wouldn't that be better? Have you ever tasted her pecan pie pancakes?"

Dean smirked at me. "I have, and they're delicious. But that won't work. This has to be public. Every shameless gossip in Hartley needs to see that we're together."

We were strolling down Main Street, nodding hello to people we knew. Curious eyes followed us, taking in the ways Dean kept touching me. Whispering in my ear. The gossips were going to be all over this. No question.

He reached over, grabbed my right hand, and lifted it to his lips. Shivers rolled in a wave along my skin and settled in my stomach, all weird and fluttery.

Dean was being so normal about this bizarre situation. I, on the contrary, was about to throw up these stomach butterflies all over the sidewalk.

We were scheduled to meet Mom, Stephie, and Brynn for brunch in about ten minutes. Dean had insisted on parking way at the opposite end of Hartley's downtown, just to make sure we could take a nice, long walk of shame.

Putting my arm around Dean's waist and feeling him up a

little was a *slight* benefit. But I couldn't even enjoy that fully. Not after what he'd confessed the other day.

If I could've stayed forever for anyone, it would've been you.

How could I ever be mad at him again when he said something like that?

I'd mostly been holed up in the guest room at Dean's house the past couple of days, trying to get settled. It was hard to wrap my head around what he'd said. That he'd really felt the same way I did. And those kisses in his truck… *Ugh*, after the pure passion of those kisses, I had to believe it. He really had wanted me.

Was it better, knowing it hadn't been some unrequited crush on my part? Or was it worse, realizing that Dean had wanted me, but too many other obstacles stood in our way.

We were never going to work out. As a couple, we'd always been doomed.

And yet, here we were. About to step into Jessi's Diner and pretend to be happily in love.

The bell jingled as Dean opened the door, holding it for me. Mom and Stephie had already claimed a booth. My sister's hair was newly done in box braids with extensions, looking so cute.

They smiled and waved, jumping up as we walked over.

"It's so wonderful, seeing you two side by side again!" my mother exclaimed. "Dean, it's been too long. We missed you."

"Thank you, Mrs. Marsh. It's good to see you too."

"Oh, enough of that." She patted his arm. "You call me Regina."

After hugs, we all sat down again, Dean and me next to each other on one side. Dean draped an arm around my shoulders and pressed closer to me with his thigh sandwiched against mine. Stephie got this excited gleam in her eyes, exchanging a knowing glance with Mom.

Great. They'd already been talking.

"So, what's the big news you wanted to tell us?" Mom asked.

I squirmed, trying to get comfortable. "We have to wait for Brynn."

"Hello, everyone. Can I get you something to drink?"

I looked up to see Jessi Shelborne holding a notepad, pen poised over paper. "Hey, Jessi," I sputtered. "Didn't know you'd be here."

Usually, Jessi was at Last Refuge running the inn. She, Aiden, and their little daughter lived up there. They still owned the diner, but they'd hired employees to run the day-to-day operations.

"We like to take the odd shift at the diner now and again. For old time's sake." She nodded toward the kitchen, where her husband was cooking. Aiden caught us watching and lifted his chin.

Aiden and Jessi first met in this diner. Fell in love here.

I had pleasant memories here too. This was the place I stopped for a hot breakfast in the morning after a night shift on patrol or for a slice of pie during a quiet afternoon.

I'd sat in these booths at least a hundred times with Dean, too. Wishing to have his arm around me. But I'd never imagined it would happen like *this*.

"What brings all of you out today?" Jessi asked. "Just in the mood for brunch?"

Mom nudged against Stephie's shoulder. "Keira and Dean's idea," my sister said. "They have some news for us." Stephie pumped her eyebrows.

Jessi's eyes lit up too. "Do they, now? How intriguing. Whatever could it be?"

Ugh, this kept getting worse. Except it was exactly what Dean wanted. Everything nice and public. We were going to cover every busybody on Hartley's Main Street *and* the crew at Last Refuge in one fell swoop.

And nobody seemed the least bit surprised.

We ordered coffees. Brynn arrived next—more hugs all around—and we focused on food for a bit. I couldn't imagine eating with my stomach so twisted up, but I ordered a Colorado eggs Benedict anyway, smothered in green chili.

"So." Stephie plunked her elbows on the table. "Get on with it. Tell us."

I glanced at Dean. He nodded for me to go ahead.

Crap.

"Well, it's about Dean and me, and…" The words got stuck, refusing to come out.

Thankfully, Dean took over.

"I came back to Hart County after hearing Keira was hurt. It made me realize some things." His smile was so tender it made my eyes burn. "We talked, and it turns out we both want the same thing."

"*Finally*," Stephie cut in. "You're dating! Took you long enough."

Mom was beaming, and Brynn gave me a wink. Jessi, clearly eavesdropping, flashed a thumbs up from behind the counter.

Had *everyone* known how I felt for Dean all this time?

"It's a little more than that," Dean added. "I asked Keira to move in with me. I know it's fast, but—"

"It's so exciting!" Mom gushed, hands waving in front of her. "I should probably tell you two not to rush this, but you've been waiting so long already. And with the attack on Keira, well…" She nodded, getting choked up. "This is a good thing."

"You mentioned you'd been staying with Dean," Brynn asked. "Where is that, exactly?"

Dean shifted around on the bench, making the vinyl creak. "I have a house I've been fixing up."

Stephie clapped her hands. "When can we see your new place? After this? I can't wait!"

"Hold on. No. We're not ready for that." I had to get them to calm down. I'd figured they wouldn't fight us too much on our relationship story, but *really*? They sounded ready to marry Dean and me off.

Once again, Dean swooped in to explain. "The house needs a lot of work. We're just trying to keep things low key. No visitors for now, not until we're sure the people who attacked Keira aren't going to bother her again."

"You're taking care of her." Mom's eyes teared up.

"I'm also capable of taking care of myself," I muttered. Not that anyone was listening.

"Dean, I need to give you a better hug. A momma hug." Mom shooed Stephie and Brynn out of the way, making them get up so she could bear-hug Dean in the middle of the diner. People were staring.

"I'm just so glad you came back for her," Mom said, voice thick. "You've always been welcome in my house, but now you're really family. You two were meant to be."

Dean smiled patiently. No dimples.

This was excruciating.

CHAPTER TWENTY-ONE

Keira

AFTER BREAKFAST, Mom and Stephie insisted on dragging us down Main Street to buy us a housewarming gift. They were on either side of Dean, talking both his ears off.

Brynn hung back with me. "Moving in." She whistled. "That's a big step."

Thank you, I thought with relief. Someone was going to point out how ridiculous this was.

"Do your worst, B. Tell me what you're really thinking. Brutal honesty."

She laughed. "You sure?"

I made a beckoning gesture with my hand.

"I'm thinking... I didn't actually expect Dean to get his shit together. But he did. You've been inseparable since he showed up at your place with that groveling basket. It's clear a lot has happened in the last few days since I saw you."

"You don't think I forgave him too easily?"

"That's not my call. If you think the timing's right, then it's right."

"But in just over a month, I went from telling him to get out of my hospital room to moving in with him."

"Do you *want* me to have an issue with this?"

Yes. Yes, I do.

"No. I'm just nervous."

"Of course you are. It's been a rough month. You're still healing, the sheriff's department still doesn't have any suspects in your shooting, and Dean's suddenly back confessing his love for you." She stopped walking, pulling me beneath the shade of an awning. Nobody else was around. "You're worried about your mom and Stephie too."

I'd texted with Brynn about the broken window at my house. The implicit threat against my family. She'd promised to arrange discreet protection for them through Last Refuge. But as for the rest of what Dean and I were up to, she had no clue. It wouldn't be right to ask her to lie for me or drag her into this revenge plan.

"I am," I said. "You're right. I've been really stressed. But doesn't that mean I should slow down with Dean?"

"Let me ask you this. Are you happy with him?"

How could I answer that question with a straight face? How could I lie to one of my closest friends about something like this?

"I want to be," I said.

Her face scrunched. "Okay. That's not very specific. Is he treating you well? Telling you how crazy he is about you? And do you feel the same about him? Does kissing him make you dizzy in the best possible way?"

"All of the above." My chest was clenching so hard I could barely breathe.

"Then that's all you need for now. It makes sense for you to stay with someone given the danger still out there, and if Dean's being the ideal guy, why not him? If it doesn't work out, everyone will go on with their lives. But maybe you'll look back someday, and there'll be an incredible happy ending to all you've gone through. Like Cole and me."

"You and Cole do have an enviable HEA."

She shrugged. "I know. It's like we're made for each other or something." We started walking again to catch up to the others. "And speaking of my handsome guy, Cole needs me back in Mexico. Now that you're spending all your time with Dean in your new love nest, I can probably head back."

Shit, how selfish was I? "Absolutely. Book your flight. Just know, I couldn't have made it through the last few weeks without you. I'm so grateful for everything."

She winked. "I've loved being here with you. I hope I don't need you to return the favor, but if I do, I know you'll be there."

When we caught up to Mom, Stephie, and Dean, he gave me a warm grin and reached for my hand. We shopped around, enjoying Main Street, but my mind was on everything Brynn had said.

Mom and Stephie would take it hard when Dean and I eventually "broke up." But they'd survive.

I had to figure out how *I* was going to survive this.

It wasn't even about me or my heartache. Not anymore. Now, I knew that Dean had been hurting too.

Maybe it wasn't true at all that he'd broken my heart two years ago. I'd broken my own heart by expecting something that Dean wasn't able to give me. And that just made me sad for *him*.

Where Dean was concerned, it was time to finally let my romantic hopes go.

He had come back to Colorado for me. So I was going to be here for him, too. As a partner in this mission. A friend.

That was all I could ever be.

———

"We'll start with the basics."

Dean set a long, narrow case on the floor, using a small

key to unlock it. Then opened the lid, unveiling the disassembled pieces of dark metal nestled into custom-cut foam.

My gaze moved eagerly over the barrel and the scope. I crossed my arms, feeling a slight twinge in my shoulder, but I was free of the sling now. Thank goodness.

I nodded. "Let's do it."

He looked up at me from where he was kneeling, a hint of a smile pulling at his lips.

In the last two weeks, I'd settled into a new routine as Dean's roommate, strange as that sounded. The armoire in the bedroom was full of my clothes and belongings. The downstairs bathroom had shelves laden with my hair and skin products, and I'd been putting my mark on the rest of the house too.

I refused to live in a place with nowhere to sit in the living room and no table to eat. It had actually been fun picking out a few items at secondhand stores. Another glimpse into the friendship Dean and I had shared before, when things had been so easy between us.

Also, Mom and Stephie had *loved* helping. I swear, they liked Dean even more than they liked me.

Now, I was six weeks into my recovery. More than ready to get training again. As much as I could, anyway. Still no actual shooting allowed.

And no word yet on the pictures we'd shared with River from our visit to Donny Phelan's mansion. But I thought I was showing admirable patience, thank you very much.

Dean pushed back that unruly long hair of his. It kept slipping into his face, though he'd tied it back in its usual knot. "This is my Knight's Armament SR-25. The same weapon I used for Marine Force Recon missions as a sniper."

"You were Force Recon? I didn't know that." Just one more small detail about Dean's life that he occasionally dropped like breadcrumbs.

He nodded, eyes still on the disassembled rifle. "For a while. As a sniper, this weapon was my best friend. I took it with me when I became a strategic asset carrying out less official assignments."

His fingers traced across the matte black pieces in their foam nests.

We were in the living room, and this space was much cleaner than before, all the tools and sawhorses put elsewhere. But aside from the addition of a couch, it was still sparsely furnished. Plenty of room to move.

Room for the memories that were no doubt filling Dean's mind, too.

"You *are* okay with this, right?" I asked. "I want to learn, but…" As far as I knew, he still hadn't actually held a gun in years.

But holding a weapon wasn't the same as firing it. Firing it wasn't the same as aiming a kill-shot at a living person.

Loopholes, right? These days, I was living in the loopholes. Sharing a home with Dean, though we couldn't ever really be together. Touching him when we were out in public, while knowing it meant nothing.

"I'm good, Keira. I promise." With no further hesitation, Dean lifted the barrel from the case. "Let's go over the architecture of this fine precision weapon, piece by piece."

He showed me the upper and lower receiver, the bolt carrier group. The Leopold Mark 4 scope and the suppressor.

It sure was *something*, watching Dean smoothly assemble and take apart the rifle. Everything the man did was sexy to me, but when he was using his warrior jargon and being all proficient?

Maybe I had a competency kink.

"Keira? Did you get that?"

"Um, yep. Clockwise. Got it."

"I'm not boring you, am I? Should we break for lunch?" He was smirking, so I smirked back.

"Nope. I can keep going. I can go as long as you can."

His smile turned more devious for a second, heat flaring in his eyes. Then it was gone. He cleared his throat. "As I was saying."

After Dean finished my introduction to the KAC SR-25, he opened up a second case. The contents of this one were more familiar to me.

A Glock 19 and a SIG Sauer P226, both with threaded barrels for suppressors. And a whole bunch of wicked-looking knives.

Dean lifted the knives and identified them, one by one. "Benchmade Nimravus fixed blade. Gerber Mark II. Folding Emerson CQC-7."

"You'll show me how to use them?"

"When you're ready. I'll show you anything you want."

He'd said that in a husky, deep voice. Dean's eyes were intent on the knives, so I didn't think he was flirting or making some kind of innuendo. But my brain still wanted to make it dirty.

Just friends, I reminded myself.

Just. Friends.

CHAPTER TWENTY-TWO

"HEY, YOU TWO. HOW'S COUPLEDOM?"

River was sitting in front of his computer at a desk in a dark room, because hackers hated daylight, apparently. Or just wanted to uphold the mystique.

"It's great." I reached over and squeezed Keira's hand, but she untangled our fingers.

River had messaged us this morning that he had news. That was why Keira and I had taken a break from training to sit on the couch in the living room with a tablet propped in front of us.

It was now three weeks and counting since she'd moved in with me, and I knew she was anxious for some kind of movement on our investigation.

Yes, I wanted news too. But the sooner we tracked down her attackers and punished them, the sooner I'd have to say goodbye to her.

And if I fucking *ached*, having her this close to me every single day, yet off limits... Well, that was my issue to deal with.

I forced myself to pay attention to River.

"How's Denver?" Keira asked him. "You're still there, right?"

River was currently spending time with his wife, Lieutenant Governor Charlotte McKinley. They split their time between Denver and Hartley, and from what I knew, they were often apart. I wasn't sure how they managed it. But River and Charlie seemed to be going strong.

"Scenery's not as nice as Hart County, but the internet speeds are top-notch." He kissed his fingers in an exaggerated gesture, which was River Kwon in a nutshell. Always over-the-top. "Which is why I'm in touch. Sorry it took me this long, but some things can't be rushed."

Keira laughed. "Trust me, I know." She pointed at her left arm.

"Healing well?" River asked.

"I am. Slowly but surely."

"I'm going to share my screen." River tapped his keyboard, and an image came up. A heavy gold ring with a large, flat blue stone in the middle. "Keira, you snapped a photo of a ring like this one at Donny Phelan's place."

She leaned forward. "That's definitely it. The same ring those guys were wearing. First was the man I met at the bar the same night I was shot, and the second was at Phelan's mansion."

Our *only* real lead.

After that broken window at her house, there hadn't been any further incidents. No sign of anyone bothering her sister or Mom, as the Protectors had confirmed. Seemed like the bad guys had bought our cover story and believed we'd given up our investigation.

They had no idea we had a guy like River on our side.

"The photo you took was a bit blurry, but enough for me to go on. I started with a reverse image search, of course, but your photo wasn't zoomed in and there were too many false positives. So I—"

"Less detail, River," I said.

He shrugged. "Okay, if you want to rush to the ending, fine. I found this image of the ring on a subreddit, and after more research, I concluded it's the right one. You'll understand why in a moment. If you look closely, you can see the word *Crosshairs* etched beneath the stone. And if you zoom in on the stone itself…"

The picture expanded, revealing the faint lines visible beneath the stone. Literal crosshairs, like those on a rifle scope. A design I'd spent far too much of my life studying.

"They call themselves Crosshairs Security." River's face reappeared on the screen. He adjusted his black-framed glasses. "I've come across the name before. The Protectors actually have a file on these guys."

"Are they legit?" I asked.

"On the surface, sure. Crosshairs was founded by a man named Harris Medina." A new face appeared on the screen. A guy in his sixties with graying temples and a stoic expression. "He's retired Army Special Forces. Spent two decades after that as a PMC. Private military contractor. Medina keeps his nose clean. The company provides highly discreet security for wealthy individuals here in Colorado. Donny Phelan employs them as personal security for his business."

Ah. So that was our connection.

"There are rumors about Crosshairs Security greasing the wheels for their clients. If you need a deal done, Crosshairs can help you push it through. Using quiet but effective means."

"They're enforcers," Keira said.

River's head moved side to side. "Seems likely. There's been no proof of them crossing legal bounds, nothing for law enforcement to bust them on. Like I said. Legit on the surface."

I rubbed my jaw. "But what is Crosshairs doing for Donny Phelan? I assume he's up to something shady. Is his media empire a front?"

"I'm working on finding out. I've tapped into the surveillance feed around the Phelan property. Aside from selling shoddy vitamin supplements and peddling backward ideas, I haven't seen evidence yet that he's doing anything illegal. Or that Crosshairs is helping him do it."

"But why does he need that level of security?" Keira mused. "A couple of bodyguards is one thing for a famous person. This is something else. They were talking about shipments."

He swiveled in his chair. "That's the question, isn't it?"

"What about someone named Ryan?" she asked. "Is there a Ryan working for Crosshairs? Could be a first or last name. Supposedly he was angry about a late shipment, so he could be important."

"I haven't come across any Ryans affiliated with Crosshairs, but they don't publicize their employee lists." River tapped his keyboard again. "I did find *him*, though. Do you recognize this man?"

Another image. This one was a mugshot. I noted the man's features. Thick neck, sharp nose, nasty scowl. A tat peeked out from the collar of his T-shirt.

Keira inhaled. "That's the guy I saw at the Phelan property wearing the Crosshairs ring. He's the one who confronted me in the hallway."

"His name is Nox Woodson. Went to prison for running a meth lab. Got parole a couple years back."

"Harris Medina hired a drug dealer as a bodyguard?" I asked incredulously.

"Yep. Not great for the shiny image Crosshairs tries to

maintain. But by all accounts, Woodson is just the right kind of ruthless to make him an ideal enforcer. He was also suspected of gunning down four people who were edging in on his meth lab territory. There wasn't enough evidence to connect him to that shooting."

This time, when I reached for Keira's hand, she didn't let go.

River went on.

"Here's the kicker, though. There was one survivor of the massacre at the competing meth lab. The survivor described the shooter as wearing a demon mask."

Keira's eyes went hard as she stared at the face of Nox Woodson on the screen. "How do we get to him?" she asked.

River leaned back in his desk chair. "Woodson's been spending a lot of time at the Phelan property. I can give you access to the security cameras there. You'll be able to find him yourself. After that, however you want to deal with him... I'll leave the decision up to you."

CHAPTER TWENTY-THREE

Dean

NOX WOODSON HAD to be one of the shooters who'd attacked Keira. He could lead us to the second.

We needed to know all we could about him. Had to know where he went, who he spent time with, what he was hiding. But it was too risky to show up on Phelan's doorstep again. Even if it would've been funny to see the look on that asshole's face.

The access to the security cameras at Phelan's place, provided by River, was a good first step. From watching the feed, we noticed Woodson now had a limp. Keira swore he hadn't been limping the day she saw him in person. Which suggested Woodson had been the driver of the car that followed us and tried to force us off the road.

No matter what, I would *not* put Keira in danger again. Not until she was actually healed and ready to fight back.

So stealth would be our friend. Like a sniper roosting in a nest.

One Friday night, I parked us on a dark, deserted stretch of road, concealed by some trees. Keira and I were both dressed in dark, nondescript clothing.

"I've got him." She tapped at her screen. "Woodson's

talking with his buddies in the hall. Should be leaving soon for the night."

"Good. We're ready."

Woodson would have to drive this way as he was leaving Phelan's property. From there, we were going to follow him.

Our plan was to stick a GPS tracker on Woodson's vehicle to find out where else he liked to spend his time.

It had taken over a week to get ourselves set up and ready for this op. River had arranged for me to pick up some gear from Last Refuge, no questions asked. The rest of the Protectors weren't aware of the specifics of our investigation. Simply because we wanted to involve as few people as possible.

My truck was too recognizable, so I'd borrowed a vehicle from River with the guarantee that I wouldn't leave a scratch on it. I'd already switched out the real license plates for some decoys. As usual, the Last Refuge Protectors had a lot of different toys to play with.

But where Keira was concerned, over the past week I'd been on excellent behavior. No more heated looks. Minimal touching. Absolutely no kissing. I'd been all business. Which probably explained the dour mood I'd been in.

"And there's Phelan. Huh. Look at *that*." Keira held up the screen for me to see the camera feed.

It looked like Woodson was giving Phelan a lecture. The podcaster had his shoulders slumped, head down as he nodded at whatever Woodson was saying.

River's access to the security feed lacked any sound, but from what we'd seen, it was clear Phelan was *not* a fan of his bodyguards. Every time he was around them, he cringed away. Natasha, his assistant, also gave them a wide berth.

Supposedly, Crosshairs Security was working for Phelan. But the podcaster acted like *they* were in charge.

Made no damn sense.

"Do they have something on him?" Keira mused. "Or…"

"Or there's something very weird going on," I finished.

"Too bad we can't see every room in Phelan's mansion. Like the room Woodson and his friends were sitting in when I overheard them talking about the shipments."

I nodded. But the security cameras were only fixed on the entrances and main hallways. Enough to see the comings and goings of people there, but no eye-in-the-sky to see these mysterious shipments. Or whatever else Phelan and Crosshairs might be doing there.

We now had profiles of several more Crosshairs Security employees, but no match with the Ryan name. One face had also been conspicuously absent: the man who'd offered to buy Keira a drink at the roadhouse the night of the shooting. He'd been wearing a Crosshairs ring.

All these pieces, and we were nowhere near fitting them together.

"I'm not even sure we can call Phelan a suspect anymore," I said. "If he was pissed off at you, why would Crosshairs agree to risk exposure by trying to kill you in the first place? They had to know you're a cop. Maybe Phelan would be that stupid, but Crosshairs doesn't seem to be. Especially with an ex-Special Forces guy like Harris Medina as their leader."

"But then why *did* Woodson go after me? I've never met him before in my life."

Exactly what bothered me. The attack on Keira seemed personal. Not random. Woodson and his buddy had wanted to kill *her* specifically. But if Phelan hadn't been behind it, what was the motive?

"Okay, Woodson's on the move," Keira said. "Heading toward the exit."

I checked the clock. We'd timed out how long it would take for someone to drive past this spot after leaving the Phelan residence. About six minutes.

I set my stopwatch.

Six minutes and five seconds later, headlights swept past us. I gave Woodson another 30-second head start.

Then I turned over the engine and pulled out onto the highway, following the direction Woodson had gone. His taillights were just visible on the straight stretch of road ahead.

Keira put the tablet away. "Have you done anything like this before? Tailing someone?"

"Sure. Never in the USA, but I sometimes had to track my targets overseas. Study their movements. Figure out how they were most vulnerable."

"Want to share with the class?"

I heard the smile in her voice. I didn't know how she managed that. Being so unaffected by the details I confessed about my old life. I was talking about assassinating people, and she always shrugged it off. Maybe because Keira and I had been plotting to destroy the men who'd shot her.

But the things I'd done? They were different. There was no way she'd ever understand it fully.

Keira would never be a cold-blooded killer deep down, and thank fuck for that.

"You don't want to hear about this stuff," I muttered.

"Are you kidding? Yeah, I do. I want to learn. And it's fascinating. You were like a spy."

"I was *not* a spy. I didn't gather information or develop intelligence assets. I murdered people, Keira."

"You didn't kill them because you enjoyed it."

"You think I didn't?"

She turned sharply toward me, skin tinged blue from the dashboard lights.

Dammit, why had I said that?

We kept driving. I thought she'd dropped it, but then she said, "You could tell me, you know. What that necklace is really about. The rifle round."

Fuck. This woman had a way of cutting my rib cage open and reaching inside with just a few words. I felt torn between wanting to tell her the entire ugly truth about me and wanting to protect us *both* from that forever.

"Maybe I will someday," I said softly. Knowing that was a lie.

"That's what friends do. They talk to each other."

"So we're friends again? I hoped so, but you hadn't said it."

"You know we are. I couldn't stand eating so many meals with you otherwise."

I felt the corners of my mouth lifting. "Your friendship means the world to me. It's the best thing I've got going for me at this point."

"Asshole," she said with a laugh.

"That wasn't sarcasm."

She had no idea how sincerely I'd meant it.

Keira rolled her shoulders, stretching them. "Anyway. I'm glad you know what you're doing, at least. Otherwise, I would insist on doing the driving. I'm allowed now, you know. Not my first stakeout or mobile surveillance of a suspect either."

"Yeah, I know, Deputy. Next time, it's all you."

"Dean," she said a little while later. "Do you honestly think you're a bad person because of the things you've done?"

"Yes." The word came out rough. Like something scraped up and bruised. "I know I am. Good people always have a tiny moment of hesitation about taking a life, however brief, even when it's their job. That means you still have a soul. I don't ever want you to lose that."

"What about you?"

"I lost my soul a long time ago."

"Let's say for a moment I believe that's true. Just because you've lost something doesn't mean you can't get it back."

Her words echoed in the quiet of the cabin, answered only by the faint rush of the tires as we drove. I didn't know what I could possibly say in response.

But I wanted her to be right.

CHAPTER TWENTY-FOUR

Dean

WE KEPT FOLLOWING Woodson until he pulled into the parking lot of a strip club. A neon sign with a naked woman flashed at us from the roof.

"A nudie bar," Keira deadpanned. "Why am I not surprised?"

We were way out near the county line. I pulled our vehicle into the lot, picking a spot within view of Woodson's truck and the entrance, and watched him go inside. Loud music spilled from the door, and a row of motorcycles was lined up out front with men chatting beside them.

"We'll wait for the right opportunity," I said, "and then I'll put the tracker on Woodson's truck."

"No, *I'll* put it on his truck. My hands are little. I'm much more nimble."

"I'm nimble," I protested.

"You're big and tall and you've been putting on weight. Nobody will notice if *I'm* sneaking around a parking lot."

"Are you calling me *fat*?"

"I meant muscle." She poked my side. "You've been training so much. You're like a solid brick wall."

Good thing it was dark, because I was probably blushing.

My damn pale skin, even though I'd picked up my usual warm-weather tan.

Way back when I'd first returned to town, I'd set up an outdoor obstacle course on my property. I ran it religiously every morning, then spent several rounds with a heavy punching bag I'd suspended from a tree branch. Keira still wasn't allowed to run or do anything too physically taxing, but since she'd moved in, she'd joined me outside for her physical therapy exercises and stretches.

It just so happened I usually stopped for a water break during her stretch times.

Keira waved a hand at the club's entrance. "You could go inside. See the local sights."

"I'll pass, thank you."

"Getting shy on me, Reynolds? You've never been to a strip club before?"

"Didn't say that," I chuckled. "But it's not my scene."

I'd been a Marine enjoying my time off-base in my younger days. But that was a while ago. *Long* before I'd met her.

"Were you seeing anyone in Switzerland? The ski bunnies at those resorts must be gorgeous."

I tilted my head, studying her profile. "Is this more *friends* talk? We're sharing secrets?"

"This is you entertaining me. Stakeouts are boring 90% of the time."

"Fair point. No, I wasn't seeing anyone. I haven't dated for a while. What about you? Boyfriends?" My fingers clenched into a fist, and I forced them to relax.

"No dates. No boyfriends."

"Why not?"

She shrugged.

There were still people lingering outside the bar's entrance, and someone walked out onto the gravel of the parking lot, talking on a phone. Too much activity for us to make our move.

"Want to know what really made me want to join the Protectors?" she asked.

I glanced at her profile again, lit up in bright colors from the neon sign. "Tell me."

"I'd wanted to join pretty much since Owen told me about them. But after you left Colorado, I gave up for a while. I was kind of...down, I guess."

Guilt and shame reared their heads. Like always. I kept my mouth shut and waited for her to go on.

"Then I was out on patrol one night on a quiet road, and a woman ran out into the street, limping and bloody. She'd been beaten within an inch of her life."

"Geez. That's awful. What happened?"

"Her name's Hadley. She'd reported her brother to her local police department for stealing their mom's disability checks. Hadley was sure her brother was into other stuff, too, but she chose to mind her own business until it involved her mom. Unfortunately, the brother got a tip-off somehow about his arrest warrant. He skipped town. To get back at Hadley for betraying him, her brother sent his friends to punish her. She was too scared to press charges or even tell me their names. So, after she got out of the hospital, I took her to Last Refuge."

"They helped her?"

Keira nodded. "Aiden and Jessi made sure she had a place to stay and meetings with a therapist. I met with Hadley every week, too. We became friends. After a while, Hadley and her mom moved away and started fresh with the Protectors' help. I'd brought other people in trouble to Last Refuge before that, but Hadley was the one who got to me the most. I was so proud of her."

"You should be proud of yourself too."

Keira rested her arm on the passenger door. "I was. I decided I was going to become a Protector no matter what. Being a deputy has been an honor, but as Deputy Marsh, I couldn't do as much for Hadley as I wanted. With the Protectors, I could."

"You *did* help Hadley. Does it really matter if you're officially one of them?"

"It matters. To me."

I felt a rush of tenderness for her. Keira was so sweet and compassionate, but she matched those qualities with a fierce sense of justice. Kinda pissed me off that Trace hadn't brought her into the fold already.

Yes, she was young, and she didn't have military experience. Wasn't former CIA or FBI or special forces. But Keira had more guts than some of the Marines I'd served with. She'd changed so much in the last couple of years.

I remembered something Brynn had said about Keira, weeks ago. *Sometimes we're forged through fire.*

"I'll talk to Trace. See what I can do."

Her chin angled toward me. "No, I'm going to do this myself. But thank you for saying that. And for listening."

I couldn't even see her that well, but her beauty hit me square in the chest. Her strength. I'd been spending every day with her, yet she could still do that to me.

This woman was *everything*.

I probably wasn't ever going to get over her, and maybe I didn't want to.

"It's quiet," she said. "I'll go now."

After what she'd just told me, I wasn't going to tell her no. Reaching into the backseat for our gear bag, I handed her a tiny black square. "Attach the transmitter to the underside of his vehicle and press this button."

She nodded. "Got it."

Her door clicked open, and she slipped out. The seconds

passed. I tried not to fidget. I figured it should take less than ten seconds for her to make her way to Woodson's truck. Another five to get the transmitter in place.

I watched the app on my phone, waiting for the device to connect.

There. A blinking red dot appeared. The GPS transmitter was active.

Headlights turned into the lot. At the same time, a drunk couple stumbled out of the club and lit up cigarettes. I held my breath, watching the activity. Keira should've been on her way back, but maybe she was keeping out of sight until the lot was clear again.

Then the door to the bar flew open, and Nox Woodson stepped out. *Fuck*.

There was someone with him. A guy with a beard. He was more slender than Woodson but taller. Had a more cunning look in his eyes as he glanced around. He and Woodson stood there, talking.

And now a full minute had passed. I didn't like this. Where the hell was she?

I had to find Keira. *Now*. No way was I just going to sit here.

Reaching for the glove compartment, I unlocked it and took the gun I'd stowed inside. It was my unregistered SIG Sauer, and I'd brought it only in case of emergency. But this certainly had the makings of an emergency.

Clipping the gun holster onto my waistband, I quietly got out of the vehicle. Woodson and his friend were in my peripheral vision. Weaving between cars and keeping my shoulders hunched, I scanned the shadows for Keira.

Woodson and his buddy were moving now. Heading this way.

Shit, shit, shit.

"Dean?" Keira whispered. She'd just stepped out of the shadows between two cars.

Heavy footsteps crunched in the gravel not far behind us. It was dark, but if those men got a good look at Keira, they could recognize her.

I had to do something fast.

So I wrapped my arm around her waist and slanted my mouth down on hers.

Her body was stiff against me. But she kissed me back, moaning around my tongue. My hands groped at her hips, squeezing her curves. Backing her up against another random vehicle, I put every bit of longing into that kiss. We had to make this look real.

Keira grabbed hold of my shirt, pulling me closer. I lifted my hands to her face to hide it as much as I could.

Woodson paused briefly and huffed a laugh. "Y'all have fun tonight," he said gruffly. Then he and the other man got into Woodson's truck and drove off.

I broke the kiss. Keira's eyes were round.

"You good?" I asked, panting for breath.

"Um. Yep. Mission complete."

I rubbed my eyes, separating our bodies, though I wanted the opposite.

She pointed in the general direction of our vehicle. "We should...um, car..."

Right.

Nice going, Marine. Get your damn act together.

We returned to the borrowed car and got in. "What happened?" I asked as I replaced the gun in the glovebox.

"You were armed? You might've mentioned that to me earlier."

"I didn't know it would be necessary. Keira, tell me what happened out there. What took so long?"

"Drive. Let's get out of here. I'll tell you on the way."

I pulled us onto the road, heading back toward my place. The drive was going to take a while. But that was good. We had plenty of time to talk, and I could make sure we weren't being followed.

Also plenty of time to calm myself down. Three times now I'd had my mouth on Keira, and not once had it felt like part of a mission.

"The man who left the strip club with Woodson tonight," she said. "That was *him*. The bearded guy who offered to buy me a drink the night of the shooting."

I cursed.

"But I got a photo of him. That's why I didn't come right back after planting the tracker."

"We should send the photo to River, see if he can identify the guy." I exhaled. "You scared me to death disappearing like that, though."

"You don't trust me to be careful?"

"I do trust you. But you're still not physically able to defend yourself. I can't let you get hurt again. You're too important to me."

"Make up your mind, Dean. Are we in this together or not?"

"We are." On the other hand, I'd promised her mother I'd take care of her.

And if I brought that up right now, Keira might smack me.

"A few minutes ago, you were saying you'd help me become a Protector. Now you're getting upset about me being in danger when it was *nothing*. I was staying hidden. Woodson and his friend wouldn't have seen me at all. Of course, then you charged over there, guaranteeing they'd notice us."

"I had no idea what was going on. What was I supposed to do, just sit around?"

"Yes. You were supposed to wait for me. Instead, you had to manufacture a make-out session to get us out of it."

"I'll be sure to avoid kissing you in the future."

"Good." Keira touched her lips. Like she was thinking about it. Replaying it. "No more kissing. Or...any other stuff."

"Like walking in on me naked?"

"That was weeks ago! I said I was sorry. There won't be any repeats."

"*Good.*" Even though the memory of that particular moment had become fodder for my shower-time fantasies daily. I also didn't bring up the fact that she'd kissed me back, every single time.

I was tired of resisting this pull. What if we gave in to the attraction? Would it really be so bad?

Yes, my conscience responded. *Yes. It would.*

I had to keep Keira safe. And that included keeping her safe from me. Even if it took every last fucking ounce of my willpower to do it.

CHAPTER TWENTY-FIVE

Keira

LIVING with Dean Reynolds was quite possibly going to kill me.

Day after day, we trained together. Sat down for meals together. Tracked Nox Woodson's movements together. We laughed and argued and sat in silence together.

And every single day, I wanted him more instead of less.

This whole *just-friends* thing was not working.

Take, for example, his training on the obstacle course he'd built. Every single morning, he was out there as the temperatures warmed. Getting all sweaty with his shirt off, hair plastered to his face and his skin getting more tanned by the day. His muscles were more prominent too. Leaner. His reaction times faster.

Lately, watching Dean on that obstacle course had become a pastime of mine. A guilty pleasure.

For the first part of each morning, I would do my own training. I'd been taking longer walks, doing light cardio and stretching. Drilling my physical therapy exercises like it was my job, and arguably it was. But I still couldn't lift anything. Couldn't run or spar. Couldn't do pushups or planks.

Despite my limited routine, I usually tired out fast. Then I liked to grab a drink, sit on the back deck, and make notes on Woodson's daily movements using the GPS tracker we'd placed on his car.

Every few minutes, I would let my eyes wander to Dean pummeling the heavy bag. Or doing a zillion pull-ups.

Dean jogged up the steps onto the deck, pouring a bottle of water over his head. Rivulets spun down his neck, shoulders, and chest. A drop of water clung to one pink nipple.

Really? Was that necessary?

"Hey. What's Woodson up to today? Anything new?"

"The usual." I showed Dean my notes.

Woodson spent most of his time at the Phelan property. At least, his truck was parked there. His other usual hangouts were his home, a dive bar, and the strip club. The man didn't vary much on his routine.

Unfortunately, after a stakeout with a pair of binoculars outside Woodson's home, we'd learned it was surrounded by cameras. River hadn't been able to gain remote access to the cameras, so there was no possibility of sneaking a listening device inside undetected.

Another option was a listening device at the Phelan place. But Dean thought it was too risky to try going back there.

I wanted to get Woodson alone on a deserted road. Force him to answer my questions using any means necessary. And I didn't have a single ounce of guilt about the thought of torturing the guy. I was sure he'd been there the night of the shooting. The demon mask connection was enough for me, and I had no doubt Woodson also tried to run Dean and me off the road after I saw him at Donny Phelan's mansion.

Woodson had tried to kill me twice. He didn't deserve my mercy.

But Dean refused to make any big moves against Woodson until I was fully healed. That would be at least another *month*. I wasn't sure I could take it.

I just wanted to hurry up and finish healing. I wanted to know who'd shot me and why. What Donny Phelan and Nox Woodson and Crosshairs Security had to do with this whole strange conspiracy.

But for now, all of that was going to take more time. More patience.

More ogling of the sexy man I couldn't have.

At night, it meant more dreams about Dean, when all my resolutions about *just being friends* went out the window, and my subconscious played out my deepest desires.

In my dream last night, we'd been sparring together, getting all sweaty and tangled up until we were suddenly kissing. I'd licked along his salty skin until I reached the erection tenting his athletic shorts. The rest of the dream had progressed in filthy images and imagined sensations. His hard cock in my mouth. The fullness when I sank down on his thick shaft, starting to ride him...

"I'll shower and make us some sandwiches," Dean said. "I was thinking we'd spend some time in the sniper's nest this afternoon."

I sighed. "Yep. Sounds good."

An hour later, we crawled into the sniper's nest we'd made on a hillside. The vegetation was thick enough here to break up the sight lines. We were dug in to keep below the ridgeline, with stones reinforcing the depression and netting woven with branches and native grass to camouflage where we lay.

I could now take apart the sniper rifle in a matter of seconds. Reassemble it. Clean and inspect it. Almost every day I practiced aiming through the scope, often with Dean lying pressed against me, correcting my body position and teaching me the right way to breathe. To wait and watch for a shot.

Of course, I couldn't actually take a shot with a live round yet. It would be a long time before I was ready for that. Even lying in a prone position was hard for me, since I had to be careful about putting pressure on my injuries.

But I hadn't seen Dean fire the rifle either, not even to calibrate it. He'd said there was far more to being a sniper than pulling a trigger.

Through the rifle scope, I watched a family of deer grazing unaware in the meadow below. The deer had no need to worry. I was only observing. The rest of me was all too aware of the man beside me.

I was *almost* used to lying this close to Dean without getting distracted. Not quite, but almost.

I'd never spent so much time with someone just being quiet. Sometimes those silences were comfortable. Sometimes fraught with tension.

Okay, there was always tension.

"What are you thinking about?" I asked today. Because I still wanted to know him, even just as friends. I wanted anything of Dean I could get.

"How I swore I'd never pick up a weapon again, but it was easy. Feels like I never left."

His tone was even. I remembered the conversation we'd had the night we followed Woodson to the strip club.

You didn't kill them because you enjoyed it.

And his response: *You think I didn't?*

But if Dean had thought I would be horrified, he was wrong. I'd accepted his past the same day he told me. He was the one who couldn't accept himself. Couldn't let himself stay in one place. Be happy.

Couldn't give us a chance.

"Do you ever have regrets?" I asked.

"About leaving that life? No. Not about that."

"What do you regret?"

Dean's arm shifted, and I knew he was touching the

leather cord he wore on his neck. Then he blew a stray hair from in front of his face. "For one, letting my hair get this long. It's out of control. It's starting to bug the shit out of me."

I laughed, pushing away the disappointment of his changing the subject. "If you have clippers, I can cut it for you. Did you know Stephie wants to go to beauty school after she graduates? She wants to be a hairstylist."

"No kidding." His grin was soft in the dimness. "Good for her."

"She makes me watch all these online videos with her. I picked up a few things. I'm not saying it'll be a great cut, but your hair would definitely be shorter."

"Do *you* like my hair long?"

Ugh, what a question. Of course I liked it long. It was hot. "Yeah. But I like it short too."

I felt him looking at me. I checked the scope, watching the deer again as they snacked on meadow plants and heat spread up my neck.

Was it weird of me to offer to cut his hair? That was a thing friends did for each other, right?

Of course, not like I'd let him anywhere near *my* hair with a pair of scissors, but…

"Okay," he murmured. "After dinner. You can give me a makeover. But go easy on me."

A tremor went through my hands. Hell. So we were doing this.

CHAPTER TWENTY-SIX

Keira

AFTER DINNER and cleaning up the kitchen, Dean went upstairs for another shower. I tried really hard not to imagine him naked under the spray of the water. But it was way too easy to picture, since I already knew what he looked like naked and all.

I'd taken a shower right after we came in from training, so I paced around in my bedroom, waiting for him. Maybe he'd change his mind and decide we shouldn't do this after all.

But no. Dean appeared a few minutes later, dressed in sweatpants and no shirt, a towel draped over his shoulders collecting the water droplets from his damp hair. My heart stuttered.

My gaze was desperate to drop to that hollow between his pecs, like it always did when I was watching him run the obstacle course. But I managed to refrain.

"Brought these." He sheepishly held up some scissors, a cordless clipper, and a comb. "You sure you know what you're doing?"

"We'll work it out," I said, portraying a confidence I definitely didn't feel. "Come into my studio."

I'd set up a dining chair in front of the dresser, which had a mirror. I'd also laid out a painting drop cloth underneath.

Dean sat down, his eyes meeting mine in the mirror. The rifle round on his necklace sat between his collarbones. He never took that thing off.

I adjusted the towel, spreading his hair out. Then carefully combed through, pulling it back from his face. The strands were slippery.

Dean made this low sound in his chest, almost a grunt, but it didn't sound like he was in pain. His eyelids had gone half-mast.

This was the best excuse I'd had in a while to touch him. Dean and I had spent just about every day together since I'd moved in, but it wasn't like *this*. My hands on him and his heavy eyes on me in the mirror.

Focus, I told myself. This isn't a thing. Just cut the man's hair. The silky, damp hair that was now tangled in my fingers and leaving my skin wet…

Ungh.

Grabbing the scissors, I gathered the length of Dean's hair into a ponytail and cut it. "There goes a bunch of it. No going back."

He smiled in the mirror. "I don't want to."

The strands were above his chin now. "How short do you want it? A fade on the sides, longer on top?"

"That works. But I think it should be drier before we use the clippers, right?"

I narrowed my eyes. "I thought you didn't know how to do this."

"I've given myself trims. I like having your help though. If you still want to do it."

"I do." I shrugged. "You do a lot for me, after all. Letting me live here. Spending months on this mission with me."

"I like doing things for you, Keira."

185

Why was it suddenly so warm in this room?

My chest was tight as I dried his hair with the towel.

I grabbed the clipper next and switched it on. Moving the clipper upward, following the contours of his head, I managed to get lost in what I was doing.

Finally, after trimming the longer layers on top, I said, "What do you think?"

He was looking at me instead of his hair. "Best haircut I've ever gotten."

"That's nowhere near true. It's decent. I mean, I think you look great, but—"

"Yeah? You do?" There was something in the tone of his voice. All husky and deep. My stomach spun.

He did look good. I could see the lines of his face better. His eyes. The skin of his neck was all pink, contrasting the brown tone of mine, and I wanted to dip my head and kiss him there.

"Yep." The word shook on its way out. "It's good. There's hair everywhere. Better get this cleaned up."

Dean grabbed the vacuum to help. Once we'd tidied up, he still stood in my room. Shirtless. Hands on his hips just over the waistband of his low-slung sweats.

And I realized what a mistake I'd made.

Dean with that long, messy hair had been hot. But with this style, short enough to show off the undeniable handsomeness of all his features? He had nothing to hide behind now, and the way he was looking at me was naked with desire.

I'd told him there would be no more kissing.

I'd told *myself* we were just friends.

But a girl could only take so much.

I stepped closer to him, and my fingers met his stomach. Walked their way up the ladder of his abs. Then I pressed my palm flat to one round pec over his nipple, which made me gasp.

I couldn't believe I was doing this. But there was no way I could stop.

"*Keira*," Dean groaned.

My lips found his jaw and brushed over the rough stubble there. His arm closed around my waist, drawing me right up against him. Our bodies met like we were dancing, except the way we were breathing was so much more intense. We panted like we'd both just run Dean's obstacle course.

Like we were already making love.

He was warm, and he smelled like soap and himself, and I wanted him to surround me. Blot out the rest of the world like my own personal eclipse. That was how much space Dean took up in my head and my heart.

But when I lifted my chin, he was looking away from me.

Dean took my hand from his chest and pressed a kiss to my palm instead of my lips. "I want to, but I can't," he rasped. "I'm sorry."

When he backed toward the doorway, I didn't stop him. Then my door clicked shut, and he was gone.

I fell back onto my bed, the mattress bouncing under me. "This is so bad," I muttered, covering my hands with my face. "Why did I do that?"

I'd made things so much more awkward between us. He wanted me, but he wouldn't let himself have me. It broke my heart that Dean was so hard on himself.

But this was probably for the best. I could already tell if Dean and I *did* wind up in bed together, there'd be no coming back from it.

I'd had a couple of boyfriends in my life. I wasn't a virgin. But since the day I'd met Dean, I had barely looked at another guy. I hadn't been with anyone in so long that I'd forgotten what actual sex was like, not that my few sexual experiences were anything to brag about.

This wasn't a dry spell. More like a dry *era*.

If I finally had Dean in my bed, he was going to ruin me forever for anyone but him. But what the hell? Maybe I wanted to be ruined by Dean Reynolds.

There was a knock at my bedroom door.

"Keira?" a rough voice said on the other side.

Leaping up, I reached for the bedroom door handle. Then paused. My heart thumped a chaotic rhythm.

When I yanked the door open, Dean was there.

He stood with one arm braced against the frame. Sweats hanging below his hip bones. His chest and stomach on display, like before. There were a couple of tiny stray hairs on his shoulders from the haircut.

He'd just been here moments ago, but still. The sight of him stole my breath.

"I thought you went upstairs," I said.

"I meant to. But I've been standing out here." His blue eyes were guarded, but heat and want showed through.

"Why?"

"I couldn't leave." He took a step toward me across the threshold. I moved back the same distance to let him inside. "I'm not a good man, Keira."

"You're *you*. That's all that's ever mattered to me."

He brought his hands to my face. "Tell me to stop."

"Never," I whispered.

"You're sure you want this? Want me?"

Yes, yes, yes, my heart shouted. My whole body wanted to shout it. "I am. I do. What about you?"

"I'm sure I'll lose my fucking mind if I don't have you."

CHAPTER TWENTY-SEVEN

Keira

"THEN HAVE ME," I said. "I'm yours."

Dean's lips parted, the tip of his tongue moving along the inside of the bottom one. His rifle round pendant lay just below the hollow between his collarbones.

For several long seconds, he didn't move. It was agony.

Then Dean held my face and brought his lips to mine.

Unlike our previous kisses, this one didn't feel illicit or rushed. He was deliberate. Waiting for me to open up to him, then delving his tongue into my mouth. Pulling back to nibble at my lower lip.

And unlike the other times, I leaned all the way into him. Trusting Dean to hold me up as his tongue stroked inside my mouth. He angled my head. Brought one hand lower to cup the side of my neck, fingers teasing along my hairline like he somehow knew how sensitive my skin was there.

Those hands that were so deft with the sniper rifle. That had once pulled the trigger and ended more lives than he wanted to tell. How could he be so gentle with me if he'd done the things he claimed?

When I pressed my hands flat to his smooth back, I felt

his muscles twitching fast. Like he was barely holding on to control.

He started walking me deeper into the room. Toward the bed. I went willingly because that was exactly my idea too. Reaching between us, I tugged at the drawstring of his sweats, but that made Dean stop kissing me.

"Not yet. You've already seen me naked. It's my turn. I want to look at you."

I tried to swallow down my nervousness. I liked my body, even if I didn't have a ton of curves. But this was Dean. The guy I'd been fantasizing about and dreaming of for *years*. What if he was disappointed?

He sidled past me to sit on the edge of my bed. *His* bed, really, since this was his house. My breaths came faster as I stared at the thick length straining along his thigh.

My mouth watered, wondering how he would taste.

"Eyes up here," he said. "Come closer."

I took a few steps until I was between his open knees. Dean caught the edge of my tank top to pull me forward. His fingers went to the exposed skin above my neckline.

"Always wanted to touch these freckles," he murmured. "Kiss them. See how far they go."

Was this really happening?

I was half hypnotized as he lifted the hem of my top. I still wasn't supposed to put my left arm above my head too much, but the fabric was stretchy and easy to get off.

Now I was in my bra and baggy sweats, and his calloused fingertips were tracing lazy patterns from one freckle to the next.

"So pretty."

Not the scars, though, I thought, fighting the urge to cover the mangled skin on the left side of my chest. But Dean wasn't looking at the scars at all. Maybe he was choosing not to see the ugly parts of me, and that was fine. I was thankful.

I wasn't ready when his mouth dipped to suck one of my nipples through the cotton of my bra.

With a breathy whimper, my hands clapped onto his shoulders. Smiling, he went to suck the other. There was something so blatantly sexual about the feeling of it. We'd kissed before because of our fake relationship cover story. And he'd touched me before as a friend. Even held me close.

But *this*. Dean's lips sucking and teasing until the white cotton over my breasts was wet and translucent... I felt a pulse of lust between my legs. He could do anything to me, and I'd let him. I would beg for it.

Then he pressed his face between my breasts and inhaled, hugging me around the waist. I rubbed my fingers over his newly short hair.

Raising his head, he pulled me down into another kiss. "I've been waiting a long damn time for this."

"How long?"

"Since the moment I laid eyes on you."

I took a shaky breath. "Really? I can't believe I never knew."

Dean tugged me by the hips and eased me onto his lap, straddling him. The tip of his nose bumped my temple affectionately. "Did my best to hide it."

He'd already explained his reasons, but it was still difficult to accept. How could Dean not see how wonderful he was? I didn't care about his past. He'd been so good to me throughout our friendship, at least until he left town. That was why I'd fallen for him.

I couldn't help but fall for him.

When I shifted in his lap, I felt his erection under my behind. His hips moved to thrust against me. That wasn't what had my thighs clenching though. It was the way he stared at me. Like he wanted to wrap himself around me until the lines between us lost any meaning.

"Keira, I haven't been with anyone else since I met you. Haven't slept with anyone. Haven't even kissed anyone."

I went completely still.

"Wait, *seriously*?"

He laughed softly. "It's true."

"You haven't been with anyone in that long? We met years ago. Like, four years!"

"I know." He drew his thumb down my chin. "Trust me, I know. Probably shouldn't be admitting that, but just in case I last all of two seconds..."

Oh, no. I wasn't letting him distract me from this subject. I was surprised, but also, my inner possessiveness liked the sound of it a lot.

"There hasn't been anyone else for me either. There's *never* been anyone else for me but you."

"No one?" he rasped. "Even after I left, and you hated me?"

"I could never hate you."

I'm in love with you, I almost said, but that would without a doubt scare him away. Dean had just barely convinced himself to be here with me.

Maybe this was just for tonight. He'd told me over and over that he would leave Hart County again when this was finished. But I didn't care.

Okay, now it was my turn to crack a joke.

"You're way too good-looking for me to hate you," I said with a small smile.

Dean laughed. Kissed me again as he gently tipped me on my back onto the mattress. He slid my sweatpants past my hips and down my legs. "I've been dreaming of doing this. Fantasizing."

"So have I." Everything he was saying was straight out of my fantasies. Was this even real? "Especially after I saw you naked."

192

"And I *still* haven't seen you. That's not fair."

"I'm not stopping you."

"I'm not in a hurry." He left my bra and panties in place as he kissed down my body like he wanted to taste and admire every inch of skin. Find every freckle. Drag this out until neither of us could stand it another second.

While he kissed the inner hinge of one knee, his hand sneaked higher. His thumb brushed the crotch of my panties right over my clit, shocking a gasp out of me.

"Wet." His eyebrow raised. "Are you excited for what I'm going to do to you?"

"Yes," I breathed.

"Do you want my cock first? Or should I give you my tongue?"

Shivers of pure lust burned through me. I was shaking. Still trying to get my brain to process the fact that Dean was saying these things to me.

"I want all of it. *Everything*. Please."

Suddenly his expression shifted, and he sat up. "Hold on. You said there's never been anyone else. Did you mean... Literally no one? Are you a virgin?"

I clapped my hands over my face. "Dean, I'm twenty-eight years old."

"So? It's fine either way. I just—"

"I'm not a virgin."

He crawled up my body and lay close to me, gently moving my hands from my face. "I don't want to mess this up. Or hurt you. You're so special to me, Keira." His Adam's apple bobbed just above the leather cord as he swallowed. "Fuck, I shouldn't be doing this at all."

"Yes, you should. We both want this." I rolled and draped myself on top of him. "I'm far from innocent. But there are things I've never done. Things I want to do with you."

Blue flashed as his eyes flared wider. "Yes? Tell me."

My hand found the thick ridge in his sweats and massaged him there. He groaned. I remembered how Dean told me once that I was too young for him. He saw me as some shy, naive girl who would be shocked and disgusted by his history as a killer.

I wanted Dean to *see me*. See the woman I really was.

"I want your cock in my mouth. Want to taste you and make you come."

"You're going to be the death of me." His nostrils flared, pupils dilating. "You've never given a blow job before?"

I shook my head. "Saved it for you."

He rolled us so he was on top of me. Staring down at me with a predatory gaze. "What else have you not done? You said *things* plural, so I assume there's more than one. Unless I'm just greedy."

"There's more." I wrapped my legs around his waist. "No one has ever gone down on me. I want your tongue inside me."

"Then I know exactly what I'm going to do to you first. Been wanting this too long and I can't wait anymore."

"Anything," I breathed.

He kissed me as a growl rumbled from his chest. "It shouldn't matter, but the thought of being the first man who's tasted your sweetness... Fuck, Keira. That drives me wild. I have to have it."

My panties were soaked. I started pushing them down while Dean was kissing me, but then he shoved back onto his knees. He grabbed both sides of the thin fabric and *tore*.

Hell. Yes.

I wanted this side of him. Not treating me like I was too young or delicate. I wanted him rough and feral. Losing control.

He shimmied his body down the mattress. A couple more

rips had my panties gone. "Spread your legs," he commanded, voice barely recognizable.

Don't get shy, I told myself. But it had been a long time for me, and no guy had ever done this. And it was *Dean*.

I opened my legs. His eyelids went heavy as he looked his fill, but only for a couple of seconds. Then his stubble was tickling the sensitive skin of my inner thighs again, his big hands sneaking beneath to shove my legs open wider, holding them in place.

His head lowered. His warm tongue slicked over my core, and I had to bite my lip to keep from screaming.

I couldn't believe how good it felt. So raw and intimate.

Dean's tongue flicked back and forth over my clit until I was crying out. "*More*. Oh, please."

When his tongue pushed deep inside my pussy over and over, I turned into a rambling mess. His eyes rose to give me a heated, intense look.

I was glad for the haircut because otherwise his hair would've been hanging into his face. I loved being able to see exactly what he was doing and how he was enjoying it.

Had I ever been this loud in bed? He was making me feel shameless.

It hadn't even been that long and I was already barreling toward the most intense orgasm of my life. I could feel it building. Ready to shatter me apart.

I almost sobbed when his mouth slid away to kiss my inner thigh instead.

"But—I want—*Please*, Dean."

"Shh. Not yet, sweetness. Not yet."

He started licking my clit slowly again. Going all the way back to the beginning, like he could do this all night. Dean worked me up again until my thighs were quaking and sweat prickled all over my skin. I couldn't take it. The pleasure was too good.

My hand found the top of his head to keep him right there. My hips rocked against his tongue, and his fingers rhythmically squeezed my ass as he feasted on me.

I moaned as an orgasm crested over me. He sucked my clit between his lips and my whole body shuddered with the climax. It went on and on. One cry after another filled the room with sound and that was coming from *me*. His tongue didn't stop until he'd wrung every last gasp of my orgasm, and my thighs tried to close.

Dean sat up, wiping his mouth. I was *wrecked*.

"Not bad for a first time, huh?" he asked.

I smiled languidly.

He dropped one more kiss to my knee, then got up. Shoved his sweats down and off, followed by his dark blue boxer briefs. I'd seen him naked before, but it was *very* different with him being hard. His erect cock was thicker and longer and looked desperate to be touched.

"After tasting you, hearing you scream, I'm already about to go off." He fisted his shaft and started to stroke as he sat beside me.

I propped on my elbow and reached for him. I had to know how he'd feel in my hand. It was better than I'd imagined. Hot and so firm, but at the same time, his skin was velvety soft. I loved it.

"Keira—fuck, I'm going to—"

Quickly lowering my head, I wrapped my lips around the salty tip of his cock and sucked while he took over stroking his shaft. Dean shouted. His cock pulsed into my mouth. My eyes fluttered closed as all the different sensations overwhelmed me, and I tasted his release on my tongue.

I'd made Dean come. He'd done the same for me. And it had been *perfect*. More than perfect.

I couldn't wait to do it all again and do everything we hadn't tried yet. Just a few tastes, and I was so needy for him.

He pulled me up into his arms. All the tension and stress had vanished from his expression. "Come here so I can kiss you," he said.

"Are you sure? I taste like you."

"I taste like you too. C'mere."

I sprawled on top of his big body, and Dean held my face as he kissed me softly. It felt like coming home.

CHAPTER TWENTY-EIGHT

I DOZED for a little while with Keira in my arms. The reality of what we'd done was plenty evident, but the guilt hadn't hit me yet. I didn't want it to. There was no way I could regret being with Keira.

I'd told her I wasn't a good man. Yeah, perhaps that sounded dramatic, but that was my truth. She hadn't blinked. She still wanted me. While she didn't know *everything*, she knew enough to make an informed decision.

Or maybe I was lying to myself and being selfish. Either way, there was no going back to what we'd been before.

I'd fought this temptation for so long. Denied myself what I wanted most. But I could no longer deny *her.*

Was it terrible that I got off on being the first man to have his mouth between her legs? Or his cock between her lips?

She wiggled on top of me like she was trying to get comfy. At some point, I'd pulled her blankets over us, and she'd taken off her cotton bra. We were skin to skin. This bed was the best place in the world, and I had no plans to leave it anytime soon. At least until morning, and that was a long time from now.

Don't think about tomorrow, I instructed myself. *Just be with her. Right here, right now.*

"You're beautiful," I murmured.

"I thought you were asleep."

"I was a little asleep."

She lifted her head and smiled. "You're either asleep or not asleep. It can't be a *little*."

"Sure it can." I yawned, stretching my limbs out and relaxing. Her body on top of me was sweet and soft. "I never sleep very deeply. I'm up half the time most nights."

Keira frowned at me. "Nightmares?"

"No. Just a light sleeper."

I felt her assessing me, so I let my gaze wander around her room. I hadn't checked it out much earlier when she was cutting my hair. It had been impossible to focus on anything else but her.

Who knew having Keira give me a haircut would be such a turn-on? Going to the barber definitely didn't do a *thing* for me.

"You brought over the lavender candle I gave you," I said, pointing at her nightstand. "And the blue throw blanket." She'd draped it over the chair in the corner.

She tucked her head against my neck. "I packed everything from your care package and brought it here. Didn't want to leave any of it behind."

"I did well? Even the fuzzy socks with the cats?"

Keira snorted. "You know you did well. You knew exactly what you were doing. Like you haven't seen me wearing those fuzzy socks."

Grinning, I smoothed my hand down her back beneath the covers. "Had to do everything I could. You'd thrown me out of your hospital room. I was afraid you'd never forgive me."

She propped her head on her hand. "I was mad. But there

wasn't really anything to forgive. Well, that's not true. You were a crappy friend."

"I was."

"But there was never any question that I'd forgive you, even when I was trying to stay angry. I've always had a soft spot for you. Never could resist you."

Warmth spread through my chest. I kissed her hairline. "That's how I felt about you. You've got no idea how many times I almost kissed you over the years we were friends."

"Clearly you *could* resist me." Her tone was light, but we were getting close to harder topics.

"I thought I was doing the right thing." I'd told myself it would be easier on us both if we didn't know how good it would be.

Now, we did.

"You really didn't date *anyone* while I was gone?" I asked.

"You think I was lying?"

"No. But you're gorgeous. Sweet and strong and amazing. I'm sure men have wanted you. Asked you out." My gut swirled with nausea at the idea of her with someone else, but facts were facts.

"Some did."

"And you said no?"

"I said no," she whispered. "Even when you were gone, you were the only man I wanted. No one else came close."

I lifted my head to kiss her. "I never felt a thing for any other woman. I'm the idiot who refused to acknowledge why."

"Were you lonely?"

"I would've said no," I said softly. "But I think I was. No one could ever replace you."

Sorrow crossed her beautiful features. "Did you ever think about coming back here?"

"All the damn time. At the end of every season, when I

had to pick a new place, I thought about Colorado. Deep down, I probably knew I'd end up back here eventually."

"I guess I was holding on to that hope too. Stephie kept telling me two years was enough time to move on and get over you. I'm glad I didn't." She flinched. "Not that I think this is permanent or something. I know what this is. I don't expect anything."

"Keira, you *should* expect more than I can give you. You deserve someone who'll give you everything."

"But I want *you*. So I'll take what I can get, and I'll keep enjoying every second of it. And I do mean *seconds* because that's how long you lasted."

"Hey, now!" With a growl, I flipped us so I was above her, still careful of her healing injuries. "*Years*, Keira. Nothing but my hand for years. I was pent up."

"It wasn't just that I'm a natural at blow jobs?"

"Your mouth had a lot to do with it." I kissed her, sucking on her tongue when she offered it to me. "I blame all of you though. You're an extremely sexy woman. In my fantasies, you've made me come at least a thousand times. The reality is even better."

My cock was firming up against her thigh, eager for more attention. She meant more to me than I could ever tell her, but at least I could give her pleasure and show her how irresistible she was.

She shuddered, eyes dreamy. We kissed some more, and I rubbed my swelling cock on her thigh.

But then Keira pushed against my chest. "Wait."

I lifted up onto my elbow. "You okay?"

She sat up against the pillows, and I shifted so I was sitting beside her. My erection rested against my stomach.

"I need you to be honest with me. Is this a one-night-only thing? We wake up tomorrow, and you have a million excuses for why we can't do this again? Some line about *protecting my heart* or that I *deserve better*."

I took her hand and kissed it. "What do *you* want?"

"For this to not be over yet. Not when we've just started. There's a lot more I want to do with you." Her fingers brushed down my chest. Then all the way to the swollen head of my cock, where she dragged a fingertip over the slit. *Fuck*. I tipped my head back and groaned. She was playing dirty in every sense of the word.

"But if this ends when the sun comes up," she went on, "I guess we could stay up all night for a sex marathon. If you can get it up that many times."

Laughing, I pulled her into another deep kiss. "I'm happy to prove my mettle. It's hardly a challenge with you around. I plan to take you in every possible way."

Now that we'd crossed this line, I couldn't go back.

I playfully nipped her lips with my teeth, and she sighed against my mouth. "But we don't have to rush," I said. "If we stay up all night, I want to talk too. Laugh with you. See you smiling and feel you cozy and happy against me. And I'd like to do that tomorrow and the next day too. However long we can. How does that sound?"

Her eyelashes had drooped, blinking fast, and her expression was doing some complicated dance I couldn't interpret. "It sounds perfect."

Her voice was sad, and I couldn't even bring myself to ask why. Because I knew. I knew.

I just had to make this so good for her that we'd both have the memories to keep us warm when it ended.

———

Bacon sizzled in one skillet, and butter melted in another. I wasn't much of a cook, certainly not compared to a guy like

ONE LAST SHOT

Aiden Shelborne, but I had a few tricks. Breakfast was one of them. We usually had cereal or toast, so Keira hadn't seen my skills yet.

She wandered into the kitchen just as I was cracking eggs into the butter. "It smells great out here." Her voice was adorably rough from sleep, and she had a few lines on her cheek from her pillow. She'd thrown on a sweatshirt, but I was fairly sure there was nothing underneath.

With a spatula in one hand, I sidled over to kiss her. "Hey, sweetness. Coffee's ready. Food will be up in a couple minutes."

Keira grabbed a mug and filled it. Then took a sip, blinking at me over the rim.

"You okay?" I asked. "How's your chest and shoulder?"

"I'm fine. Just...getting used to this. Last night, I wondered if I was going to wake up to you being all broody, saying you'd changed your mind about us."

I pushed at one egg with the spatula. "I told you I wanted more than a night with you."

Her brow wrinkled as she sat on a kitchen stool. "Yeah, but I was half convinced I'd dreamed all that sweet talk of yours."

"So, I'm a dream come true."

She laughed into her mug. "You're so corny. I missed how corny you used to be. You've been pretty serious since you came back."

I shoved the bacon strips and the eggs into a serving dish, then crossed over to her for another kiss. "There's been a lot to be serious about. But I'll be corny for you. If you like it."

She tasted like coffee and temptation. But I didn't have to say *no* to this anymore, and that was pretty wild to me too. She'd told me last night she planned to enjoy every second we had together. Made sense to me.

After I made her a plate, complete with toast, sliced

bananas, and a side of hot sauce, I sat beside her with my own mug of coffee.

She stared at her food. "Sunny-side-up eggs are my favorite."

"I know. I remembered."

Keira broke off a shard of crisp bacon and popped it in her mouth. "Aren't you eating?"

"Can't eat much before my workout. The obstacle course is waiting."

"Isn't this a day off? I declare a sex holiday."

I grinned. Fuck, she made me happy. "Sex later. Training first."

Tension drew tight in the room, like an invisible string being pulled. I'd just reminded us both of why we were here. We had a mission.

Keira shook hot sauce on her eggs and took a bite. "Speaking of sex. Did we…last night…"

"Bad sign if you can't even remember."

She bumped me with her elbow. "I remember the best orgasm of my life and your cock on my tongue. I remember *that*."

My skin glowed with pleasant heat. "Good. I was hoping to leave an impression."

"But then we were working on round two, and my mind goes blank after that."

"You fell asleep before anything else could happen. It was very cute." I kissed her temple, my hand on her back. "You were drooling on my chest."

"I left you hard? I'm sorry." Her smirk had sarcasm all over it. So I had to kiss her lips some more.

"I survived."

After she finished eating, I put away the rest of the spread to eat later and did the dishes. Keira offered to help, but I said no. "Go get dressed for your morning training."

"You're worse than my physical therapist," she grumped.

After she'd changed into workout clothes, with her curly hair tied back, Keira returned to the kitchen. I was wiping down the counters. Her arms went around my waist, her cheek resting between my shoulder blades.

I closed my eyes and savored the contact. This was what I'd always longed for with her, and it was so perfect it hurt.

Then her hand sneaked into my shorts and brazenly squeezed my cock. "We have time for a quickie, don't we?"

"Keira..." I groaned, turning around.

But she was already sinking to her knees. Damn. Tugging at my shorts and boxer briefs, she had her mouth around my soft dick in moments. *Nngh,* how was a guy supposed to resist that?

My hands gripped the counter. She sucked me, and my cock filled in no time. Hard and aching between her lips as her tongue flicked the underside.

Heaven. This was heaven, and I had no idea who'd screwed up and let me in past the gates.

When she pulled off me, I almost dragged her back. "Why'd you stop?"

"I almost forgot about morning training. Oops. I know how important it is. We'd better get out there."

My head tipped back, and I made an undignified sound that some might've called a whimper. "When did you turn evil? How am I supposed to run with this thing?"

Keira stood up, brushing off her sweatpants. "Isn't that the three-legged race?"

"Now who's got the corny jokes?"

She went onto her toes and whispered in my ear. "I'm not so innocent anymore, huh?"

"Not innocent." My arm draped around her shoulders, holding her close as I leaned back on the counter. "You're good in all the ways that matter. But not innocent."

Her face got a thoughtful look. "There's an old proverb I heard once. Passed down through generations. *A lady must be proper in the streets, but a freak in the sheets.*"

We both cracked up. "Wow. Are you sure you didn't get that from Donny Phelan and his podcast?"

She poked me in the chest. "Jerk. He wishes he was as clever as me."

I had to give her a few more kisses before training time. We were still laughing as we headed out into the sunshine.

When had I ever been this giddy with happiness?

It was almost enough to make me forget this couldn't last.

CHAPTER TWENTY-NINE

I CONTROLLED my breathing as I leaped up and over a wall, landing on the balls of my feet. Then practiced quick footwork through the tire run, grabbed a couple of heavy sandbags, and sprinted up a hill.

Keira always watched me from the back deck, and today, she wasn't even being subtle about it. She stood with her hands on the railing, head tracking my every move.

It was possible I was showing off a little. After getting naked with her last night, I somehow had even more to prove.

The temperatures were starting to climb. Sweat poured down my face and body and soaked the waistband of my shorts. I'd gotten rid of my shirt a while ago.

I felt her eyes on me as I grabbed a drink of water and caught my breath. Keira had already finished her cardio and stretching as well as her drills on cleaning and assembling the rifle.

Since our surveillance run following Woodson and planting the tracker, she'd been learning about ranging, wind reading, creating a data book. I'd given her all kinds of manuals to read too, even though becoming a sniper was about practical experience. She couldn't fire the weapon herself just yet, but I should've been showing her how to zero the rifle and make adjustments.

So far, I'd sucked as a teacher. I mean, I'd slept with the student. But that wasn't even the worst of it.

I still hadn't been able to fire a gun. It was a mental block of some kind. I hadn't been able to get past it. And the thought of *Keira* being the one behind the scope and pulling the trigger, taking an unsuspecting life, even if it was justice... My fist closed around the bullet at my neck.

Sharing her bed had only intensified my protectiveness. And my doubts.

By the time I ran the course again and returned to Keira, I was all smiles, my uncertainty packed away in a neat box. The rest of today was just about making her laugh. Making her come.

Water poured into my mouth from the bottle as I sauntered toward the deck.

I poured the rest over my head and wiped a hand over my face and through my hair. The short hair reminded me of everything that had happened last night. Arousal pooled in my low belly as I remembered thrusting my tongue inside her. How she screamed my name.

"How's the haircut?" Keira asked. She folded her arms on the top railing and smiled down at me.

"Much easier. I don't miss the strands hanging in my face. But how did I look out there on the obstacle course?"

She rolled her eyes. "Like all that shaggy hair was hiding a big head."

"There are other big things about me." I loosely cupped my junk through my shorts.

"Corny as hell," she muttered.

I went up the steps to the deck. "Can your returning hero have a kiss?"

Her eyebrow arched as she gave me a once-over. "You're sexy when you're sweaty. But that doesn't mean I want that all over me."

"Damn. Because I have some very specific ideas about getting all over you."

Her dark eyes gleamed with humor. But that look turned a lot more interested as I stood next to her and braced my hands behind me on the railing, pushing out my chest like I was putting myself on display.

"How about you call the shots right now," I said. "What do you want me to do?"

"Strip."

Mmmm. I liked where this was going. That bossy, official-sounding tone in her voice emphasized how much Keira Marsh had grown up in the years I'd known her.

With slow, teasing movements, I hooked my thumbs on the waistband of my athletic shorts and eased them down over my hips. The slick fabric dropped to the deck, and I stepped out of them. I followed the same routine with my boxer briefs. Which left just my running shoes and the leather cord on my neck.

I spread my legs a little and leaned back against the railing again. My cock hung heavy. With her gaze on me like that, I was already getting hard.

And Keira just kept staring, like the vixen she apparently was, as my shaft filled and lengthened without a single helping stroke from me.

I was throbbing. Aching. My cock pointed at her like it knew exactly what it wanted.

The sun beat down on my bare skin. A slight breeze had picked up, cooling me off a little as it whistled through the trees. This property was all ours. Nobody else around for miles. Though if anyone had been watching, I wouldn't care. Like I'd told Keira before, I wasn't modest.

If she asked me to, I'd bend her over the railing right now and thrust inside her. With the great outdoors as our witness.

I was like a starving man who'd been offered an all-you-can-eat buffet. Despite my doubts, I wasn't going to say no to her again. I wanted it all.

The tip of Keira's tongue followed the curve of her upper lip. "Go inside and shower."

"Yes, ma'am." My voice was laced with all the innuendo I could fit in those two words. "You planning to join me?"

"If you're lucky."

Smirking, I toed off my shoes and went inside with my cock bobbing in front of me.

In the downstairs bathroom, the rush of water filled the room with noise. After testing the heat with my hand, I stepped inside and closed the shower curtain.

Renovating this bathroom was on my long list for the house. Some new tile, a glass enclosure, and a framed mirror would make it much nicer and more modern. Keira deserved the best.

Fuck. I closed my eyes under the spray, realizing how stupid that thought had been.

Keira and I wouldn't be living here longer than another month or two, depending on how long it took to finish our investigation into Woodson and his buddies at Crosshairs Security. I would make sure she had her vengeance. And then...

The rings on the shower curtain jangled. There was a burst of cooler air, followed by soft, small hands on my back. "Hi," Keira said.

"Hi." I glanced at her over my shoulder, happy to see she was naked. "I was just getting washed up."

"Good."

With a handful of body wash, I lathered myself, then

washed Keira too. Which led to us kissing with her back against the tile. Holding her by the hips, I lifted her up. Her legs wrapped around me. My erection was trapped between us as we made out, tongues and lips sliding.

"Dean," she said between kisses. "I need your cock inside me. I can't wait anymore."

A flush passed over my skin. A burn from within me that had nothing to do with the hot water of the shower. "Soon. I want to make you come first. And then I'll make you come again on my cock."

Setting her on her feet, I kissed her some more, sucking on her tongue with long pulls. At the same time, I brought my hand between her legs and gently teased her clit.

"How does that feel?"

"Good," she moaned. "So good. Keep going."

My fingers circled her clit, drawing out whimpers and pleas. Then moved lower to tease her opening. Keira's hand jacked my cock at the same time until she lost concentration, her head falling back against the shower wall.

"Show me how you like it," I said low in her ear. "How do you touch yourself?"

"Here." Keira guided my hand. "Like this." I knew I'd gotten it just right when she made a desperate sound, eyelids fluttering.

"Do you think about me when you make yourself come?"

"Only you," she panted. "Every time. No one but you."

My fingers moved faster. A sob wrenched from her throat. Keira grabbed for my arm, her face pushing to my chest, and then she was shuddering. I felt her clench around my fingers.

Only you, Keira, I thought. No one else had ever made me feel the things she did.

I needed more. Had to finally claim her.

Switching off the water, I pulled a couple of towels from

the hanger outside the curtain. Wrapped one around her shoulders, the other around my hips.

"Your room," I said, taking her hand and lacing our fingers together. Just that small amount of contact, and it was everything to me.

I was so gone for this woman.

"It's your room more than mine," she pointed out.

"I guess right now, it's ours."

Keira's eyes went soft, and she nodded quickly.

The lights were off in her room, with daylight streaming around the curtains. Keira turned to face me and dropped her towel to the floor. I couldn't get over how stunning she was. So much gorgeous, flawless skin. Her perfect small breasts and the slight curves of her hips. And those freckles. I'd mapped them out last night, but those were going to need more extensive study.

She reached out to flick open the towel on my hips. The terry cloth pooled at my feet. There was no secret about how my body was reacting to her. My erection had gone down a bit earlier, but now it was back in full force. The head of my cock almost purple and the veins prominent.

Then our hands were on each other. I cupped her breasts. She dragged her short nails down my abs, just enough sensation to drive my arousal even higher. I was dizzy with it.

I reached up to touch the tiny hairs along her hairline. "You're so beautiful to me. Every bit of you."

She inhaled sharply. "The scars are ugly."

My gaze moved to her side, where a bullet had grazed her, and then to her chest and shoulder, where the scar tissue was more extensive. I'd avoided those areas last night because I hadn't wanted to hurt her or make her uncomfortable. But now, I traced my fingertips as lightly as possible over the healing wounds.

Rage, consuming and dark, took me over for a second.

Squeezing my throat and blurring my vision. Because the men who'd done this were still walking free.

"No part of you is ugly," I said, tamping my anger down. It was just Keira and me right now, and I didn't want anything else tainting that. "I don't want to hear you talk that way. Every inch of you is beautiful to me. Including your scars. No other woman comes close."

She shrugged with a small smile on her lips. "I guess scars are pretty badass."

I grinned. "Damn right. I've got a few myself."

"Hmm, I should get a better look."

I twisted and fell back on the mattress, making it bounce, while Keira laughed. She crawled on top of me and started kissing my skin randomly. My oblique, a bicep, my pec. She paused as she eyed the rifle round. But she didn't ask about it. Not today.

Instead she crawled upward and sucked on my lower lip.

I circled my arms around her to switch our positions. She spread her legs to make room as I stretched over her. My eyes met Keira's. Held. "Do we need protection?" I asked.

She shook her head.

"Tell me you want me," I rasped.

"Always. Do you want me?"

I kissed the tip of her nose. "Keira, you're all I've ever wanted."

That sounded so messed up given how many times I'd put distance between us. Told her no, tried to let her down easy. But this was all I'd wanted. Keira in my arms, skin to skin, knowing she was safe and cared for. Happy, because I'd made her happy.

I wished with every tattered remnant of my soul that we could've had this forever.

But at least we had it for a little while, and that would have to be enough.

I guided the tip of my cock to her opening. At the first push, she gasped, and I froze, just barely inside. "You okay?"

"I'm just… It's been a long time for me, and you're so… Never been with anyone as big as you. What if it doesn't fit?"

Smiling, I dropped my head to nuzzle her cheek. "I'll go slow. I won't hurt you."

Holding my upper-body weight on one elbow, I rocked my hips while I caressed her face and body with my other hand. When I was finally all the way inside, the tight grip of her on my cock made me lightheaded. She was shaking. Breathing hard.

"You okay?" I asked.

Her palms were on my chest. Her pulse thrummed at her neck, and she had to feel the way my heart was beating. Beating just for her. And she probably felt the way the vein in my shaft was throbbing inside her too, with every hard thump of my pulse.

"I want you to be rough with me. Make me feel like I'm yours."

"You've always been mine."

I started to move. She arched into me, sighing, and hooked her ankles behind my waist. With every thrust of my cock into her sweet, perfect body, I was losing a little more of my control. This was *Keira*, the woman who meant so much to me, who I would do anything for. *Kill* for.

I was inside her. We were finally connected, with everything else stripped away.

Sweat gathered on my upper lip, my brow, my chest. I could feel my muscles flexing. Tight, hot pleasure throbbed low in me, building and building. My groans sounded primal.

"Want you to come, Keira. I need to feel you come on my cock."

She gasped and moaned like she was close. I leaned back

so I could reach between us and rub her clit the way she'd shown me in the shower.

The moment she cried out, I gave in too. Basking in waves of pleasure that I felt everywhere, taking me over. My hips kept rocking into her to draw it out. To keep that connection between us for as long as possible.

As I started to soften, I lowered myself to the mattress beside her and kissed her forehead. Her cheeks. "How do you feel?"

She smiled and hummed. "Like I got what I always wanted."

That made me smile too, though the feeling was also bittersweet.

"How about you?" she asked. "How do *you* feel?"

"Like I want to do that again as soon as I'm hard."

CHAPTER THIRTY

Keira

LIVING and training with Dean was a wholly different experience now that we were lovers.

Mornings started off with kisses and caresses in bed. Smiling and flirting as we made coffee together. Dean finally let the sunnier side of his personality show through after it was absent for so long. I loved how he would sneak up and hug me from behind as I poured my cereal, as if he couldn't stand not to be touching me.

Dean was still serious about getting out early to complete our drills and training, but sometimes I succeeded in distracting him. Like when I sank to my knees in the kitchen and sucked him off until he shouted and came hard down my throat. No more teasing like that first day.

Or when I worked him up so much he set me on the kitchen counter, tugged off my sweatpants, and licked and sucked my clit until I was a rambling mess. Other times, he bent me over that counter and slid his thick cock into me, pumping until an intense orgasm left me gasping.

But we always got outside eventually, where Dean ran the obstacle course. I pushed myself a little harder each day too. As soon as the three-month mark since the attack passed, I started practicing with my service weapon on the outdoor range we'd set up.

No, my doctor hadn't *technically* given the okay yet, but I felt strong. I was ready. Each day, I warmed up my shoulder carefully and kept the targets close, using lower-recoil ammo.

After a few days of watching my progress, Dean brought his handguns out of their case and joined in the daily target practice. He didn't say a word about it, but I could tell it was a big deal for him. Firing a gun again after so many years.

But it was just practice. Not firing at a person. Still in loophole territory.

Some afternoons, Dean showed me knife techniques for hand-to-hand combat, though we couldn't spar full-out. I was relieved to feel more like myself again, brushing up on the skills I would eventually need to go back on patrol. I hadn't been cleared to return to duty, of course. Except on a desk, which I'd been able to avoid so far.

I much preferred spending my days with Dean.

"Are you ever going to show me how to shoot this thing?" I asked one afternoon in the sniper's nest.

Because as much as I loved being here with him, being *anywhere* with Dean, this aspect of my training had completely stalled. I had a long way to go before I could handle firing the rifle myself because of the level of recoil. Even *I* wasn't stubborn enough to risk re-fracturing my collarbone.

But I could learn a lot from seeing him do it. I didn't understand his reticence. Probably because he wouldn't talk to me about it.

"Soon," he said. Same thing he always said. "You've got plenty of room to improve on ranging and target ID, and a dozen other things that don't involve firing."

I held back my grumbling.

Dean turned his head to look at me. "The problem is,

halfway through any lesson I try to give you, you start kissing the teacher."

"*Me*? Who was just grabbing my ass like five minutes ago when I was making a wind call?"

"You have to learn to ignore distractions."

Pushing into Dean, I rolled him half onto his back and draped my leg over him. It wasn't easy in the narrow depression we were in. But he went willingly, laughing as I kissed him. We were all tangled limbs and heavy breathing and heat. The butt of the rifle bumped me.

His hard cock was bumping me too, through the stiff canvas of his cargo pants, but there wasn't enough room to get too vigorous in here. After a couple of minutes, our kisses slowed, turning softer and sweeter.

It made me think of the way he'd fucked me from behind in bed last night, rough and raw and dirty, then traced soft patterns on my back with his fingertips until we both fell asleep. How could those hands be so lethal and yet so gentle?

Sharing a bed with Dean every night was an indulgence. One I never wanted to end, though of course it would eventually.

"Since we're distracted anyway," Dean said, "I was thinking we should do something else the rest of the afternoon."

"Like what?"

"Been a while since we've gone into town, except just to get groceries."

I reached up to run my palm over his lightly stubbled cheek. "What should we do?"

"How about some clothes shopping? I saw you looking in a store window the last time we were down for groceries. That place with the dresses."

"Okaaay." I dragged the word out. "You really want to do that? Shop for clothes?"

He shrugged. "Not like I mind it. Especially when it's for you. And I want to take you out to dinner afterward. There's a new place that just opened on Main Street, right? Looked nice."

The light was too dim in here to see his expression well, and what I could see gave little away. But my heart was thumping a fast rhythm, lurching up into my throat.

It almost sounded like he was asking me on a date. A very boyfriend-y date.

Even though we were sleeping together, the whole *dating* part was still a cover story, and it had been working well enough without us making appearances at romantic restaurants.

That brunch with my mom and Stephie had been awful. Pretending to have everything I wanted when I didn't.

Now, Dean and I were *sort of* together for real. I loved what we shared. Kissing him and getting to explore his body and sleeping next to him at night. But wouldn't a romantic dinner be even *worse* now? It would just emphasize the fact that our "relationship" was a lie. We had no future.

"I don't know," I said hesitantly.

"You deserve something special. You've been cooped up here with me for weeks. We haven't learned anything new about Woodson or Crosshairs in a while. I know you're frustrated."

His fingers touched my chin and moved up the side of my face, like he was trying to map out my bone structure. To see me better, even though it was dark.

"Let me do this for you," he murmured.

My heart was in so much trouble. Dean was going to leave again, and the poor, battered muscle in my chest was going to get torn to shreds.

"Okay," I choked out.

If he'd already ruined me for anyone else, why not enjoy every last bit of Dean that I could get?

————

Hartley's Main Street was bustling that afternoon. It seemed like everyone was out to relish the summer sun. Some kids ran past us with ice cream cones, and there was a pick-up game of soccer in the park as we passed.

"That boutique you like is up this way, isn't it?" Dean asked.

"Yeah. Next block."

Dean held my hand as we walked, and his thumb traced lazy circles on my palm. We looked like any other couple enjoying the day together. The thought made my chest ache.

I'd taken extra care styling my curls into a loose braid, draping it over my shoulder, and I'd worn a cute pair of shorts, a stylish top, and sandals. A little dressier than my usual, even though this wasn't *really* a date. It was... I didn't know what it was.

Dean and I had grabbed dinner together countless times as friends. But he'd never been holding my hand or possessively touching my back.

I hadn't known what his kisses tasted like or that sexy, growly grunt he made when he first pushed his cock inside me.

The bell chimed as we stepped into the boutique, and the shop owner looked up from behind the counter, her mouth forming a shocked O shape.

"Keira! Just imagine seeing you here today. And you've brought Dean with you? What a treat! Looking for anything special?"

"Hi, Lorraine," I said. "Just doing some browsing."

Lorraine had lived in Hartley since forever, but the

boutique was a new venture after getting divorced. She'd gotten a makeover too, complete with pink-dyed hair and a little butterfly tattoo on her shoulder.

Lorraine came around the counter, her flowing caftan trailing behind her. "How are you feeling these days, hon? Back on duty soon? We'll have to get used to calling you Deputy Marsh again."

I shrugged. "I'm feeling all right. But I'm not back at work just yet."

"Well, I'm *sure* you're enjoying your time off." With a knowing smirk, Lorraine pointed a pink fingernail at Dean. "Your man might like to know about our new jewelry collection. Is that why you came in today? Shopping for a gift?"

Tensing my jaw, I grabbed Dean's arm and tugged him toward the dress racks. "Actually, my *man* was going to help me pick a new dress. He has some strong opinions on fashion."

"Do I?" he muttered.

"This was your idea."

While I sorted through a rack of sundresses, Dean kept glancing back. "Lorraine's staring at us," he whispered.

"She's just curious." She'd probably heard *all* about Dean and me and helped spread those rumors around too. But she meant well.

After all, Dean and I were the ones lying to everybody. We'd wanted people to talk.

"Did you hear those people gossiping behind us in the grocery line last week?" Dean asked under his breath. He was standing right behind me, murmuring into my ear. "They said Lorraine bagged herself a younger boyfriend. The new mail carrier. He's not a day over fifty-two, so they say."

"Stop it." I elbowed Dean's stomach, snickering.

"Ow! I'm impressed, that's all. Go, Lorraine."

I turned my head and kissed him, both of us grinning. It

was such a simple moment, so *normal*, and I could almost believe it was real. That we could really have this. Braving the small-town gossip together, shopping, just living.

"Aren't you two precious!" Lorraine gushed. "Now that's what true love looks like."

I broke away from Dean, blinking. His blue eyes were wide, radiating discomfort. Which told me everything I needed to know about Dean's opinion of the L word.

I'd been in love with Dean for years, but he was never going to love me back. He was never going to stay. A few weeks of hot sex had not changed that basic truth.

Why did it hurt so much when I'd always known it?

Averting my gaze, I turned back to the rack of dresses, grabbing a few in my size without paying much attention to the styles. I just wanted to get this over with.

In the dressing room, the hangers rattled as I shoved them onto a hook. "Let me know if you need any other sizes!" Lorraine called out. "Or Dean can come find me! I'm sure you'll be doing some modeling for him."

"Thanks," I said, trying to sound cheerful. I slumped onto the little stool next to the mirror.

Outside the dressing room, Lorraine was saying something else to Dean, and he was laughing politely. Acting like my patient, perfect boyfriend.

Why had I ever agreed to this stupid outing?

When Dean and I were alone at his house, it was like nothing else existed but the two of us and the mission. Out in public, reality came rushing back. After Dean left, I would have to tell everyone we broke up. I'd have to deal with the gossip and their pity and their questions about what went wrong. *Poor Keira. She couldn't get her man to stay.*

So much for true love.

After a few minutes, there was a soft knock. "Find anything you like?" Dean asked.

Shit. I hadn't even taken a single dress off a hanger. Sifting through them, I found one in a coral color with a subtle abstract pattern. "Just a sec!"

I wriggled out of my clothes and pulled the sundress over my head. Then opened the door. Dean stood with his hands in his pockets, grinning when he saw me. "That one's pretty. You look great."

The dressing area was at the back of the store, next to a storage room, and a wall blocked me from the view of the register. Which was good. Lorraine wasn't watching our every move.

Self-consciously, my fingers traced the contours of the scars on my left shoulder and upper chest. "I don't know why I picked all sundresses. I should find something with sleeves. Nobody wants to look at this while they're trying to eat."

Dean's eyes moved over me, lingering on my face, then my shoulder. Then he stepped into the small dressing room, crowding me back, and closed the door behind him.

"I told you before. I don't like it when you talk that way about yourself."

"But it's true. Everyone at the restaurant is going to be talking about me. They'll be staring." And feeling sorry for me. Which would only get worse later when they heard Dean had left me.

I hadn't felt this down in a while. Yet I couldn't seem to break out of it.

He put a hand on the mirror behind my head. "If they talk, they'll just be saying how gorgeous you are." He leaned in. "And *I* will be thinking about how sexy you are. How I can't wait to get you home and watch you riding my cock with that dress still on. I'll definitely be staring."

I inhaled, and Dean's crisp scent filled my nostrils.

"Why are we even doing this?" I asked. "I don't need a new dress."

"And I say you do. Turn around. Look how beautiful you are."

Slowly, I rotated to face the mirror. Dean crowded behind me, hands going to my hips and massaging me through the thin fabric. Then his touch moved upward, his fingers brushing gently over the scars visible on either side of the skinny left strap of the dress.

"Lorraine's going to wonder what we're doing in here," I said.

He shrugged. "Let her wonder. She's hardly going to call the cops on Deputy Marsh."

His right hand slipped downward and started pulling up the back hem of my dress. My eyes went wide in the mirror. "*Dean*," I warned.

"I want you to feel good about wearing this dress." He pressed a kiss to my scars and whispered, "Let me make you feel good."

Dean's fingers trailed up my inner thigh and slipped inside the crotch of my panties. I had to reach out and brace myself against the mirror, biting my lip. I couldn't believe I was letting him do this to me in a dressing room. On Hartley's *Main Street*. The gossip that could spread about this…

But would it be worse than anything else they might say? At least my sweet, innocent reputation would be in tatters. That wasn't me anyway.

"It has to be quick," I said quietly, gasping.

His grin in the mirror was wicked.

Dean started out with slow, teasing strokes of his fingers. He rumbled with a quiet groan. "There you go," he murmured. "Getting nice and slippery wet for me. Wish I could pull my cock out and fuck you right here up against this mirror. Or maybe I'll do it later in the restaurant bathroom. So the whole town knows who you belong to. They'll know how much you love taking my cock and my tongue and my fingers."

While he kept whispering dirty things, those fingers stroked faster and faster over my core in exactly the way I craved. The way he'd learned would push me over the edge. I felt wanton as the pleasure built.

Then two of his fingers thrust inside me, and I pressed my lips together to keep from making a sound as wave after orgasmic wave shuddered through my body.

I sagged, going limp. Dean wrapped an arm around my waist to catch me. He tugged his other hand free, carefully moved my panties back into place, and kissed my temple.

"Need any other sizes?" Lorraine's cheerful voice chirped. I startled, but Dean just smiled in the mirror.

"Nope, we're good. I was helping Keira pick her favorite. I think we found a winner."

CHAPTER THIRTY-ONE

Keira

LORRAINE'S FOOTSTEPS MOVED AWAY, and I straightened the hem of my dress. "Guess I'm buying this one."

"No, I'm buying it. You should wear it tonight to dinner."

That orgasm had my blood full of the good kind of chemicals. I watched as Dean adjusted the very visible ridge in his jeans, tucking his erection against his waistband. I was tempted to take care of that problem for him, but I'd rebelled enough for now.

"Okay. I'll let you buy it for me on one condition."

"That is?" he asked with a smirk, pulling me closer to kiss me.

"You have to let me pick something for you to wear tonight, too. Lorraine's got a whole rack of shirts for men."

He grimaced. "Keira."

"You got all bossy over this dress. It's my turn. Far as I know, you only have one nice shirt. The one you wore to Jessi and Aiden's wedding and to every fancy occasion since I met you." I paused. "Unless you bought another shirt in Switzerland or something. With some other woman."

Dean touched my chin. "There have been no other

women, not for a long time. You know that. There's only you."

Warmth rose to the surface of my skin. "Do we have a deal or not?"

He huffed a laugh. "Fine. I could probably use a second nice shirt. Also, you look amazing, so I'd better at least try to look decent."

Yes, he looked *terrible* in that snug T-shirt right now. But he'd agreed, so I was taking the win.

We went out to the main area of the boutique and browsed the rack of menswear. Lorraine perked up. "Looking for something for Dean, too? I might have just the one."

She came over and picked up a folded shirt from a shelf. It was a button-down, charcoal gray, in a soft fabric that toed the line between casual and dressy.

"You're a genius, Lorraine," I said.

"Well, aren't *you* in a good mood. Must be that man of yours." She gave Dean a wink, and I really hoped that didn't mean she knew what we'd been doing in the dressing room.

Ugh, she probably knew. At least she didn't seem mad.

Dean looked like he was holding back a laugh.

"Just need to decide on a size," Lorraine added, picking up a second shirt. "This one is a slim fit, so it'll hug all those muscles of yours. Depends on how daring you want to be."

I smiled at Dean, thinking of how daring we'd both been just minutes ago. He cleared his throat, neck flushing red, and took both shirts. "I'll try them on. Be right back."

While Dean disappeared into the dressing room, I went with Lorraine to the register. "Could you snip off the tags for me?" I asked. "I'm going to wear the dress to dinner."

"Of course, hon." Lorraine produced a pair of scissors and did the honors. "You know, I was just thinking about you earlier today. Wondered if your ears had been burning from how often your name's mentioned in town."

My smile turned careful. "I have no doubt."

"There was a *very* flirtatious young man at the market just yesterday, asking the checkout girl about you. Fellow with a cowboy hat and a flashy diamond earring."

A jolt of cold dashed my happy mood. Was she talking about Donny Phelan?

"Do you know him?" Lorraine asked. "Perhaps another suitor, vying for your heart? Does our Dean have competition?"

"Um, *no*. Definitely not." I reached unconsciously for my scarred shoulder, rubbing at it. Lorraine's eyes followed the movement.

"You've certainly been through a lot in the past few months. But with Dean coming back, well... I believe it all happens for a reason."

I nodded along, even though I wasn't so sure I agreed.

"Has the sheriff caught the culprits yet?" Lorraine asked in a stage whisper. "There's been almost no word about suspects. Everyone's been concerned. Gunmen roaming around Hart County, shooting an innocent sheriff's deputy in her own home? We've had our issues over the years, but I thought that was behind us. What's this place coming to?"

She reached over to grasp my hand. I managed to keep my expression pleasant.

"At least you have Dean. I just know he's taking care of you. The way he looks at you? That's a man who cherishes the woman he's with. Trust me, my ex-husband didn't look at me like that even on our wedding day. But Dean? That's a man head-over-heels in love. You two have such a bright future ahead of—"

"Thanks, Lorraine," I said, cutting her off. "I'm going to do a little more shopping."

I moved away from the register, pretending to browse

through a rack of blouses just to escape any more comments about Dean's epic love for me.

That wasn't love she was seeing. It was lust, mixed with affection and friendship.

I believed Dean when he said he cared about me. But if I let myself believe, even for a second, that Dean truly loved me? My damaged heart wouldn't be able to survive that. Once, I'd been full of hopes about him, and I'd learned better. I would never let myself be so foolish again.

Sighing, I wandered over to a display near the shop's front window. Then goosebumps rose all over my skin.

I lifted my eyes and found Donny Phelan just outside. Watching me through the glass.

Cocking my hip and raising an eyebrow, I glared back. To my surprise, he averted his gaze, dipped his blue cowboy hat, and slinked away down the sidewalk.

Now *that* was strange. Especially if the man had been asking people about me. What on earth could that be about?

When I'd first met Phelan, that night months ago that I was shot, he'd been brash and arrogant. Same when Dean and I had visited his house. But the man I'd just seen on the sidewalk had seemed...small.

Not like I'd ever feel sorry for him. But Dean and I were less sure all the time that Phelan was involved in my shooting. Nox Woodson and the other people at Crosshairs Security seemed to have the guy on some kind of leash.

We hadn't figured it out yet, but we would.

When I returned to the register, Dean was there in the charcoal shirt. The neutral color made the blue of his eyes even more brilliant, and the fit hugged his chest and the trim lines of his torso.

"Looking good, Reynolds. Is that the slim fit?"

"I figured you'd like it." He hooked my waist and kissed my cheek, then pulled back, scrutinizing me. "You okay?"

I thought about reporting the Donny Phelan sighting. But I didn't want to mention it if Lorraine might overhear. "Yeah. I'm good. Happy."

He kissed my forehead. "Then I'm happy too."

Lorraine was tapping on a tablet screen. "He looks handsome, doesn't he?"

"He does," I agreed.

"While I'm paying, why don't you grab us some drinks at the coffee shop next door?" Dean asked. "They have the really good chai there, right?"

I narrowed my eyes at him. "Yeah. But why does it seem like you're up to something? I already agreed you could buy the dress for me."

"Oh, go on, grab a drink, Keira," Lorraine said with a knowing smile.

"Now I think you're *both* up to something."

But I agreed to play along. Lorraine had already picked up my shorts and top from the dressing room, folded them up, and tucked them in a bag for me. She handed my clothes over, and I headed next door to the coffee shop while Dean did...whatever he was really doing.

This coffee shop wasn't as nice as Silver Linings Coffee over in Silver Ridge, but they did make an excellent chai.

While I ordered, I said hello to a couple of people I knew. Answered the inevitable questions about how I was healing, how my mom and sister were doing. When I would return to duty.

But my mind was still on the man I'd left next door.

The date tonight, the dress, the way Dean had of sweeping me away and making me forget everything else... It was too much. Every day, I fell deeper in love with him. But Dean would never truly be mine, no matter how many sweet things he did or said. No matter how intense our connection.

I'd never known love could hurt like this. A tear welled at the corner of my eye, and I brushed it away.

"Keira?" the barista said, setting my chai on the counter. "Anything wrong?"

"Nope." I laughed. "Sorry. Allergies. Um, I need to run to the restroom. I'll be right back for the drinks."

Turning quickly to hide my face, I hurried down a short hallway toward the restroom.

Then someone grabbed my arm from behind. I dropped my bag and spun, instinct taking over, my hand already moving to where my weapon should be. But of course, it wasn't there. Just the thin fabric of my sundress.

"*You*?" I spit out.

It was Donny Phelan. "We have to talk."

"I don't have to do anything." I wrenched my arm free, anger flashing hot through my chest. "You're following me?"

"I saw you come in." His eyes darted around the hallway, wild and unfocused. "This is urgent. They're watching me all the time. I have nowhere else to turn."

"What're you—"

I didn't get to finish.

Dean appeared, moving so fast I barely registered it. He shoved Phelan away from me and against the wall, his forearm pressed across the man's throat. Phelan's hat toppled to the ground.

The look on Dean's face was cold. Brutal. Every muscle in his body was coiled tight. This wasn't the man who'd kissed me just a few minutes ago.

This was the sniper. The assassin.

"Give me one good reason," Dean said, his voice dangerously quiet, "why I shouldn't break your neck right now."

"Dean," I said carefully.

"I told you what would happen if you didn't leave Keira alone."

Phelan's face had gone pale. "I'm sorry. I'm sorry. I just need help. *Please*."

Dean's forearm pressed harder. "Don't *Real Men* handle their own shit? Take charge of their own lives? You sound pathetic."

Phelan was shaking now. "They're watching me," he hissed. "Constantly. I can't go anywhere, can't do anything without them knowing. I barely slipped away today. Then I saw *her*, and I thought if we could just talk…"

"Talk about *what*?" I demanded.

"I think I know who attacked you that night a few months back. Shot you. If you help me, I'll help you."

CHAPTER THIRTY-TWO

"THIS PLACE GIVES ME THE CREEPS," Keira muttered, eyeing the deserted park through her binoculars.

"No kidding." I glanced around the parking lot, where the only other car was a decrepit, abandoned van with two flat tires.

"Lots of places for people to hide in the trees. But Phelan really did seem scared. Not sure he's that good of an actor." She handed me the binoculars, and I took a look from the passenger seat.

We were in Keira's car. She'd insisted on being the one to drive us into town this afternoon, even though *I'd* asked her on the date.

I was already losing patience with this whole situation. We should've been walking down Main Street right now toward the restaurant. Not scoping out a clandestine meeting spot, hoping Phelan actually had information and wouldn't screw us over.

I'd wanted to do something special for Keira tonight. Wanted to give her just a little bit of what she deserved, even though I couldn't give her everything. Shopping with her had felt so normal. She'd seemed like she wasn't enjoying it at first, but after I showed her how sexy she was in that dress, well…

Danger had been the last thing on my mind. I'd told Keira to head to the coffee shop while I bought her a present. It was still in my pocket, wrapped up in tissue paper. But I shouldn't have let her out of my sight. Keira was far stronger now, and she'd been working her ass off in training, so it wasn't about her ability. I didn't *want* her to have to defend herself.

Fucking Donny Phelan. He'd snuck up on Keira and ruined our afternoon, so I wasn't feeling very sympathetic to the guy. Certainly didn't trust him.

The ambiance of the park didn't reassure me. A tall chain-link fence surrounded an ancient playground full of rusty equipment. Looked like the county was going to replace the old jungle gym and swing set with newer stuff, but the construction hadn't started yet.

There were some picnic tables scattered among the pines, fire rings dark with ash, and a single restroom facility that had seen better days.

We still had fifteen minutes before we were supposed to meet. Phelan had suggested this spot, all nervous and paranoid, before he dashed out of the coffee shop.

"You think it's a trap?" I asked. "Say the word, and we're out."

If Phelan had genuine info, then of course I wanted to know what it was. But another part of me just wanted to go back to Main Street with Keira. Have our dinner out, an actual date, as if I had nothing else to worry about except making her smile.

Lately, I'd been wishing for an alternate reality more and more. A different version of our lives where Keira and I could be together without any complications. Where I'd never left

Hart County at all, and she'd never been shot, and I wasn't…
me.

"I want to meet with him," Keira said. "I want to know what Phelan is up to. Every other lead has dried up."

"Then we'll stay."

"But I'm going in armed." She reached over to her glovebox and pulled out her concealed holster and service weapon.

"You brought a gun on our date?"

Keira smirked. "Like it's that strange. I'm still a cop. You're just annoyed we didn't take your truck. I know you keep your SIG Sauer in there all the time now. And a knife or two as well."

I shrugged. She wasn't wrong. "Might be hard to keep a Glock concealed in that dress."

Neither of us had changed out of our new clothes. There hadn't been much chance. And I did have a small hope of getting dinner with her after our chat with Phelan.

Keira dug in the back seat and produced a cardigan. After putting on her concealed holster, she pushed her arms into the light sweater. It was just loose enough to obscure the weapon. "See? I've got all kinds of stuff in here. Betty's a very good car. I missed her when I couldn't drive."

"*Betty*? You named your car Betty? How is this the first I'm hearing of it?"

Keira arranged her braid. Soft curls framed her face. "You don't know everything, Reynolds. You think you're mysterious, but I've got some mysteries to me too."

Grinning, I cupped the back of her neck. "I know you do. I'd love to solve every one." I leaned in for a kiss. Then another.

Fuck Donny Phelan, I thought to myself. We could stand him up. Drive away right now and enjoy our evening together. I would give her the gift I'd bought and, *maybe*, we could try to make this work for real.

But that was just a fantasy talking. The only reason Keira and I were together right now was the mission.

So I reluctantly pulled away. "Let's take a closer look before he gets here," I said.

She nodded.

We checked the bathrooms and the perimeter of the park until we were satisfied. No sign of anyone else waiting or any surveillance. We chose the picnic table with the best position and waited.

Right on time, another car pulled into the lot. A door opened. Phelan slunk toward us.

He'd left the cowboy hat somewhere, probably in his vehicle, and his dishwater brown hair was lank. Even the diamond stud in his ear seemed dull, lacking its usual shine.

Keira sat on top of the picnic table, sandals resting on one bench, while I hovered beside her. "Out with it, Donny," I said. "What's this about?"

He kept glancing around. "I told you they've been watching me."

Keira crossed her arms and lifted her chin. "Crosshairs Security?"

Phelan sucked in a breath. "You know them?"

"We know they work for you," she responded.

"It started that way." He rubbed his eyes. "I moved here last year to expand my business. People love the rugged cowboy, Marlboro-man persona, you know?"

I held back an eye roll as he kept talking.

"I met a guy at a strip club one night. Nox Woodson. He told me he worked as a bodyguard for a company called Crosshairs Security, and if I ever needed anything, I should give him a call."

Keira and I exchanged a glance.

"Then a few weeks later, I started getting threats. Anonymous messages claiming to be from disgruntled customers who were going to tell everyone I was a fraud. Ruin me."

"Because of your shady supplement sales?" Keira's tone was cold. "Or the coaching scam?"

"It's not a *scam*." But Phelan couldn't meet her eyes. "Okay, look. The whole Real Man Formula thing, the podcast, the coaching… It's just marketing. A way to sell product. Nobody else out there believes what they're selling either. It's all just noise to move merchandise."

"You're a piece of work," Keira said.

Phelan bristled. "I didn't come here for a lecture."

"Then get to the point," I said. If he started saying shit to Keira or called her *little girl*, the rest of this conversation wouldn't be nearly so friendly.

"After the threats started, I called Woodson. He said Crosshairs could find the people making threats and take care of the problem without any authorities getting involved. He and his friends would shut it down."

"You weren't concerned about the methods they were using?" Keira asked.

Phelan's jaw tightened. "Crosshairs seemed legit, based on my research."

"Did you meet with Harris Medina?" I asked. "The head of Crosshairs Security?"

He shook his head. "No, I've never spoken to the guy. Woodson said he had clearance to do whatever was necessary to keep my business safe. I didn't really care how they did it."

"Meaning you didn't care if they did anything illegal," I said flatly.

"I just wanted the threats to stop. I wanted to protect what I'd built. Looking back, I think Woodson was behind the threats in the first place. He set me up. Played me to get access to my business, all so Crosshairs could take it over."

237

I could just imagine a guy like Woodson, former drug dealer and ex-con, meeting Donny Phelan. The podcaster was probably throwing cash around the strip club, bragging about his media empire. Woodson saw an opportunity for his company.

But for *what*, exactly? And how far up the chain at Crosshairs did this go?

I crossed my arms. "What do you mean, take it over?"

Phelan pushed his hair back. "I don't know. Deliveries come in. Shipments go out, but it's not just my supplements and coaching materials anymore. Crosshairs took over my finances too. I can't access half my own accounts."

"Money laundering," I said, thinking it through. "Or they're using your shipments as cover for drug distribution."

Phelan flinched. "I didn't sign up for any of that."

"What about Natasha?" Keira asked. "Is she in trouble too?"

"Natasha was smarter than me. She saw how bad things were getting and took off a couple weeks ago. Quit on me, no notice. I haven't got anyone in that house on my side anymore. I've been switching out my Porsche for friends' cars just in case Crosshairs is tracking me. They talk to me like a fucking dog, order me around inside my own house, and I won't take it anymore."

I took a step toward him. "Then you saw Keira in Hartley today and—*what*? What did you think she could do?"

"Keira has law enforcement connections. She can help me and keep this discreet. Since she's on leave, nobody would assume I'm narcing if I'm seen talking to her. I know we've had our disagreements before, but..."

Keira scoffed. "Disagreements. That's an interesting way to put it. You've been a complete asshat every time we spoke."

"But I didn't report it when your boyfriend *attacked* me. I could have pressed charges!"

"Thanks," I said sarcastically. "Let's get back to the point. You said you know who shot Keira. Were you involved?"

Phelan hesitated, nervousness flickering across his face. "I had nothing to do with your shooting, Keira. I swear. I don't know who did it for sure."

"But?" she pressed.

"But I have suspicions." Phelan's voice dropped. "Nox Woodson is vicious. Sadistic. But there's another guy from Crosshairs who's even worse. Ryan Garrett." He shuddered as he said the name.

At the same time, Keira went rigid beside me, as if she'd stopped breathing.

I looked at her sharply. She shook her head, a clear signal not to say anything in front of Phelan.

I filed that reaction away for later. Was it just the fact that the guy's name was Ryan? We'd been trying to find a Ryan who worked for Crosshairs for a while now.

Or was it something more?

Phelan seemed oblivious to Keira's response. "The night of your shooting, Ryan Garrett was at the roadhouse. I'd gone out for drinks with some friends, and Garrett showed up, lurking at the bar like he was watching me. There's always somebody from Crosshairs showing up near me, even when I don't want them to. It's intimidation. A reminder that they think they own me now."

"But they have no problem with you harassing innocent servers?" Keira asked. "Like Misty at the roadhouse?"

"That's not something they'd concern themselves with. Trust me, they do worse than I'd ever dream of. Besides, Garrett was my minder that night, but he took off early."

"Garrett left early," Keira repeated, eyes distant.

I leaned into her. "Could this Garrett be the man who

offered you a drink that night? The one wearing a Crosshairs ring?"

She nodded slowly. Then reached into the pocket of her cardigan, where she'd stowed her phone. Thumbing the screen, she jumped down from her seat on the table and held up the phone to Phelan.

"Is this him?"

It was the photo she'd taken of Woodson and his mystery buddy outside the strip club. Phelan glanced at it and nodded.

"Yeah. That's the two of them. Woodson and Garrett."

"You think Ryan Garrett was involved in Keira's shooting?" I asked.

"Maybe. Garrett didn't show up anymore at my house after that night. Someone mentioned he'd been injured, but nobody would give me details. They told me to shut my mouth about Garrett ever being around me. But after I heard about the shooting, I wondered if Garrett was involved somehow. Because he'd been there at the roadhouse too."

On the night of the shooting, Keira had returned fire on her attackers. She'd hit one of them. The police hadn't found any DNA matches, which meant it couldn't be Woodson's blood. He'd been convicted of a felony, so Woodson's DNA was definitely in the law enforcement databases.

But we didn't know anything about this Ryan Garrett guy. River hadn't even turned up Garrett's name while researching Crosshairs Security.

It sounded like Keira had shot Garrett. It must've been a minor wound. He was healed up now. He'd looked perfectly healthy outside the strip club several weeks ago.

"I could go to Sheriff Douglas with what I know," Phelan said. "If you can clear the way first. Guarantee my safety. If Crosshairs finds out I'm talking, they'll kill me. Help me so I can help you."

"I don't know if it's worth my time yet." Keira had her arms wrapped over her middle, fingers tapping at her side. "Tell us more about Woodson. The day Dean and I came to see you at your home, someone followed us in an SUV. Tried to run us off the road. Was it Woodson?"

Phelan opened his mouth to answer.

Then his head snapped back, a spray of blood erupting. The crack of the gunshot registered a split second later. Then another.

Fuck. We were under fire.

I grabbed Keira and pulled her down beneath the picnic table as Phelan collapsed. My mind was already moving, calculating angles, trying to locate the shooter. Clearly, Keira was doing the same, because she drew her weapon and returned fire.

Movement in the trees. Someone running through the brush. But they were moving away. Trying to escape.

I launched myself up and toward the sound.

"Dean!" Keira shouted behind me.

"Call the police!" I shouted back. "Try to help Phelan!" She had her gun, and she could defend herself if necessary. Leaving her behind went against every instinct, but I had to trust that she was ready for a fight.

I had to stop that shooter. No way would I let him get away. Not this time.

The forest was a blur around me as I ran. Branches whipped at my face. The sleeve of my new shirt snagged on something and tore, but I didn't slow down. The shooter was ahead, weaving through the trees. I caught glimpses of movement, the flutter of dark fabric.

And a demon mask. A swirl of colors and grotesque features, turning back to look at me.

The shooter raised a gun and fired. I threw myself sideways, bark exploding from the tree beside me.

The shooter fired again. And again. He was panicking, firing wildly.

Then there was a loud *oomph* as the guy tripped and fell.

I sprinted to close the distance between us, my lungs burning. As he rolled over and tried to get up, I launched myself at him. Drove him into the ground.

The gun flew from his hand, skittering out of sight on the forest floor. We rolled, grappling. The guy was strong, but I hadn't run that obstacle course a thousand times in the last couple of months for nothing.

A fist connected with my jaw. I returned it, felt cartilage give under my knuckles. The shooter tried to get free and scramble away, but I caught him and slammed him back down.

The guy's arm raised. A blade glinted in his hand.

The knife came at my ribs. I twisted, felt it scrape across my side instead of plunging in. I caught the wrist holding the knife, wrenched hard. Bone cracked, and the shooter screamed behind the mask, the sound muffled and distorted.

I pulled the knife free and didn't hesitate.

The blade drove into the shooter's side, finding the soft space between his ribs. Once. Twice. The body beneath me went rigid, then slack. I stayed on top of him for a moment, breathing hard. Then I reached down and pulled off the mask.

Nox Woodson stared up at nothing, his eyes already glazing over.

CHAPTER THIRTY-THREE

Keira

"DEPUTY MARSH, do you have anything else to add that you haven't told me already?" Owen said. "Anything at all about today's events?"

"No, Sheriff. I don't."

The interview room was small and windowless, with beige walls that had gone dingy over the years and a table bolted to the floor. I'd been in this room countless times before, but only a couple of times on this side of the table. I wasn't a fan.

Owen reached forward and pressed the button on the recording device. "Concluding interview with Deputy Keira Marsh at 20:47 hours." The red light blinked off.

He leaned back in his chair and rubbed his face, looking as exhausted as I felt. "Dean's waiting in my office. Meet me there. We need to talk."

"We just spent the last hour talking."

Owen gave me a sardonic look. "Yes, on camera. Now it's time for you and Dean to explain what the hell is really going on."

Without another word, I got up and left the room, heading down the hallway toward Owen's office. The station was buzzing with activity, people moving with the kind of heightened energy that came after a major incident.

I kept my eyes forward, avoiding the curious glances of my coworkers as I passed. I felt sick. Tired to my bones.

Woodson was dead. The very thing I'd wanted. I'd wanted *revenge*.

But this feeling in my gut wasn't triumph.

Dean and I had been having fun just a few hours ago, acting almost like a real couple. Now the dress Dean had bought me was evidence, sealed in a bag somewhere in this building. Covered in Phelan's blood. There'd been no way to save him, though I'd tried.

I suppressed a shudder.

Reaching Owen's office, I went inside and shut the door behind me. Dean stood up from the chair where he'd been sitting.

"Hey, sweetness. I missed you." He came to me immediately and pulled me into his arms, kissing my temple and squeezing me against him almost too tight. But it was such a relief. The sheriff had separated us to take our interviews, doing everything by the book. But I'd needed Dean.

He's not yours, I reminded myself. *He doesn't love you.* But right now, I needed his comfort.

"You good?" His voice was low.

No. No, I'm not.

Tears rose in my throat, but I pushed them back down. I was still a deputy, kind of, and there was no way I was going to cry here at the station.

There was one small benefit to my title as Deputy Marsh, though. I'd left some toiletries in my locker here, and I'd been able to clean up and change back into my clothes from before our shopping trip. Dean had showered and changed in the men's locker room, since his new shirt had been ruined.

Nodding against Dean's chest, I pulled back slightly to

talk. "I kept my interview as dry as possible. Didn't tell Owen we already knew Nox Woodson's identity before Phelan mentioned him."

"Same here. I said Phelan contacted us today on Main Street out of the blue. We went to meet with him, and he said he needed help from the police but was afraid of his security company. Then he got shot."

"You didn't mention Ryan Garrett, right?"

Dean nodded. "Figured I shouldn't. You knew that name, didn't you?"

I nodded. Garrett was the *Ryan* I'd heard Woodson talking about, who'd been angry about some shipment. But I hadn't made the connection to the last name Garrett.

It was a name I'd heard before.

Ryan Garrett had to be the second shooter. And I knew *exactly* why Garrett had gone after me.

"Who is he?" Dean asked.

I hesitated. There was something else I needed to know first. Owen could be back any second.

"I'll tell you later. What happened after you chased Woodson?" In the chaos of the ambulance arriving and Dean returning dazed and covered in blood, we'd only had time for him to tell me the shooter was Woodson and that he was dead. But little else about exactly what happened.

Dean didn't blink. "I killed him. He lost the gun. Went after me with a knife, and I took it from him. Made sure he could no longer use the knife against me. It was self-defense."

"Of course it was." I'd assumed that was what happened, but was Dean okay? Physically, he seemed like it. A bandage covered the knuckles on his right hand, and there was a bruise blooming on his jaw. I'd also seen a scrape on his side earlier through a slice in his shirt, and I assumed he was patched up.

"You're all right though?" I asked, gripping his biceps.

"Yep," he murmured. "Just fine."

Wasn't so sure I believed him. Then something else occurred to me. "You ran after a gunman while you were unarmed. That was so *stupid*, Dean. You could've been killed."

He caressed my face. "But I wasn't. It's not always about the weapon, Keira. It's about the person using it."

The office door opened. Owen came in, closing it behind him and heading to his desk. He took off his hat and rubbed his fingers through his cropped, dirty-blond hair.

Dean and I both took our seats. "Hey, Tex," Dean said. "You look tired."

Owen sat heavily, his chair creaking under his weight as he glared at us both. "At least you don't look like a hippie anymore. You had the sense to get your hair cut. As for what happened today, though? I'm not seeing the sense at all."

"Sheriff, we already told you—" I started.

But Owen cut me off with a wave of his hand. "You're both going to tell me what you left out of your official interviews."

I kept my face neutral, even as my mind raced. Owen had no idea that Dean and I had gone to confront Phelan at his home weeks ago. Or about the masked assailant who'd tried to run us off the road afterward. Or about the rest of our investigation.

There was a *lot* Owen didn't know.

"Let's start with this one. Why on earth would Phelan suddenly contact *you two* after he hid behind his lawyers since the shooting?"

"He wanted help," I said. "Exactly as I told you in my interview. He was afraid to make an official report against Nox Woodson and Crosshairs Security. He thought I would be discreet."

Owen's eyes narrowed. "Out of all the law enforcement he could contact, Phelan picked the same deputy he argued with at that roadhouse three months ago? The same deputy who was later shot by masked assailants, with Phelan as our top person of interest?"

"Maybe he came to Keira simply because he thought his bodyguards wouldn't expect it," Dean chimed in.

Owen ignored him. "And then there's Nox Woodson. The guy was wearing a demon mask today. Like the shooters who came after you several months back. Did Phelan offer to trade information about Woodson, Keira?"

Neither of us responded.

But yeah, my boss was on the right track.

Owen sighed, shaking his head. "Today's really the first time you heard Woodson's name? Are you sure? Did Phelan tell you *anything* about what happened the night you were shot?"

Chills raced along my skin. Dean and I glanced at one another.

Owen cursed. "No answer, once again. What the hell are you up to? That was a rhetorical question, by the way. Since I can't imagine you'll tell me." He picked up a pen from his desk, fidgeting with it between his fingers. "Here's another interesting little detail. Something else I need to keep out of my official report. I found a tracker on Nox Woodson's vehicle. Exact same kind of GPS tracker we use at Last Refuge. Do either of you know anything about *that*?"

Shit. The tracker.

When Dean and I had been shopping on Main Street, Nox Woodson had been one of the last things on my mind. We hadn't checked it during our meeting with Phelan either.

But it did make me wonder how Woodson had known Phelan's location. Phelan had worried about his bodyguards tracking his Porsche. Maybe they'd bugged his phone, too.

Woodson must've realized Phelan had tried to slip away. Then he followed. Spotted Phelan talking to us.

If Woodson hadn't aimed that first shot at Phelan instead of us? If Dean hadn't pulled me down with his lightning-quick reflexes, and I hadn't returned fire with my concealed Glock?

All of us would probably be dead right now, not just Donny.

And Woodson... I hadn't wanted to show him mercy. But I hadn't wanted Dean to be responsible for his death, either.

"Not sure what you want us to say, Tex," Dean said.

"Look, I'm ashamed of how little progress I've made on bringing your attackers to justice, Keira. Based on the demon mask, I would bet Woodson was one of them. But there's a second one out there, and if Phelan wasn't behind it, we have no clue why they went after you. Unless you've learned anything to enlighten me?"

I felt Dean's eyes on me now. But I wasn't about to tell Owen everything we'd learned about Ryan Garrett. And what I'd realized.

Not yet. Maybe not ever.

Owen sat back and tossed the pen onto the desktop. "I'm not trying to be a hardass here. We're in my office, but I'm not speaking to either of you as the sheriff. I'm your friend. Just tell me, all right? Is all this part of a secret Protectors op that I don't know about?"

"I'm not a Protector," I said tightly. "Dean isn't either."

"But the moment Dean got back to town, he was demanding answers about my investigation into your attack. I thought you'd both backed off, but now I see I was wrong. I *know* you're still trying to find the attackers. And the truth is, I can't blame you. River's involved, right? He provided the GPS tracker?"

I crossed my legs. "No comment at this time."

Owen snorted. "Fine. Keep it to yourself for now. But for the love of all that's holy, bring in the rest of the Protectors. Let Trace and the others help you. Especially if this involves Crosshairs Security or Harris Medina."

Dean tensed. "What do you know about Medina?"

Owen gave him a look. "Enough that I'm extremely concerned to hear his company surface in relation to Keira's attack. If you want to know about Crosshairs, go talk to Trace and the Protectors."

Ugh, Owen was really getting on my nerves with that constant refrain.

"Better yet," he added. "Go stay up at Last Refuge for a while until this blows over."

"I'll think about it," I said, intending the exact opposite. But Owen looked relieved.

"If anything happens to either of you, I won't be able to forgive myself."

Owen walked us out of his office, and we headed toward the exit.

Outside, the night air was cool and clean. I took a deep breath, trying to clear my head. My bag was slung over my shoulder, holding my belongings.

Before we got to my car, I reached for Dean's hand. The parking lot of the station was brightly lit, and there was no one else here.

"Dean, I'm sorry," I said softly.

He stepped in closer. "Why? Why should you be sorry?"

"I feel like I'm coming between you and your best friend. You're lying to Owen because of me."

"Tex and I will be fine."

"And you killed a man today." Bile rose in my throat.

"Which we knew would happen eventually," he said, far too calmly. "I won't shed a tear for Nox Woodson. Would you? He tried to kill you. He *did* kill Phelan."

"I'm not sorry he's dead. That's not the issue."

"In my mind, Woodson signed his death warrant the night he hurt you."

My emotions tipped over, refusing to be held back. "But I didn't want his death on *your* conscience on top of everything else!"

From the moment I'd agreed to work with Dean, I'd always meant to be the one to deal out vengeance. I hadn't wanted any more blood on his hands. Only on mine. Maybe that was unrealistic.

Dean kept insisting he was a killer, but he'd tried to change. He'd given up violence. Yes, Dean had raced back to the States saying he wanted to destroy my attackers, but *I* was the one who'd insisted we work together and train together. I'd kept this thing going.

He shrugged. "It was self-defense. Loophole, right?"

I wasn't in the mood to joke around or pretend this was nothing. The more I thought about everything that had happened, the worse it seemed.

One of the men who'd tried to kill me was dead. Why didn't I feel some sense of satisfaction? Why did I have this hollow echo in the pit of my stomach?

Tears burned again in my eyes, so damn close to falling.

"Do you still think I'm worth all this?" I asked, tripping over the words.

"Are you kidding?" Dean said fiercely. He held my face in his hands. "For you, I would tear this whole world to pieces, including myself. That's what you're worth."

But I don't want you in pieces, I thought. *I want all of you. Your heart. Your love.*

The one thing Dean couldn't give me.

"I would never want you to destroy yourself for me. Or to take stupid risks for me either. Like running after a shooter while unarmed."

"Are we back to that again? Really?"

I pulled away from him and marched toward the car, digging my keys out of my bag. After beeping the lock, I threw open the door.

There was a business card sitting on the driver's seat. It had *not* been there before. Reaching down, I picked it up.

Crosshairs Security, it read. Along with a crosshairs symbol.

I glanced around the parking lot, but it was quiet, and beyond the bright security lights, everything else was dark.

Dean came up behind me on my side of the car. "What is it?"

"Someone left this in the car."

"*Inside* the car? While it was locked?"

"Yep." I flipped over the card, showing Dean. The back had the name *Harris Medina, CEO*, printed on it. And there was a handwritten note.

Lunch tomorrow. Last Refuge Tavern, noon.

"Of all the fucking nerve," Dean said. "This guy is summoning you?"

After the meeting with Phelan and how badly it had gone wrong, I wasn't eager to meet with someone else. But assuming this was really from Harris Medina, the head of Crosshairs Security, it had to be important.

And the location was no accident. He'd chosen Last Refuge, a place with a serious security presence of its own. A place where I felt completely safe.

"I'm going to check over the car," Dean said. "Make sure they didn't mess with it."

"That wouldn't make sense. Medina wants to talk. Maybe we'll finally get some real answers, and we can do it on our turf." Even if Dean and I weren't Protectors, I knew Trace and Aiden and the others would be on our side. Always. If this was a trap, Crosshairs would encounter serious armed resistance. Medina had to know that too.

"And if Medina was behind your attack all along?" Dean asked.

"No. I don't think it was him. There's a lot we don't know, but I'm pretty sure of that."

"Keira—"

"I'll explain everything. But I think we should take Owen's suggestion and get a room at Last Refuge. At least for tonight. We won't have to worry about anyone following us to your house."

Dean seemed to think about it, and then his lips curved in a half-smile. "You're the one driving. I'm just riding shotgun. I go where you go."

I tried to smile back, but it felt like another lie.

CHAPTER THIRTY-FOUR

JESSI HELD up a pair of jeans and a soft, silky top. "Will this work? These jeans are short on me, so they should be okay for Keira."

I stood just inside the hotel room, while Jessi was on the other side of the threshold in the hall. Her little girl, Zoe, peeked out from behind her mom.

"Uh, yeah. I assume so. Thanks." I waved at Zoe, whose big eyes disappeared as she hid behind Jessi's legs.

"And these are Aiden's. They should fit you."

"Appreciate it." I took the clothes from her.

"Let me know if you or Keira need anything else?"

"Thanks, Jessi. I think we're good."

She picked up Zoe, kissing the girl on the head, and then hesitated. "I didn't mention it last night, since you were both tired, but if you want to talk to Trace or Aiden, they're around. They're worried about Keira. We all have been."

"I'll mention that to her." Though I doubted she would take Jessi up on the offer. Keira wasn't too eager for help from the Protectors, aside from River, and he was still in Denver with his wife.

When we'd shown up last night, Jessi had found us a room. They always kept a few open at the inn for last-minute needs. Everyone had already heard about the podcaster who'd been shot and how I'd killed the shooter. And about the likely ties to Keira's attack several months ago.

There were a lot of questions and rumors swirling around.

Since Donny Phelan was famous in some circles, media requests had been coming in on Keira's phone and mine. We'd been ignoring them. Good thing I didn't waste my time on social media platforms, so I didn't have to worry about that.

The media interest would die down soon. I wasn't thrilled about having my name out there, but any threads between me and my former career were pretty tenuous at this point. Apart from the basic facts of my military service, the government had scrubbed the rest clean a long time ago.

As for the meeting today with Harris Medina and what he might reveal, well...we'd just have to see. Interesting that he wanted to meet in public right here at the home of the Protectors. If he'd wanted something more secretive, I wouldn't have been comfortable with that after yesterday's mess with Phelan.

After saying goodbye to Jessi and Zoe, I changed into the borrowed jeans and a fresh tee, courtesy of Aiden. Then set the clothes for Keira on the bed. She'd been showering before, but now the water was off.

When Keira stepped out with a towel around her, I crossed the room and rested my hands on her arms. I always felt compelled to touch her, but that urge was especially bad after what happened yesterday.

I kissed Keira's damp forehead. "Jessi brought clothes for you."

"Sweet of her."

"You feel all right? Still want to do this?"

"Yes." Her expression was serious, as it had been since we'd walked out of the sheriff's department the night before.

She tilted her chin, and my next kiss was on her lips. I was truly going to miss this. Felt like we were on a countdown now. And every tick of that clock wrenched my heart.

We knew the identity of the second shooter: Ryan Garrett. Keira had explained it all to me last night. I understood now why Garrett had targeted her.

One thing was certain. I was going to kill that fucker.

"I'm almost ready," she said.

"Take your time." I reached for the bullet at my throat as she got dressed and fixed her hair.

Keira had been stressing over the fact that I killed Woodson. She'd thought I might feel some kind of conflict because I hadn't killed anyone in so long. But the truth was far worse.

I felt *nothing*. No remorse. Technically, I'd acted in self-defense, but I would've done the same to Woodson even without that flimsy justification. He'd hurt Keira, so he'd earned his bad ending. I wouldn't lose any sleep over him. I supposed I did have some kind of conscience left, but it was hardly worth protecting the way Keira thought.

That was the difference between me and Keira. She had a good, pure heart, and mine was tainted.

Together, we walked into the tavern just before noon. A hostess greeted us, but Keira told her we were meeting someone.

A quick scan of the tables didn't reveal anyone resembling Harris Medina. But as soon as we stepped onto the deck outside, there he was. Sitting alone at a table, with one leg crossed over his knee, wearing khakis and a polo. Smiling confidently like he'd expected us to walk out at that very moment.

"Deputy Marsh." Medina stood. "Thanks for being here."

He shook Keira's hand, then pulled out a chair for her. I frowned as he turned to me. "And Dean Reynolds. Pleasure to meet you in person."

"Already knew my name, huh? Is that supposed to intimidate me?"

"Knowing your history, I doubt it would." He held out his hand, and I shook it.

My history? I wondered what he meant by that. How much did he know? "I've heard a few things about your history as well."

"Then we're on an even playing field. Just the way I like it."

I didn't believe that for a second. But Keira wanted to talk to this guy, so I sat in the chair beside her.

We were in a quiet part of the outdoor seating area, and some families sat on the other side with kids running around. The beefy men sitting at a nearby table were certainly Crosshairs bodyguards. Neither Keira nor I was armed.

I really hoped this wasn't a mistake, meeting Medina with innocent people around, but he'd be a complete fool to start trouble here. The man was probably capable of plenty, but a guy who'd been Army Special Forces and a PMC for two decades was no fool.

Then again, we probably should've told the Protectors about this meeting as a courtesy. Keira hadn't wanted to. She'd worried Trace or Aiden would show up and try to take over, which probably wasn't too far off.

"I ordered a few things from the menu for our table already," Medina said. "Hope you don't mind. But I assumed you'd like to talk sooner rather than later."

Keira nodded. "Definitely. I'm not that hungry, actually."

"Understandable, given yesterday's events. Though I do love the food here."

I reached for her hand under the table and tangled our fingers together.

After a server brought glasses of water and iced tea, Medina clasped his hands on the table. "I'll get right to it. I heard last night about the tragic death of Donny Phelan, a Crosshairs client, at the hands of one of my men. I assure you, I was shocked and outraged when I found out. It's a mess, and I do not like messes."

"You didn't order Phelan's death?" Keira asked.

He didn't flinch. "No, ma'am. I did not."

"What about *my* death? Did you order that?"

Damn, my woman had nerves of steel. I was proud of her.

"Certainly not. But I've just become aware of a number of things, some of which concern the attack on you, and that's why I wanted this chat. To clear the air."

Keira waved her hand. "Go right ahead."

Smiling, Medina took a sip of iced tea. "Nox Woodson brought in Phelan as a client, so I gave him leeway. My trust was misplaced."

"You had to know Woodson was a convicted drug dealer and suspected of a multiple homicide," I pointed out, keeping my voice down. Luckily the kids on the deck were drowning us out.

"I was aware, yes. My bodyguards need a range of skills."

Keira snorted. But Medina just kept smiling.

"A range of skills," he repeated, "like your boyfriend has."

I held his stare when he glanced at me. Okay, so he knew *that* part of my past. Given his likely connections within the higher levels of the military and government, it wasn't that surprising.

The server brought a couple trays of appetizers, and then Medina went on.

"Overnight, I spoke with some of the lower-level

Crosshairs employees working under Woodson. They confessed the whole plot to me."

"*Spoke* to them?" Keira interrupted. "And they just decided to come clean?"

"I'm very persuasive."

Yeah, we all knew Medina had probably used more hands-on methods.

He shrugged. "Apparently, Woodson was running a side hustle of his own. Prostitution, drugs. He operated out of a —" He cleared his throat, casting a look at the families enjoying lunch. "Strip club."

"They laundered the money through Phelan's Real Man Formula business?" I asked.

"Indeed. I had no knowledge. No part of it."

That would explain the odd shipments going to and from Phelan's home. And it explained why Woodson would kill to keep the truth quiet. Keira had seen Woodson at Phelan's house and potentially overheard something incriminating, so he'd tried to run us off the road that afternoon. Then yesterday, he'd killed Phelan to keep him from talking.

Woodson had feared the police *and* Medina finding out,

But Medina hadn't even gotten to Ryan Garrett's part in this yet. Did he know?

"The reason I've contacted *you*, Deputy Marsh, is that I understand Nox Woodson and a close friend of his targeted you as well. It's a...regrettable situation."

That nonchalant tone of his set me off. "Are you fucking kidding me?" I hissed. "They put on demon masks to terrify her, broke into her home, and meant to kill her."

Medina's bodyguards at the nearby table shifted.

"Calm down, Mr. Reynolds. You don't want to draw attention." Medina took a bite of a French fry. "I hear the staff at Last Refuge can be sensitive about such things."

Gah, I did not like this guy. Keira squeezed my hand

258

under the table, and I commanded my heart rate to drop back down.

"Do you know where Ryan Garrett is?" Keira asked.

"So you already know his name."

"Phelan mentioned Garrett yesterday before he died. But I knew that name before."

Keira had told me last night: she'd known Ryan Garrett's name because his sister was Hadley, the woman Keira had saved. Ryan's buddies had nearly beaten Hadley to death after she reported her brother to the police. Keira found her and brought her to Last Refuge. But Keira never knew what Hadley's brother looked like.

She was trembling. "Somehow, Garrett knew that I'd once helped his sister escape him. He must've recognized me when he saw me at the bar the night of the shooting. Garrett wanted revenge on me. This was personal."

"You have my sympathies."

"Fuck you," I muttered. No, I wasn't helping. But it had felt good to say it.

Medina dabbed his mouth with his napkin. "Garrett doesn't work for me. Woodson brought him in separately."

"But I saw Garrett wearing a Crosshairs ring. Phelan thought Garrett was part of your company."

He glanced to the side, toward his guards. "It turns out Woodson and Garrett were plotting something else as well. They wanted to oust me as head of Crosshairs in favor of Garrett. As if he could waltz in and screw me over, and I'd simply sit here and let him do it."

Damn. So this involved an internal power struggle within Crosshairs too, something that never had anything to do with us.

Keira leaned forward, dropping her voice. "Do you know where Ryan Garrett is?"

"If I did, I wouldn't tell you."

"Excuse me?"

"I know you and Mr. Reynolds have been running your own investigation, separate from the sheriff's office. Your boyfriend probably wants to do to Garrett what he did to Nox Woodson."

"That was self-defense," Keira protested.

Medina lifted an eyebrow and glanced at me like he knew the truth. That I could've left Woodson alive if I'd wanted to.

"We're not running any investigation," I said. Opting for a different lie.

"I'm aware you went to question Donny Phelan without Sheriff Douglas's knowledge. You didn't report that Nox Woodson chased after you in an SUV and, I assume, tried to kill you. Nor did you tell the sheriff about Ryan Garrett after Phelan must've given you his name."

Hell. He knew way too much.

Medina placed his elbows on the table, tenting his fingers. "Here's what's going to happen. I will see to Ryan Garrett. I'll make sure he never bothers you again, Deputy Marsh."

"You're admitting that in a public place?" she asked.

"I'm admitting nothing. All I've said is that I won't let him get away with what he's done. Garrett is *mine*, and I won't tolerate any interference. As I said before, I don't like messes. If you or Mr. Reynolds gets involved, *especially* Mr. Reynolds, I have no doubt things will get messy."

I held the man's gaze. "It sounds like you're making a threat."

"On the contrary. It's an offer of friendship. You would both be wise to accept it."

A shadow appeared over the table. "They've got friends already."

Medina's eyes shifted upward. "Trace."

"Harris." Trace Novo, the leader of the Protectors, crossed

his arms over his chest. "I hope you've enjoyed your lunch. It's time for you to leave."

Medina grinned. "I was just about to ask for the bill."

"It's on the house."

After Medina and his goons had left, Trace sat down in the man's place. "Keira, Dean," he said softly. "Good to see you both. I was sorry to hear about what went down yesterday. You're mixed up with Crosshairs Security, somehow?"

Keira looked deep in thought. I had no clue what was going through that beautiful head of hers. "What do you know about them?" she asked.

River had already told us the Protectors had a file on Crosshairs, but neither of us were going to mention that to Trace.

"Enough to urge caution. This world is rarely black and white, but Medina dabbles in darker shades of gray than I'm comfortable with." Trace looked from me to Keira. "Do you need us to get involved?"

Us, meaning the Protectors. Which only emphasized that she wasn't one of them.

"No," Keira snapped, getting up. "I don't need anything from you, Novo. I'm going to say thanks again to Jessi before we leave. Dean, I'll meet you in the lobby."

"Geez, what did I say?" Trace asked after she stomped off.

"You're a fucking idiot," I muttered.

"Still don't know what I said."

"You're an idiot for not seeing what's in front of you. You shouldn't be offering Keira the Protectors' help. You should finally be asking her to join you."

He rubbed his jaw. "I know that's what she wants. But Aiden, Owen, and I have known her a long time. Longer than you have. In some ways, Keira still seems like a kid. You really think she's ready?"

"*She* thinks she's ready. That's what counts. And I...I want to see her happy. More than anything in the world."

"Spoken like a man in love."

Shit. "It's not like that." It couldn't be like that.

"Then *you're* the idiot who's not seeing what's in front of you."

CHAPTER THIRTY-FIVE

Keira

"WHAT'RE YOU THINKING?" Dean asked as I drove us home.

"I'm thinking that...I don't know what to think."

First it was the revelation yesterday about Ryan Garrett. A couple of years ago, his friends had almost killed his sister Hadley on Ryan's orders. I'd seen her right afterward, broken and bloodied. Her story had gotten under my skin. She'd become my friend. Her strength had been an inspiration to me. Lit a *fire* underneath me to join the Protectors someday, as I'd explained to Dean that night we were surveilling Woodson outside the strip club.

Hadley deserved justice as much as I did.

She and her mom lived in another state now, and thank goodness. They had new identities. Ryan Garrett could never touch them again.

But somehow, he must've known about my involvement. He'd seen me at the roadhouse. Maybe even followed me home and then called his buddy Nox Woodson to join him.

Why hadn't Ryan gone after me before that night? I had no idea. But I finally understood the motive behind the attack.

I didn't just want to take down Ryan Garrett for *me*. I wanted it for Hadley too. And now, Harris Medina had decided to show up, telling me to stay out of it. It was bullshit.

Then again, if I made Ryan Garrett suffer the way he'd made me and Hadley suffer, would that give me peace? Would it make me happy?

"We don't take orders from Medina," Dean said. "If you want Garrett, we'll find him. We don't have to give up."

"I need time to consider. A lot's happened."

Dean reached over to caress my shoulder. "Take all the time you need."

I couldn't believe we'd been shopping together on Main Street just yesterday. It had seemed like we had plenty of time. Now, I wasn't so sure.

When we got home, I changed out of Jessi's clothes and put them in the laundry. I would return them whenever I saw her next.

After that, I checked my messages and reassured Mom and Stephie once again that I was fine. They'd been understandably upset after hearing about the shooting yesterday afternoon.

STEPHIE

Kiki, are you going to come by soon? Mom is so stressed. She's driving me nuts

ME

I can't today. Really tired and a lot on my mind. But I'm with Dean, and I told Mom that. She knows I'm safe.

You're never around anymore

I know. I'm sorry.

> Is this what it's gonna be like now? You've got Dean, so you don't need us? 😂 Jk I'm giving you shit but also we miss you and you suck

> What about you? Still dating the cute ranch hand? What was his name? Cody? Colton?

> If you come around more, you might find out

> OK, message received

I smiled at the phone. It was a relief to know the Protectors still had an occasional detail checking on my mom and sister, and Mom had a security system that I always bugged her and Stephie about using.

Maybe after the craziness died down, and we got another bedroom fixed up, Dean and I could invite Mom and Stephie over here to stay a few days and…

What was I thinking? I wouldn't be living here that much longer.

Dean and I would have to "break up" soon. But Mom and Stephie would survive the bad news. *I* would survive it. I could visit Stephie often enough that she'd be begging me to go away. We would all go back to normal.

I would get over Dean. Somehow.

Sure. Keep on lying to yourself.

I really was exhausted, so I lay down to nap for a little while. Until the enticing smell of food woke me, and my stomach started making demands. I'd barely eaten anything all day. My appetite was back, and hanger was only a matter of time.

When I went to investigate, I found Dean bent over the oven. There was jazz playing from his phone, and a couple of candles were lit on the dining table already.

"What's all this?"

He turned around, tossing an oven mitt onto the counter. "We didn't get to have our date last night, so I figured I owed you another try. Except it's frozen pizza and garlic bread instead of a nice restaurant."

"Garlic? On a date?"

"It's no foul if we're both eating it. I'll still kiss you." His arms circled my waist, pulling me closer. "Yesterday got derailed in pretty much every way possible. The dress I bought you got ruined. I could call Lorraine and see if she has another in stock."

I shrugged. "It's not necessary."

"But I still want to give you something special."

"Like garlic breath?"

He grinned. "Yeah. Garlic breath and a whole lot of kissing. And maybe more. If you're lucky."

My heart ached even as his mouth met mine in a tender, perfect kiss. Why, oh why, did Dean have to be everything I wanted? I had him, right here, and he would always be out of reach.

"Any new insights about what Medina said?" Dean asked. "Decisions?"

"No." I put my head on his chest. "I can't think about that anymore tonight."

"Okay. You don't have to. Let's just be together."

That was all I wanted.

We had dinner by candlelight at the table. Cheesy pizza with extra marinara on the side and bread swimming in garlic butter. After eating so little the past day, it tasted like the finest cuisine. The bottle of red wine didn't hurt either. My chair was right next to Dean's, and I wound up with my legs draped over his lap, his arm tight around my shoulders.

I hardly had any pain anymore in my injuries. I would never take my health for granted again. The simple privilege of having a body that didn't hurt and an arm that could lift over my head.

Now, I knew I could survive just about anything. Including a broken heart.

Dean tugged on my hand. "Come on. Stand up. We should dance."

The jazz playlist had shifted into R&B. I was just tipsy enough to make me loose, but not so much he had to hold me up.

With my arms around his neck, his hands at my hips, we swayed and kissed lazily, no rush to be anywhere else. Like we'd never have to stop.

It was so, so perfect.

Then he dropped one of his hands and dug into his back pocket. "I bought you something else at the shop yesterday. Didn't seem like the right time to give it to you until now."

I unwrapped the tissue paper. A silver bracelet lay inside with a tiny charm of the letter K engraved on a heart.

It was pretty and delicate and my own heart was frozen in my chest. "This is why you made me go to the coffee shop? Lorraine talked you into perusing the jewelry, huh?"

"It was my idea. Do you like it?" He seemed nervous. The man who was never afraid of anything.

"I love it."

Dean fastened the bracelet onto my wrist, and my body came to life again. Pulse thrumming and stomach fluttering.

A new song came on. Dean pulled me close and started swaying again. My mind was all over the place, wondering what this meant. A man didn't buy jewelry like this for a woman who was just his friend or friend with benefits. Or a fake girlfriend, either.

The shopping trip and the date yesterday. The bracelet...

I wanted so badly for it to mean something.

Dean's lips brushed over my temple. "I think a lot about

the night we danced at Jessi and Aiden's wedding. How close I came to kissing you."

I pulled back, frowning. "I wanted you to kiss me. More than anything. Why didn't you?"

"You know why," he said softly.

Because he'd already gotten that new job and decided to leave. Because he hadn't wanted to hurt me. All those ridiculous reasons he'd told me before.

And nothing had changed in two years, not really.

Clarity hit me. Knocked me right upside the head. I almost laughed at how incredibly stupid I'd been. The exact same thing was happening as two years ago, and I hadn't seen it.

I let go of Dean and stepped back. "You're about to leave again, aren't you?" I lifted my wrist, feeling the metal slide coldly against my skin.

"Keira, I was always going to leave. That was the plan."

"Well, plans change! And I didn't think you were going to leave *now*. Not yet."

"It's not today or tomorrow, but…" He put his hands on his hips, looking at the floor. "Yesterday, when I took you into town, I wasn't thinking about leaving. But now, Nox Woodson is dead. Ryan Garrett is the last loose end. I don't care what Harris Medina says. I *will* make Garrett pay for what he's done, and then…there's nothing else keeping me here."

A tear streaked down my cheek. "*Nothing?*"

"You know what I mean. It would be selfish of me to stay. I'm not what you need."

"Bullshit. Why do you get to decide what I need?"

Two years ago, I'd been afraid. I'd stood on that dance floor and let Dean walk away from me. I'd been a coward.

But I wasn't that same girl anymore. So why was I making the same exact mistake?

The truth was racing at me, refusing to be denied. Another tear slipped free and left a trail down my face, but really? I'd never felt so damn strong.

"Dean, I'm in love with you."

He stared. Blinked. Ran his fingers through his short hair. His skin had gone ashen. "Don't say that."

"It's true. I wasn't brave enough to tell you two years ago, but I should've been. I loved you then, and I still love you now." I'd already bared my heart, so I kept going. "I want you to stay."

"That's not what we agreed. I came here to get justice for you. *Vengeance*." He shook his head. "I never should've taken you to bed."

Ouch. That hurt. But I stood firm. "I'm just finally telling you how I feel." This time, if Dean left, at least I'd know I told him my truth. I would know that I'd tried. "I do want justice against Ryan Garrett. But I would give that up in a heartbeat if it meant I could keep you."

Dean didn't say anything. Wouldn't even look at me anymore.

So I walked away from him and got ready for bed. Slipped under the covers. Dean still hadn't come to the bedroom.

I guess I had my answer.

———

When I woke, the light on my nightstand was still on. But Dean wasn't beside me.

I sat up, rubbing my eyes. My phone said it was after midnight. I kicked off the covers, restlessness itching under my skin. Was he sleeping upstairs on the floor again? How stubborn was he? Was it really so awful that I'd told him I loved him?

The man was pissing me off.

Then I noticed the necklace on the pillow beside me, and my anger drained away. Dean had left his leather cord with the bullet pendant. He *never* took that off, but here it was, on the pillow where he'd slept next to me for weeks.

What the heck did that mean?

I picked up the necklace. The metal of the bullet was cold on my palm.

"Dean?"

The rest of the first floor was dark. I switched on the lights as I went upstairs, calling out his name.

He wasn't here.

The feeling of dread grew as I moved from room to room. Nausea coated my throat. Back downstairs, I checked the spot where Dean kept the locked cases for his sniper rifle and other weapons.

They were all gone.

No. No, no, no.

He was going after Ryan Garrett. Alone. But what did it mean that he'd left his necklace behind?

Was Dean not planning to come back *at all*?

Frustration and fear boiled over. Grabbing my car keys, I ran in my bare feet to the front door and threw it open. Dashed outside into the chilly air.

But I stopped short when I spotted the figure sitting on the porch steps.

The porch light was off, but the moon was bright enough to illuminate Dean's profile. His shoulders were slumped, elbows on his knees. The gun cases were here on the porch. A duffel sat near the porch railing.

"You *asshole*. You made me think you'd left! You almost gave me a heart attack!"

"I meant to leave," he said in a monotone.

Tears balled in my throat. "You were going to find Ryan Garrett. By yourself." I held up the leather cord with the bullet dangling between my fingers. "And *this* was all you left for me? Why?"

Dean stood up. He was dressed in his tactical cargos and a dark tee. The porch creaked as he walked toward me.

"I'm sorry."

"You should be!" I shoved his shoulder to keep him back, but he just came forward again.

Another shove, and he wrapped his arms around me, pinning me in place against warm, solid muscle. I couldn't have gotten away if I'd tried.

"You said you love me," he rasped. "Are you sure?"

"I kind of hate you right now for scaring me like that."

Dean moved his hands to my face. His blue eyes, glowing with moonlight, searched mine. "Keira, do you love me?"

"*Yes*." My voice broke. "I love you so much."

"I love you too. With everything in me."

I repeated the words in my head. *He loves me*. Had he really just said that?

Our mouths met in a fierce, desperate kiss. Heat built against the cold night air. I grabbed fistfuls of his shirt and held on.

Finally he broke the kiss and rested his forehead on mine.

"But I have to tell you the truth about me. I have to tell you what I did."

CHAPTER THIRTY-SIX

I TOOK KEIRA'S HAND, and we walked inside. "I need to bring my stuff in," I murmured.

"Okay. I'll meet you in the kitchen. Yeah? You're not going to take off and scare me again?"

I managed a faint smile. Kissed her on the forehead. "No, baby. I'll be right there. Just give me a sec."

"You've never called me baby before."

"Is it okay?"

She shrugged. "I guess I don't mind it."

Yeah, she was still mad. But that was okay. I couldn't blame her.

If Keira still accepted me after I confessed everything, then I would never leave her again.

Keira's footsteps moved away, and the faucet ran in the kitchen. Grabbing the gun cases, I carried them inside along with my duffel.

I really had almost left. I'd packed my stuff with every intention of hunting down Ryan Garrett, regardless of whether or not Harris Medina had a problem with it. Now that we knew Garrett's name and his involvement, I doubted it would be hard to track him down.

Really, all I had to do was follow Medina's men. They would lead me to Garrett. I'd wait for the right moment and take Garrett out from a distance. My sniper skills were probably rusty given my lack of real practice lately, but whatever. I was sure I could make it work.

On an impulse, I'd taken off my necklace and left it on the pillow while Keira lay sleeping. I'd bent to kiss her one last time too.

But when I walked out on that porch, my feet stopped there. Wouldn't let me go a step further.

She'd told me she loved me. That she'd loved me years ago, and she still loved me now, even after seeing the broken-down parts of me. Not all of them, but enough that she should've been running in the other direction.

She'd held her chin up when she told me, pure defiance, fucking *regal*. And I was going to slink away in the night? What kind of man was I?

Well, I knew I wasn't much. But Keira thought I was worth the risk.

If we were really going to try making this work, she had to know everything I'd been hiding.

In the kitchen, Keira was heating a pan of water on the stove and adding spices. "Chai?" I asked.

"Yeah. I could use something warm and cozy. I think we both could."

I sat on a barstool and watched, my knee bouncing up and down. Might as well get started on telling my story. It would be easier with Keira busy and not staring at me with her big brown eyes.

"I grew up in rural Oregon. I don't think I've ever told you that."

"No, you haven't." She dropped a cinnamon stick into the pot. "You've hardly told me anything about how you grew up."

I scrubbed a hand over my jaw. "It's not a very happy story. My parents never wanted me. They left me with my grandmother, and she raised me. She'd been diagnosed with MS before I was born."

Keira watched me from her peripheral vision while stirring the pot. "That's a rough start for any kid."

I chuckled humorlessly. "Very."

It had all been so long ago, and I rarely thought about those days anymore. Who wanted to admit that his own parents didn't want him? But if I was going to give Keira all of me, this was part of it. And it hadn't been all bad.

"Grams had a great sense of humor and was tough on me in all the ways I needed. Taught me how to work hard. How to fight, mentally I mean. She fought her illness the best she could. She was a grocery store clerk with inadequate health insurance, so there was only so much she could do." My fingers drummed on the counter. "Passed away when I was seventeen."

"I'm sorry," Keira said softly. "I know how hard that must've been."

"Of course you do." Keira had lost her dad in a car accident. "As a Marine, I found my family. My purpose. I tried to give all I had every day. Training as a sniper just added to that. I was proud."

"It's something to be proud of."

I nodded. The mixture was bubbling now. I watched Keira pour in milk.

"Then you joined Force Recon?" she prompted. "And...the less official stuff?"

"When some intelligence guy approached me about serving my country at the next level, I didn't hesitate. The missions got further afield. Most of the people I killed, I had no idea why they were marked. I did what I was told. It was gradual, I guess. The shift. They took away my brotherhood, my sense of meaning, left me with nothing but my orders. Nothing but the next mission. At the end, I didn't even know who I was actually serving. Not really. But I enjoyed it, Keira. I liked being good at killing. It seemed like *all* I was good for."

I got lost in the memories for a while, until Keira set a mug in front of me and sat on the barstool beside me. Her expression wasn't horrified, so I took that as a positive sign.

Even better when she placed her hand over mine. "Is there more?" she asked.

"Unfortunately."

"I love you, Dean. You can tell me."

I didn't deserve her. I really didn't.

But I wanted to.

"My last mission." My heart thumped, and I resisted the urge to reach for my rifle round pendant. Keira had left it on the counter, the leather cord limp, the clasp open.

Just say it, I ordered myself. *Get it done.*

"I was in a city in Eastern Europe. Specifics aren't important." Also, they were beyond classified. But that wasn't my top worry at the moment. "My target was a diplomat. I had a cover story as a journalist living in the building next door. My days were spent preparing. Studying his movements, making sure I had my exit plan in place."

Funny how dry these details were, when told this way. As if I wasn't confessing the worst thing I'd ever done.

"My handler had told me to wait for a certain important meeting to take place at the diplomat's home. Then I was supposed to execute everyone in attendance. Kill shots to the head with the rifle. Follow my exit route. Escape detection. The usual."

"Okay." Keira's hand still rested over mine.

"Turned out there were..." The words faltered, but I kept talking. "The diplomat's wife was there along with another couple. I watched them through the scope. It looked like a social gathering. But I had my orders. I took the shots. Killed them all."

My eyes closed, seeing through the scope. Feeling the recoil of the rifle and the low sounds from the suppressor. *One. Two. Three. Four.* Quick and efficient, before they could even react enough to escape.

"Then, through the scope, I saw a teenage girl run into the room. I hadn't even known she was in the diplomat's house. I think she was the daughter of the visiting couple. She was...screaming." I swallowed, my throat dry. "I had orders to kill everyone there. *Everyone.* No survivors."

I wrapped my hands around the mug, feeling the warmth, but my stomach was roiling too much to take a drink.

Keira was quiet. When I didn't go on, she said, "Whatever you did, I forgive you."

How could I possibly deserve her? "I almost killed that girl. But I didn't. Couldn't take the shot. First time that ever happened."

Keira exhaled slowly. "You told me before that you lost your soul a long time ago. Sounds to me like you took your soul back that night."

"But I killed that girl's parents, Keira. Traumatized her for life. And for what? I have no idea. I hadn't *wanted* to know. But that night, it was like I looked in a mirror and found a monster staring back. The monster inside me. Dealing out death as if it was my sole purpose."

"You thought you were doing the right thing."

"I suppose I do that a lot. Fuck up my life based on some twisted idea of what's right." Like when I left Keira two years ago.

"But that was your last mission," she pointed out. "You quit afterward. You stopped."

"I had to. Felt like waking up from a nightmare, and the

nightmare was me. I kept that bullet as a reminder." I nodded at it. "The last shot I would never take."

"Your superiors let you walk away?"

"If they'd wanted to stop me, they would've had to kill me. They decided not to. I tried to live a simple life after that. To make up for my mistakes. But deep down, I was still Bullseye. I didn't get rid of my rifle or other weapons. I couldn't. They were still…parts of me. I wandered around for years not really knowing what to do with myself."

I turned to look at her.

"And then I met you."

Her eyes were shining, but not with pity or fear or judgment.

"All I wanted was to be good enough for you," I said. "Never thought I could manage it."

"You *are* a good person. You're a good man."

"How do you know?"

"I wouldn't have fallen in love with you otherwise."

I knew what she was trying to say. She had faith in me. Knowing the truth, the *full* truth, about my past hadn't changed that.

"I love you, Keira. I didn't want to admit that to myself because it scared me. But I loved you two years ago. Loved you a while before that. I think…I think I probably realized it the day we took that photo in Owen's backyard. The one I printed out and kept? That day, you truly felt like *mine*, and I wanted to hold on to that. For me, it's *always* been you."

"It's always been you for me too."

She leaned into me. Our lips touched and opened to each other. Keira tasted like spices and milky sweetness. Everything soft and good that I hadn't believed I deserved.

I still wasn't sure. Maybe she could have faith enough for the both of us.

CHAPTER THIRTY-SEVEN

Keira

"TAKE ME TO BED," I said against Dean's lips.

Still kissing me, he picked me up from the barstool. My legs wrapped around his middle, arms closing around his neck. The rest of the chai was going to get cold, but I'd worry about that later.

I wanted Dean in our bed. Inside me, all over me. This man I loved with everything I had.

Nothing he'd told me had changed how I felt about him. Nothing had frightened me, or even surprised me that much given what he'd shared before. My clearest impression was that Dean had been searching for some bigger purpose his entire life. His superiors had taken advantage of that, but at the crucial moment, he'd broken free.

I just wanted to love him. To show him how perfectly imperfect he was to me. Dean was all I needed, just as he was.

In the bedroom, he kicked the door closed and carried me to the mattress. Every one of his kisses was deep and passionate. Nothing held back.

Tonight had been an emotional roller coaster, especially when added to the events of the last day, but giddiness bubbled inside me. We loved each other. We could be together now, and we wouldn't let anything stand in our way.

Dean lowered me gently, then stripped off his shirt. The sight of him without the necklace was surprising. Just golden skin, a dusting of chest hair. A small bandage on his ribcage, where Woodson's knife had glanced over Dean's skin. A faint bruise on his jaw from the fight.

I finally understood the meaning of that necklace. A reminder didn't have to be a bad thing at all, but for Dean, wearing that bullet around his neck meant he could never let the past go. He'd still been punishing himself for it.

I wasn't sure he'd forgiven himself just yet. That wouldn't happen overnight. But I believed he was finally ready to try.

His Adam's apple moved as he swallowed, his hands going to the button of his cargo pants. He flicked it open. Shoved the cargoes down and stripped them off.

"No boxers?" I asked.

"I was hurrying earlier. Trying to go before I could change my mind. Obviously, that didn't work." He fisted his cock and stroked it a couple of times until it was thick and straining. "My mind's made up. I'm not going anywhere again. Not without you."

"You promise?"

"I promise." He crawled onto the bed and stretched out over me. "I love you."

Every time he said those words, I inhaled them like they were oxygen. Dean *loved* me. He wasn't going to leave. There were no guarantees, but we were actually going to try making this thing real.

He kissed me again, touching my face and neck. His hand moved to my wrist and covered the bracelet. That gift meant so much to me. It had hurt when I thought it was a consolation prize or something. An apology for leaving again.

But now, it felt like another *I love you*. A reminder of our friendship and a promise for the future.

"Why are you naked and I'm still dressed?" I asked when he gave us a moment to breathe between kisses.

"You're right. Let me fix that."

Dean helped me sit up and carefully tugged the shirt over my hair. Then slid my panties over my hips and down my legs.

He wasn't rough this time. His touch was reverent. Like he was unwrapping a present or dealing with some precious object. And I knew that had nothing to do with my past injuries. I was all healed now. I could take whatever Dean wanted to give me.

He was showing his love. Touching my skin like it was the first time, and he didn't want to miss a single thing. His blue gaze wandered over me. The scars and the imperfections. But I saw nothing but appreciation.

I lay back down. Dean was kneeling between my thighs. "I'm going to worship you, Keira. I'm gonna love you all night. Love you forever."

There was so much raw desire in his tone that my eyelids fluttered, and my clit throbbed with want. We'd told each other how we felt in words, but our bodies spoke a different language. Something deeper and truer. That was what I craved now. Being as close to Dean as possible, sharing something that was only for us. No one else.

He bent down and kissed my knee. "Are you ready for me? Do you need a glass of water or something first? Because when I get started, I won't want to stop."

"Don't stop," I moaned. "Don't ever stop. I'm ready."

"Good." The word was a whisper. "Get on your hands and knees for me at the edge of the mattress."

Trembling and breathing hard, I crawled into position. Dean stood up behind me. His large hand rested between my shoulder blades, easing my upper body down and leaving my hips in the air.

"Arch your back, sweetness. Like that. Perfect."

I was completely exposed to him. Nearly vibrating with how much I wanted him.

Dean went to his knees on the rug, holding on to my outer thighs. And then I felt his tongue at my core. Lapping over my most sensitive places.

I gasped, dropping my forehead to the mattress.

Even after weeks of being Dean's lover, having his tongue inside me so many times, this still felt different. I felt like *his* in every way. I was completely in Dean's hands, more relaxed with him than I'd ever been. I trusted that he'd never leave me wanting again.

His tongue circled my clit, and then he said, "I love you," before gently sucking.

My hips rocked back against his tongue. Dean's thumbs massaged the flesh of my thighs. My heart was racing, heat prickling all over my skin.

"I love the taste of you. Can't get enough." He brought his fingers between my legs to keep up that relentless pleasure on my clit. "And I love that it's only for me. No one else will *ever* have you this way."

"No one." My mouth opened on a gasp as his tongue flicked over my clit again. "Oh, Dean. Please."

"I've got you."

He gave me everything I needed. Tongue and lips taking turns with his talented fingers. When I was close, his tongue thrust rhythmically into my pussy. I shouted and writhed. So taken over by pleasure I felt drunk with it.

I was still coming when Dean stood and pushed his cock inside me, setting off another orgasmic wave.

Dean hadn't been with anyone else for *years* before me.

Not since before we'd met. And he was all mine now too. No one would feel his passion but me. Feel his love.

Dean's cock filled me with slow strokes. He wasn't racing toward any finish line. I relaxed again, eyes half closed with bliss, my fingers holding on to the sheet beneath me. Just savoring this feeling. That smooth, perfect glide of our bodies meeting. As if we were always supposed to love each other this way.

After a while, he pulled out. His hand caressed my back. "Roll over, baby. I want to see your pretty brown eyes."

When I was on my back, legs spread for him, Dean entered me again. He bared his teeth and grunted. "Nothing's ever felt this good. You're so perfect for me."

I reached up to touch his handsome face and follow the lines of his jaw and cheekbones. This face I'd loved for years without believing those feelings would be returned. The pure wonder of it made happiness glow at the center of my chest.

"I love you," I breathed.

Dean's smile was raw and genuine. He'd smiled at me a million times before but never so full of open affection. My heart stuttered and ached like I was falling in love with him all over again. Like I could spend a whole lifetime falling deeper in love with him and never reach a limit.

Dean hooked his arms beneath my knees and bent my legs even wider. He could do anything, have any part of me. I'd felt that way about him two years ago, but now I knew how much it hurt to lose him. I knew the secrets he'd been hiding.

The way I loved Dean now was so strong, it felt like we could conquer anything.

He licked a bead of sweat from his upper lip. His chest rose and fell, his rhythm faltering as he pumped his shaft into me. Then his cock started to pulse, and he fell forward onto one hand, hips still moving.

When he stopped, he licked his lips again, breathing hard. "You're incredible."

"You were doing all the work."

Dean landed heavily on the mattress beside me, making me bounce. "I disagree. Everything you were doing was working *great* for me. Think I blacked out for a second."

I laughed and poked his arm affectionately. He retaliated by draping that arm over me, half crushing me. But I didn't mind.

"Love you," he murmured.

"I love you too." And no, I was not tired yet of hearing or saying that. Not even close.

He closed his eyes, but his soft, uneven sighs told me he was still awake.

"Dean?" I asked.

"Not sleeping. Just resting for the next round."

My lips quirked. "I know. But I wanted to say something. Ask you something."

"Yeah?" His eyes opened.

I took a deep breath.

"Don't go after Ryan Garrett. I don't want revenge anymore. Harris Medina can do what he wants with him."

"You're sure?"

"Completely. I just want to have *you*."

Nothing mattered more than that. Our future. Our happiness. We had to leave the rest of it, especially the anger and fear, behind.

Dean reached out to cup my cheek. "Alright. I won't. You have me, okay? You have me. Always."

CHAPTER THIRTY-EIGHT

Keira

DEAN DIDN'T MAKE me get up to train the next morning. He'd kept me up far too late for that.

We made love in the shower in the middle of the night, with Dean holding me up against the tile. Then later, before sunrise, I straddled his cock while we were on the couch with a blanket wrapped around us both.

In between orgasms, I reheated the chai and we got to sip mugs and cuddle and talk some more. Dean shared memories of his grandmother from growing up. We reminisced about the early days of our friendship and discovered all the moments that I'd secretly wanted him and he'd wanted me.

We finally passed out in bed, snuggled beneath the covers. The sun was bright in the windows by the time we woke.

Dean reached for his phone to check the time. "Two in the afternoon. Damn. You wore me out."

I burrowed against him. "You wore *me* out."

We stayed bundled a while longer until our other physical needs won out. Such as bathroom visits, food, and caffeine.

After getting dressed in the bare minimum of clothing and checking our phones for messages, Dean and I made a huge breakfast spread. Or make that lunch. Eggs and sausage, pancakes with sliced bananas and maple syrup, and huge mugs of coffee.

Then we took our meal outside to the back deck and sat close together at the table. He'd insisted on putting all our food on one plate so we could share, which I thought was ridiculous, but also cute.

I loved Dean like this. Cuddly and affectionate, cracking bad jokes and smiling with his dimples on constant display.

I loved *him*. So, so much.

He speared a piece of sausage with his fork. "Suppose it's time for me to get a job again. Do you think Marco's hiring?"

Marco ran the Hartley Tap & Saloon on Main Street. "I can text him and ask. What about Last Refuge? You could bartend there."

"That would be a serious drive from here."

"So? When I'm back on duty, I'll be driving all over the county on my patrols."

His mouth twitched as he chewed. "Don't remind me. It's been nice having you here all to myself. I'm going to miss that."

So would I. But at the same time, I looked forward to starting a real life together. Something I'd always dreamed of having with Dean. Sharing a bed with him at night. A home. Even a family.

I took a bite of pancake. "We can work on the house too. I'd like to invite Mom and Stephie soon, and when there's a second bedroom ready to go, they can stay a night or two. Would that be okay?"

"Of course. We owe them a visit." He hooked my chin with his finger, tilting my head to kiss me. His lips were sweet with maple syrup and salty with breakfast sausage. Then he pulled back to fix his blue gaze on me. "You want to keep living here? Instead of going back to your place?"

Heat prickled the back of my neck. "Oh. I just assumed. If you'd rather, I could—"

"I would much rather you stay here with me. If that's what you want too."

I nodded, emotion choking me for a moment.

His forehead rested against mine. "Never thought I could really have this. A home with you. A *life* with you. But this is what I want, Keira. It's all I want."

Dean didn't go out on the obstacle course that day. We didn't talk about continuing our training either. It was important to me to bolster my recovery and get fully back into shape for duty, but that could wait until later.

Maybe I would head back to desk duty soon, and we could both start making some money again instead of relying on our respective savings. We'd been living cheaply, but fixing up this house for real would take funds.

And if Dean no longer wanted to train me to shoot like a sniper, I would be okay with that too. What mattered was that he'd chosen *me* over vengeance against Ryan Garrett. Nothing mattered more than that.

We'd chosen each other. We'd chosen love.

———

That night after dinner, we watched a movie together on my tablet and then made love, slow and deep. We were both on our sides in bed, facing each other with my leg hooked over his hip as he thrust lazily into me. Kissing. Touching. Just enjoying each other.

I fell asleep with Dean spooned behind me, his even breaths warm against my ear.

Something pulled me out of sleep. Dean was already sitting up, rubbing his face. "Think it's your phone," he said gruffly. "It's buzzing."

I reached for my device on the nightstand. I'd left it on silent but still able to receive notifications.

Stephie was calling.

"It's my sister." Adrenaline pulled me to awareness. It was one in the morning. She wouldn't be calling unless something was wrong. "Hello? Stephie?"

"Kiki." Her voice was a rough, agonized whisper, and it wrenched my heart.

"What's going on?" I asked, trying to stay calm. This was not a time to panic.

Dean's hand rested on my thigh.

"I…" She sniffled. "I snuck out to meet Colby."

That was his name. The ranch hand she'd been seeing. Disappointment made my shoulders sag.

"What happened? Where are you?"

What had Stephie been thinking? But lectures would wait until later. Whatever this guy Colby had done, I would deal with him.

Dean got up, grabbing clothes. Seemed like he'd heard enough to start thinking ahead. I stood as well, still holding the phone to my ear.

"We went to a party at a house. His…his friend." She could barely speak for crying. I heard faint music in the background, but it was muffled. Like she was in a bathroom or bedroom.

"Is Vivian with you?" Stephie's best friend, who'd been dating the other ranch hand. Vivian was also Trace Novo's daughter, and if Vivian had snuck out too, I'd have to tell him.

"No. Vivian didn't know about it. People are drinking and…I want to leave, but Colby wants to stay. Please…please come get me."

Oh, I was gonna make this Colby very sorry for messing with my sister. I just hoped nothing worse had happened.

"I'm coming, okay? Dean and I are coming. But maybe I should call dispatch and have them send someone to—"

"*No.* No, Kiki, you can't. Don't tell anyone else." She cried harder, struggling to breathe before she calmed again. "I'm texting the address. Please hurry."

"Okay. I will. I'll get there as soon as I can. Just lock your-self in a bathroom or something and don't come out till I arrive."

The line went dead.

"Do you have the address?" Dean asked. I handed him my phone as I threw clothes on.

"She said she would text it."

"Got it," he said. "I'll plug it into Maps and check the directions. It's forty minutes away. Out in the middle of nowhere."

Forty minutes. A whole lot of *bad* could happen in that time. "We need to get there faster."

"Then I'll drive. My engine's a V-8."

I'd been about to suggest the same. I'd seen his high-speed driving skills.

But before we left the house, I grabbed my service weapon and holster. We headed outside. Dean eyed me as I got in the truck. "You're not going to shoot the boyfriend, are you?"

"Planning to? No. But I'll sure as hell put the fear of God into Colby for messing with my little sister." I put the holster on over my shirt.

Dean got us to the address in twenty-five minutes instead of forty. We pulled up to a rundown cabin with trees closing in on almost every side. Four trucks parked haphazardly in the grass out front.

Lights were on inside, but all the curtains were closed.

"I'll tell her to come out." But my call to Stephie's phone

went unanswered. Her voicemail picked up, the automated message garbled from the shoddy connection.

I unbuckled my seatbelt. "I'll get her."

"Want me to come in with you?"

"Nah. If you come in, Colby and his friends will just focus on the big, strong man. They'll get territorial, and that could escalate this. Colby needs to learn to fear *me*." I touched my weapon.

"You just said you *didn't* want to escalate this."

"I won't. I'll just calmly explain he will lose his balls if he comes near my sister again."

I pushed open the truck door and jumped down. As I started toward the house, Dean opened his door and leaned out.

"Keira, wait. Try calling her phone again."

"I'm not waiting. My sister's in that house, and I'm going to get her."

Loud music thumped inside the cabin, and shadows moved behind the curtains. Marching up to the entrance, I rapped on the metal screen door. It rattled.

The hinge squeaked as I yanked it open and knocked hard on the wood. "Hey!" I shouted so they'd hear me over the music.

The door wasn't latched, so the pressure of my knocking pushed it inward. I took a step forward across the threshold, and my breath caught.

My sister sat on a sagging couch facing the front door. Her eyes were bloodshot from crying. A scowling man I'd never seen before stood behind her, a thick-knuckled hand on her shoulder.

"Kiki, run!" she screamed, trying to get up, but the man held her.

Shit.

My hand had already gone to my weapon, but a strong

grip landed on my wrist that same moment, twisting my arm. I lashed out with my elbow, catching the person in the torso. He'd been hiding just behind the door. The guy let out an *oomph* of pain and shoved me hard. I fell to my knees on the carpet, and the front door slammed closed behind me. The weight of my gun in the holster was gone.

The music kept thumping.

"I'm sorry, Keira," my sister sobbed. "I'm so sorry."

Another person walked into the room. A neatly trimmed beard, ice-blue eyes.

Ryan Garrett.

CHAPTER THIRTY-NINE

I SAT in the car watching Keira head toward the house. Every instinct screamed at me to follow her, to go inside with her. But she'd said no. She was a cop, and aside from that, what she'd said made sense.

My presence could make things worse. At the very least, it might suggest I didn't have faith in Keira's abilities. She didn't need an escort.

But when it came to her sister, Keira was emotional, and that could be dangerous for anyone. Emotion made you do foolish things. I knew that well myself. Every moment that I'd been back in Hart County since hearing about Keira's injuries, emotions had been driving me.

I'd been in love with her this whole time. Fucking *years*.

I could finally admit that, now that Keira was really mine. But if anything, my nerves were even worse now. Worrying about something going wrong. Losing her.

Then I saw Keira push the door open and step through. There was a blur of movement. A shadow appearing at her side. A moment later, the door slammed closed behind her, and I sat up sharply in the driver's seat.

Nope. I didn't like that at all.

The door had slammed shut too fast. Like they'd been expecting her or were seriously pissed off at her presence.

I unlocked my truck's glovebox and grabbed my SIG Sauer, checking the magazine. Fully loaded. My Gerber Mark II tactical knife was here as well, its familiar weight reassuring in my palm. I'd been stowing both weapons in my truck since the night outside the strip club, just as Keira had noted before.

She was armed herself, and that was good. But I knew I would feel better if I at least went to the door and stood outside. Then I could hear what was going on and if she needed backup.

The knife had a sheath with straps, and I quickly placed it around my thigh. After screwing the suppressor into the barrel of the handgun, I clipped my gun holster onto my waistband.

I got out of the truck quietly, easing the door closed without latching it all the way. The cabin sat in a small clearing with trees surrounding it except for the narrow gap of the driveway. The forest pressed close on all sides, dark and silent. A breeze whispered through the pines, carrying the scent of decay and damp earth.

The air felt too still, too heavy. Above, clouds obscured the moon, leaving only the pale light from the windows to illuminate the gravel drive.

I stepped toward the cabin, my footfalls soft on the loose stones. Music filtered through the walls. The muscles in my shoulders tensed.

Something felt wrong.

Then I heard the faint scuff of a shoe against gravel. Coming from *behind* me.

Without turning around, I ducked and shoved backward into the person who'd been sneaking up on me. A gun went off, the shot cracking through the night air, close enough that my ears rang.

I grabbed the man's wrist and slammed it against my thigh. Once. Twice. His gun clattered to the ground. He tried to knee me in the gut, but I twisted, taking the blow on my hip. In a split second, I'd pulled my knife from its sheath and drove the blade into his solar plexus.

He made a wet, choking sound, his body going rigid. I yanked the knife free and let him drop.

Movement to my left. Another man was running at me, mouth open to shout. He lifted a shotgun.

This was an ambush. I had to get to Keira.

I leaped forward, closing the distance before he could make a sound or pull his trigger. My knife found his jugular, the blade slicing through flesh and artery in one smooth motion. Blood sprayed across my hand. He collapsed onto the gravel with a heavy thud.

I dragged both bodies into the trees as quickly and quietly as possible, my heart hammering against my ribs. The adrenaline singing through my veins made everything sharp and clear.

Checking the hands of both men, I found heavy rings with blue stones. Crosshairs Security.

I gathered their guns and tossed them deep into the forest. The gravel was dark from blood, but it probably wasn't noticeable given the darkness outside.

I ran between the trees along the side of the house, staying low. What was happening inside? They had to have heard the gunshot. Yet no one had ventured outside to investigate.

The answer occurred to me. The men I'd just killed knew I was coming. They were supposed to take me out. The people in the house probably thought I was dead.

And now, they had Keira.

My gun was still in place at my thigh. It had the suppressor, but it wasn't silent. If I'd used it, the distinctive noise could've alerted the people inside.

Could Harris Medina be behind this? He'd warned us not to go after Ryan Garrett, and we hadn't exactly promised to comply with his order. But Garrett seemed more likely. He and Nox Woodson had threatened Keira's family.

He probably had Stephie. The perfect bait to draw Keira out.

But right now, the question of *who* hardly mattered. These people were trying to take Keira from me.

So I would annihilate every last one of them.

CHAPTER FORTY
Keira

GARRETT WASN'T SMILING like he had the first night I met him. He'd been funny that night at the bar. Charming and even handsome.

Tonight, the cruelty of his expression turned him ugly.

"Deputy Marsh," Garrett said. "You made good time getting here. Must care a lot about your sister."

The mention of my sister just reminded me of *his* sister, Hadley, and what he'd done to her. This man was merciless. He would kill me and Stephie both. And he wouldn't make the mistake of leaving me alive this time.

I spoke over the relentless thump of the music. "My boyfriend's outside. Sheriff Douglas has already sent every available deputy. They'll be here any minute. Just let us go." There was no way Garrett could know I was lying. Yet he seemed unconcerned.

"Your boyfriend, Dean Reynolds? The one who killed Nox Woodson?"

I was still kneeling there on the floor, and Stephie was sobbing on the couch. Fury burned through me, white-hot and vicious. I kept my face blank, but inside I wanted to tear

295

Ryan Garrett apart. This man had sent people to kill his own sister because she'd defied him.

Frankly, I was surprised he hadn't done worse to me the night he'd recognized me. He'd probably offered to buy me a drink in the first place to drug me.

"Dean's armed and highly skilled. We already know you were the second shooter at my house three months ago, but if you let me and Stephie leave right now, this doesn't have to go any further. You and your friends can walk away before the police get here."

Ryan drew a gun from the back of his waistband. "I don't think so. I think you did as your sister asked and didn't tell anyone else. There are no cops coming."

"There *are*," I insisted, but he spoke over me.

"As for your boyfriend, he definitely fucked things up for me by taking out Woodson. But I figured he'd come with you tonight. I planned for him. Woodson didn't expect Reynolds to be such a problem, but I did."

There was a gunshot outside, which made me flinch and Stephie shriek.

Ryan Garrett smiled.

"And there it is, right on time." He went over to turn down the volume on a small speaker, and the music got quieter. "My guys had orders to execute your boyfriend the moment you were inside. Dean Reynolds is dead. No cops are coming. It's just us, Deputy. Time for us to have a nice, cozy chat."

The gunshot echoed in my mind. I refused to believe that Dean was dead. There was no way he would let Garrett's men sneak up on him.

Even if we'd both been unsuspecting when we arrived here, too caught up in the last couple of days and our own happiness to imagine that Garrett was still plotting against us, Dean was too good to go down like that.

But still, fear seized my chest as I thought of Dean being in danger.

Right now, there was nothing I could do for the man I loved. I had to focus on my sister. On getting us both out of here.

"If you want to know where Hadley is, I have no clue," I said.

Garrett's lip curled. "I don't give a shit about Hadley anymore."

"Liar. Of course you do. She's the reason you and Woodson tried to kill me. Because you recognized me that night at the roadhouse and followed me home."

Garrett looked down at the handgun he was holding. "All right, yes. That was my motivation. It was impulsive. I saw you sitting there at the bar and my anger got the best of me."

"How did you recognize me? If you knew who I was and that I helped Hadley, you could've taken revenge on me ages before that. I haven't seen Hadley in almost two years."

"But I didn't know who you were. Not exactly. I'd had somebody watching Hadley's place back then, waiting for her to go home after I figured out she survived the beating. You showed up with her. Helped pack up her car, and you hustled her along like you knew exactly how much danger she was in. My friend took pictures. I didn't have a clue you were a sheriff's deputy. Not then."

"Would you still have gone after me if you knew I was a cop?"

He shrugged. "Hell if I know. I just recognized you at the bar that night. There you were, smiling with your own sister like you didn't have a care in the world. Meanwhile my sister and mother were gone, in the wind, like I'd meant nothing to them."

"You stole from your mother and nearly got your sister killed. What did you expect?"

"They were *mine* to do whatever I wanted!" he roared. "I couldn't find them, but I knew you had something to do with it. Even considered getting you to answer questions first about where they were. But after we got to your house and you had a gun? Figured I should just be quick about it."

Nausea rocked me as I remembered walking into my living room and seeing masked men. Woodson and Garrett had planned to torture me for information. No wonder they'd been disguised.

I tensed as Garrett took a few steps, staring at my sister. Stephie squeezed her eyes closed and whimpered.

"After you survived and I found out you were a cop, I decided to let it go. But you showed up at Phelan's house and Woodson saw you."

And the next day, after Woodson had tried to run us off the road, either Garrett or Woodson had left that rock smashed through my window with the yearbook picture of me and Stephie.

Garrett paced back toward me where I was still kneeling. "Now, because of *you*, I'm completely fucked. Woodson is dead. Harris Medina's crawling all over my operation at Phelan's place."

"How is that my fault? You and Woodson decided to run a side business laundering money through Phelan's accounts. Making shipments in and out of his house. You used the Crosshairs name to do it. Didn't you think Medina would find out?"

"If you'd stayed away from Phelan, none of it would've happened. The whole thing is blown up because of you!" Garrett cocked the gun and aimed it at me.

Stephie screamed. "No, *don't*!"

My breath stopped in my throat. The barrel of the gun was a black void pointing straight at my face.

CHAPTER FORTY-ONE

Dean

I FLANKED the house to go to the back door. Garrett's men, assuming Garrett was behind this, would soon come looking for their friends out here.

I planned to be waiting.

I crept up to the back door and peered through a window into the cabin's small kitchen. The place looked like it was rarely used, more of a hideout than a home. A man stood inside, armed with a shotgun, casually watching the back door. He shifted his weight, the weapon resting against his shoulder.

He wore a ring with a blue stone on his hand.

I picked up a handful of pebbles from the ground and tossed them against the side of the house, away from where I stood. The clatter was small but distinct.

The man's head snapped toward the sound.

"Come on," I whispered as heady adrenaline flooded my veins again. "Come out and play."

The guard moved to the door, shotgun raised. The hinges creaked as he stepped outside. The barrel of his gun swept across the darkness, searching. He didn't see me.

But I was waiting right beside the door in the shadows.

As soon as he was within reach, I grabbed the shotgun with my left hand, shoving the barrel skyward. He tried to pull the trigger, but I'd already twisted the weapon from his grip. He opened his mouth to yell. My knife slashed across his throat before he could make a sound. He gurgled, clutching at the wound, and I lowered him to the ground as quietly as I could.

That was three down. But how many others were there?

A ringleader, possibly Garrett, would be inside with Keira. That meant at least one more guarding Stephie if she was really here. A third man if they were smart. But the cabin wasn't huge. Probably no more than one bedroom, that small kitchen, a bathroom, and a main living area.

None of the other guards had raised any alarms yet. The others had no idea their friends were dead, which bought me a little time.

I needed a better view of the inside, so I continued around the house to peer in the windows. The music still thumped, the volume slightly lower now. There were voices coming from inside.

Keira's voice.

Cold ran through me. Pure rage, so powerful I felt like it could rip me apart. The sensation burned through my chest. Turning my blood to ice and fire at once.

Maybe emotion made people careless, but when it came to Keira, I was nothing *but* emotion.

I had to turn that outward. Use it.

At the side of the house, I found a window into a bedroom. There was a light on here, but the curtain was only drawn partway. I carefully glanced in and didn't see anyone. The bedroom door, leading to the rest of the cabin, was almost entirely closed.

I wondered if I could risk breaking the window to get inside. But then I just tried pushing it open, and it slid.

Bingo.

Nobody had bothered to check if this window was locked. Or maybe the lock was simply broken. I carefully climbed inside and landed on the wooden floor in my socks. I'd slipped my boots off outside so I wouldn't make noise.

The sound of voices drifted through the door. A man talking loudly. Then Keira again.

With my gun drawn, I checked the room. A narrow bed with a sagging mattress sat against one wall. But as I inched forward, I saw a pair of legs lying horizontal in cowboy boots and jeans.

Someone was lying on the floor on the far side of the narrow bed. His ankles were bound with zip ties.

His wrists were bound too, and a gag filled his mouth. The guy was maybe twenty years old. A kid.

His eyes went wide and terrified when he saw me.

Holding my finger to my lips, I kneeled and yanked the gag away from the kid's mouth. He started coughing and shoved his arm against his face to muffle the sound. I pulled out my knife and cut through the zip ties on his wrists, then his ankles.

"Are you Stephie's guy?" I whispered.

"Yeah. Colby."

"Did you bring Stephie here?"

He shook his head vigorously. "Never. She snuck out of her house, but just to see me. We never thought somebody could be watching. They grabbed us. Drove us out here. What the hell is going on? Do you know what they want?"

There was no time for a full debrief with the kid. "This is about Stephie's sister. Keira."

"Are you Dean? Keira's boyfriend?"

I nodded. "I'm going to get Stephie and Keira out of there. You should go. Climb out the window and get in the old pickup outside. I'll meet you there when I've got them."

"No way. I'm not leaving Stephie in there. Let me help."

A man's voice rose in the living room. Someone screamed.

I looked at the kid. He was scared but determined. "If you're willing to help, here's what you need to do. But you'll have to move *fast*."

CHAPTER FORTY-TWO

Keira

MY PULSE HAMMERED in my ears, so loud I could barely hear anything else. Every muscle in my body locked up, braced for the impact.

"Stephie, it's okay," I said, fighting to keep my voice steady. "It's going to be okay."

But I wasn't sure it would be.

"What do you want from me, Garrett?" I asked. "You said you wanted to talk, right?"

He took a small step back, the gun dropping, and my lungs worked again.

"I have contacts inside Crosshairs Security. Other people who don't like the way Harris Medina runs things and who want a bigger piece for themselves, like Woodson did. I know you met with Harris Medina. I want to know what he said to you."

I scanned the room without moving my head, cataloging positions. One man stood behind Stephie on the couch, his hand still resting on her shoulder. Another was behind me near the door. And Garrett was right in front of me. All of them were armed.

Were there others elsewhere in the house? Outside?

My first priority was getting Stephie away from Garrett and his two friends in this room. I had to distract them somehow.

But I was also thinking about whether Dean was still out there and what he might be planning. I had to believe he was alive.

"You don't even work for Crosshairs," I said.

"Exactly why Woodson brought me in. Now that he's dead, our timeline has to move up. I'm taking Crosshairs for myself, and Medina's on his way out. You're going to tell me how much Medina knows. Did he mention me at your meeting yesterday?"

I wondered which answer would satisfy Garrett more. Hearing that Medina knew about his involvement? Or should I lie and say Medina didn't know his name at all? Garrett's ego probably wouldn't appreciate that. I didn't want to make him angry again. Not yet.

"Let my sister go, and I'll tell you everything Medina said. Stephie has nothing to do with any of it. She's a kid."

"How about this? You tell me everything, and I'll kill you first. So you don't have to watch your sister die."

"Bastard," I said through gritted teeth.

There was a noise at the back door. Breaking glass. Hope lifted my heart.

Garrett's head snapped toward the sound. "Go check that out," he ordered the man behind Stephie.

The thug moved immediately, heading toward the kitchen. Garrett pressed his gun against my head, the cold metal digging into my temple. "Don't even think about it."

There was a thump from the kitchen. A wet, gurgling sound. "Fuck," Garrett muttered, while the other man tensed, and Stephie's eyes darted around as if trying to decide what to do.

I had no idea what was happening, but I realized this was

the best chance I had to strike against Garrett. Maybe my *only* chance.

Just moments ago, I'd been terrified to have that gun barrel against my head. This man had tried to kill me before and almost succeeded. But now was the moment to be brave.

For my sister.

I exploded upward from my knees, driving my shoulder into Garrett's gut. He stumbled backward, the gun jerking away from my head. I grabbed his wrist with both hands and twisted hard, using my body weight to torque his arm. He grunted in pain and his grip loosened.

I wrenched the gun free from Garrett's hand and rolled away from him, going to one knee.

The thug behind me was already moving, raising his shotgun. He would've fired at me before if Garrett hadn't been blocking the shot. I aimed and pulled the trigger of Garrett's handgun. The thug jerked, red blooming from his chest as he fell and dropped the shotgun.

"Stephie, run!" I screamed. "Hide!"

Stephie scrambled off the couch, sobbing. Garrett lunged after her. He grabbed Stephie before she could reach the door. She screamed and kicked at him, but he was too strong. He yanked her against his chest, one arm locked around her throat.

"I'll snap her neck," Garrett snarled. "Drop the gun."

My hands shook. The gun felt impossibly heavy. Stephie's eyes were wide with terror, tears streaming down her face.

Then Dean stepped into the room, moving like a shadow. His SIG Sauer, complete with its suppressor, aimed squarely at Garrett. "Let her go."

Garrett's eyes were wild, darting between Dean and me. His arm tightened around Stephie's throat. She made a choking sound. "Back off or she dies."

I couldn't get a clear shot at him with my sister so close.

Garrett started to squeeze her neck harder, his face twisting with rage.

Dean fired.

The shot hit Garrett in the shoulder. He screamed, and his grip on Stephie loosened. She crouched and covered her head.

Dean fired again, this time hitting Garrett's leg. The man screamed again and collapsed.

I ran forward and grabbed my sister, dragging her away from Garrett. She was crying hysterically, clutching at me. I wrapped my arms around her and held her tight.

Stephie pulled back from me, her face pale and streaked with tears. "Colby. Where's Colby? They took him too. Please, is he okay?"

A young man dashed into the room from the back of the house. "Stephie!" She launched herself at him and they collided.

So that was the boyfriend.

Garrett was still shouting, writhing on the floor. Dean flipped him onto his stomach, yanking his arms behind his back. He produced a set of zip ties from his pocket and secured Garrett's wrists, pulling them tight enough to make the man scream louder.

"Your wounds are superficial," Dean said, his voice perfectly calm. "I could've killed you. Put a bullet right through your skull. But I knew Harris Medina would want a word with you first. And I promise you, what he'll do to you is a lot worse than dying."

Garrett cursed and spat, but Dean ignored him.

He stood. His face was streaked with dirt and blood, which didn't seem to be his own. His eyes were fierce and focused, but when they met mine, they softened.

Gesturing for me to follow, Dean went to a nearby doorway. A dingy bathroom. There, he washed his face and hands.

I waited for him by the bathroom door. Thankfully, Garrett's obnoxious music had cut out.

"Everyone else is dead," Dean said as he stepped out. "Do you want to make the call to Medina?"

There was no question about what would happen next. When it came to Ryan Garrett's fate, Dean and I were on exactly the same page.

I pulled out the business card Harris Medina had given me and dialed the number. He answered on the second ring.

"Deputy Marsh?"

Was I surprised he already knew my number? Not really. "Ryan Garrett just tried to kill me and my sister. You claimed you'd take care of it, but clearly you failed to move fast enough."

Medina didn't waste time on apologies or emotion. Not that I'd expected any. "Is Garrett alive?"

"Barely. There are other Crosshairs people here, all dead. He was talking about the plot to oust you and take over your company. We left Garrett alive for you, as a favor. In exchange, I want this all to go away. And I want your guarantee this time that nobody will touch my family *ever* again."

"Done. Would you like to witness Garrett's suffering? Because I promise you, he will suffer for what he's done."

I shivered. "No. I never want to see him again. I don't want anything more to do with him."

"Send me your location. I'll have someone there within the hour."

"I don't want any evidence left that my sister and I were ever here. Same with her boyfriend and Dean."

"I assure you," Medina said smoothly, "I will take care of everything. Your help is greatly appreciated."

I hung up and looked at Dean. He pulled me into his arms. I buried my face against his chest. He didn't smell too pleasant, but he was solid and warm and alive.

"I was afraid they'd got you," I whispered. "That gunshot outside. I didn't want to believe it, but…"

"They tried." His arms tightened around me. "But I told you I wouldn't leave you again. I'm going to keep that promise."

I laughed, the sound coming out shaky and half-broken. "You better."

He pulled back just enough to look at me, his hand coming up to cup my face. His thumb brushed across my cheekbone, gentle despite the violence still clinging to him.

"You did great in there," he said.

"So did you."

Dean kissed me then, soft and fierce at once. When we broke apart, he kept his forehead pressed against mine, and my hands stayed fisted in his shirt. Refusing to let go.

CHAPTER FORTY-THREE

Keira

MOM WAS ON THE PORCH, already crying as she saw us drive up. Which made Stephie start crying again too.

The moment I stopped the truck, my sister was out and running. She and our mom embraced.

I'd already texted to let Mom know Stephie was safe. Our mother had woken in the night and realized Stephie was gone, as if she could feel it in her bones that something was wrong with her baby girl.

I wasn't sure how many times Stephie had sneaked out before tonight, but she had a lot of explaining to do. Our mom was definitely furious. But right now, we were all just relieved. And upset and overwhelmed, and every other emotion.

I switched off the truck's rumbling engine and got out, joining them by the front door. I caught the tail end of what our mom was saying.

"—in the world were you thinking? When I woke up and figured out you were gone, I was two seconds from calling the police. If I hadn't seen Keira's messages…"

"I'm sorry, Momma. I'm so sorry."

I put my hand on Stephie's shoulder. "Let's go inside. Come on."

Mom looked up. "Where's Dean? And where is *that boy*?" Those last two words were fierce with protective momma energy. Good thing we hadn't brought Colby here, even though he hadn't wanted to leave Stephie's side.

"Inside," I said again. "I'll tell you all about it."

I knew Stephie was worried about how Mom would react to the truth. The fact that she'd sneaked out with her boyfriend was one thing. But hearing that we'd actually been in real life-or-death danger?

It wasn't going to go over well. But that was for me to worry about.

Our first priority was getting Stephie settled. She'd been awake almost all night and in fear for most of that. She was worn ragged and needed rest.

Stephie went into the bathroom for a quick shower, while Mom and I waited right outside. "Keira, what happened to my little girl?" Mom whispered.

"She had a bad scare. It could've been far worse. Someone was trying to use her to get to me."

"*What?*"

"I'll tell you all about it, but not until she's resting, okay? It's going to be a long story."

After her shower, Stephie agreed to a warm cup of tea and getting bundled up in our mom's bed. "Don't leave yet, please," she said from under the pile of blankets. "Either of you."

Mom was sitting next to her and stroking the top of her head. "Don't you worry. We're right here."

While Mom whispered reassuring words, I sat in a chair nearby, keeping an eye on my texts.

I had far more experience dealing with these kinds of situations than my mom and sister did, but I was far from calm.

Adrenaline still roared through my veins, and I probably wouldn't come down until Dean was back with me again.

I had wanted to get Stephie home as quickly as possible. Dean had stayed behind to make sure Medina's men arrived, and also to clear away whatever evidence he could of our presence there. Just in case the police eventually showed up.

We had no idea who that cabin really belonged to. Colby was going to be Dean's ride back here when everything was finished.

After Stephie was sound asleep, Mom and I crept out to the living room, leaving the bedroom door open.

"Oh, my Keira," Mom sobbed quietly, pulling me into a hug. "This is awful. Please just tell me."

Keeping my arm around her, I led Mom to the sofa. "Do you want some tea first?"

She scowled. "Do not baby me. I'm your mother. I want to know where the hell my daughters really were tonight, what kind of danger they were in, and who was responsible."

I managed a weak smile. "Okay. I'll try my best to explain."

Mom wiped her eyes. "How about you *try* the truth?"

I didn't always tell our mother everything. Far from it. Like the more gruesome aspects of my job. But this time, there were things she needed to know.

And we all needed to have our stories straight.

"Dean and I have been investigating my shooting for the last few months. Unofficially. In the last few days, we discovered who was really behind it. And why."

I told Mom as much as I could. How Ryan Garrett had wanted revenge against me for helping his sister years ago. And how, after the death of his accomplice Nox Woodson, Garrett decided to use Stephie to lure me into the open tonight.

"But in your message, you said your baby sister snuck out to be with some boy. Was he in on it too?"

"No. Not at all. The boy's name is Colby, he's twenty-one, and he works as a ranch hand. Seems he and Stephie have been getting pretty serious."

"*Twenty-one?* Does he know your sister is eighteen?"

"Mom, he tried to protect Stephie tonight, and if he'd had his way, Colby would be here right now. Getting an earful from you, no doubt. I think he's a good one. Just made some mistakes, as did Stephie, and she's technically an adult."

Ryan Garrett and his friends must've been watching my sister and Colby for days or even longer. Stephie had known about the protection detail I'd placed on her and Mom, so she'd figured out how to turn off the security system and sneak away from the house with nobody the wiser.

Unfortunately, Ryan Garrett had figured all that out too.

Last night, Colby had picked her up as usual, and they'd headed toward their favorite parking spot to look at the stars. But Ryan Garrett and his buddies had been waiting. Garrett had ambushed them, shoved them both under the cover of Colby's truck bed, and driven them out to that isolated cabin.

God, Stephie and Colby must've been near hysterical, not knowing what was happening or why.

After they'd arrived at the cabin, the men tied up Colby and dumped him in the bedroom, leaving Stephie at the mercy of Ryan Garrett. The bastard had ordered her to call me on the phone, instructing Stephie on what to say. She'd been too scared to defy him, even though she'd wanted to warn me. Thank goodness she'd done what he said.

Bravery wasn't always about defiance. It was also about being smart, and considering the situation, my sister had done the best thing possible by getting me and Dean there.

Now, Ryan Garrett was never going to hurt us again.

"You know Dean used to be in the military, right?" I

asked. "He had some high-level skills. He did a lot to save us tonight. Colby helped too, creating a distraction so I could neutralize one of the armed men guarding us."

"Neutralize? Just say it, Keira. You killed one of the men trying to hurt you and your sister?"

I swallowed. "Yes, Mom. I killed one of them. Dean killed a bunch more."

She nodded, jaw clenched. "And this Ryan Garrett? What about *him*? Is that abomination dead too, or will I have to do that myself?"

Sometimes, I wondered where my courage to become a cop came from. Well, clearly it came from this woman right here. Mom worried herself too much about us, and I tried to protect her from that, but in the most crucial moments her spine was made of steel.

"Garrett won't last much longer."

Her eyes widened. "Is that where Dean is?"

"Um...not exactly. Dean's taking care of some things. He's making sure Colby's all right, and then he's going to join us here soon." I considered how much to say about this next part. "Turns out, Garrett made another powerful enemy. Someone who'll make sure he never walks free. As for what that man does with Garrett? I'm choosing not to know the details. I've dealt with enough violence for one night. It's enough for me to know that Garrett will never bother us again."

Mom gripped my hands. "Then that's enough for me too."

I explained the official story I'd sketched out with Dean: Stephie had sneaked out tonight with Colby, his truck had broken down, and Stephie had called me for help. Dean and I had gone out to meet them.

Officially, we'd never been at that cabin tonight. Never seen Ryan Garrett or his friends. Dean was going to make sure Medina's men torched the cabin, including any remaining trace evidence inside, after they'd taken Garrett and disposed of the bodies.

I did have that phone call to Medina in my call log. I'd also met with Medina, very publicly, at Last Refuge just a couple of days ago. But if anyone asked about my connection to him, I could come up with an explanation later on. I wasn't too worried about that part.

Harris Medina seemed like a dangerous man, someone with far more questionable morals than I was comfortable with. But this time, cooperating with him had benefited us both.

In the future, I planned to steer clear of Medina and Crosshairs.

"If anyone asks me about what happened last night," Mom said, "I'll just say what I witnessed firsthand. My daughter was gone because she sneaked out to be with some boy. You brought her back. And she's going to be grounded for a *month*. But I'm just so grateful you were there, Keira. I know I haven't always been comfortable with your being in harm's way as a deputy. But you're a force to be reckoned with, and I'm proud of you. And so happy you have a man like Dean standing next to you."

"I'm happy about that too," I said softly.

Then Mom grabbed my hand, studying the bracelet on my wrist. "This is new. It's lovely."

"A gift from Dean."

She sighed, but it was a contented sound. "You two are so in love. It's beautiful to see. Even more beautiful to know he's the kind of man who's worthy of you."

"I love him very much. Having him love me back is the best feeling."

"I know it." She patted my cheek, tearing up again. "I'll always miss your dad and wish we had more time, but I cherish what we did have. You hold on to that love.

Every second you and Dean have. Never take it for granted."

"I won't." Dean and I were together, we were in love, and that wasn't a lie anymore. This was one truth I couldn't wait to share with the world.

While Mom went to check on Stephie, I sat in the living room and texted Dean, anxious for an update. We had to be careful not to say too much on our regular message thread, but I also had to know what was happening.

ME

Heading to Mom's place soon?

DEAN

Soon. Wrapping up. I love you.

Love you too 🤍

Tapping on my phone case, I had an idea. So I opened an encrypted app the Protectors used for missions and typed out a message for Trace.

Papa Bear - I have updates on Harris Medina and Crosshairs Security. I didn't involve the Protectors before for a bunch of reasons, but I'd like to tell you everything that's been going on if you're willing to listen. And then we can decide what to tell Owen. I want to work with you on this if you'll work with me.

I didn't expect any response from Trace at this hour, but hopefully I'd hear back from him soon. I still hadn't given up on joining the Protectors.

In fact, facing Ryan Garrett had only strengthened my resolve.

And now that Dean loved me back the way I'd always dreamed? He made me believe I could really have everything I wanted.

———

Dean turned up after sunrise, knocking softly on the front door. I rushed to open it, pulling him inside. He was cleaned up and wearing fresh clothes.

"Is Colby doing okay?" I whispered.

"Yeah. He's holding up surprisingly well."

He explained that Colby had driven them both out to Dean's house, where they'd showered and changed, and then Colby had dropped Dean off here before heading home to his own place.

"He's determined to drop by later to check on Stephie," Dean said. "And to face your mom. He's a good kid. Probably a keeper."

"My baby sister deserves nothing less."

"Is that our man Dean?" Mom called out, then bustled in from the living room, where she'd dozed off. "Thank goodness. I've been worried about you! Come here. You need a momma hug."

"Yes, ma'am."

"Thank you for making sure my girls got home safe. I'm so glad you're part of this family." She squeezed him tight enough that his eyes widened. "You've never mentioned a mother in your life, and I've never asked, but just know I love you like a son. You got that?"

Something intense flickered over Dean's expression as he hugged her back. "Yes, Mrs. Marsh."

"Regina," she snapped.

"Yes, Regina." He smiled, dimples flashing. "I, uh, I love you too."

"You'd better." She patted his cheek, and a blush crept up Dean's neck. It was adorable. "Now, you both need to sleep. I've got the guest room set up for you. You're staying, aren't you? I need to know where you both are. At least for a day or two. I'm sure it'll be good for your sister as well."

"Of course we'll stay." I kissed her cheek. "That's what I was planning on."

As for sleep, though, I wasn't sure I could relax enough for that. My nerves were all zapping like live wires.

Dean and I stripped down to our underwear and slipped under the covers in the guest room. I snuggled against him, grabbing onto him like a koala and resting my cheek on his bare chest.

"Did you speak to Medina?" I whispered. "Did he come to the cabin himself?"

Dean kissed my hairline. "Yep, he did. Along with a dozen guys from Crosshairs who I assume he trusts implicitly. Given the potential for a mutiny within his company, he wants to get it snuffed out as quickly and thoroughly as possible."

"Helps that Garrett is now a prisoner, Woodson is dead, and several of their allies are dead too. Thanks to us."

"Medina seemed appropriately grateful. He told me to pass on his thanks to you. And repeated his offer to give you evidence of Garrett's suffering. I assume your answer is still no?"

I shivered. "I'm done with Garrett." But there was something else I didn't fully understand. "When you walked into that room and shot him, you could've killed him. You shot him in the shoulder and leg instead."

"Either shot could've been lethal. Depending on where exactly I hit."

"But they *weren't* lethal. You knew what you were doing. They didn't call you Bullseye for nothing." I looked up at Dean and found him smirking, but that hint of a smile disappeared quickly. His arms tightened around me.

"Would you prefer that I'd killed him?"

"No, that's not what I mean. I just want to understand why you didn't."

Dean rolled his tongue over his teeth, blue eyes contemplative. "When I killed Garrett's friends, it was because they were armed and trying to kill me. Garrett was threatening Stephie, and of course I'd have done anything to ensure her safety. But you'd already taken his gun. I had a split-second to decide, and...I made my choice. Medina will ensure Garrett doesn't harm you or anyone else again. It didn't have to be me."

I brought my hand to his upper chest, where the bullet pendant used to be. Now it was just his soft skin and the muscle underneath. "You told me once that good people always have a moment of hesitation about taking a life. Even when it's justified."

"And you told *me* I'm a good person, so..." Dean rolled onto his side and faced me. "Maybe you're right."

He hadn't spared Garrett for that man's benefit. Dean had made the choice for *himself*.

"I know I'm right. You have a good soul."

"I lost it for a while, but you helped me find it again." He brushed his lips over mine. "It's probably tattered, but whatever soul I have, it belongs to you. All of me belongs to you. I love you."

"All of me belongs to you too. All my love. My future. But that future is up for discussion, you know. If you ever get the itch to wander again. If you ever get tired of Hart County and want to spend a season somewhere else, I could take time off work and..."

"No. I'm done wandering." Dean placed my hand against his heart, and then he mirrored my position, pressing his palm flat to my beating heart in turn. "I have everything I need right here."

Epilogue

DEAN, ONE YEAR LATER

GUESTS STARTED ARRIVING in the early afternoon. We heard their cars pulling up out front, parking on the gravel.

"Crap, I think we need more hamburger buns," Keira said, looking panicked. "Why didn't I buy more? Do you have time to run to the store?"

"The store that's half an hour away? No, baby. I don't."

"Do you think I made enough mac and cheese? You've seen how Colby can eat. Not to mention Vivian's boyfriend and her brother. Toby polished off half of Trace's birthday cake."

"C'mere, sweetness." I hooked her waist and tugged her to me, leaning my hip against the kitchen island. "You're adorable."

"I am *not*. I'll have you know I can be very scary."

"Yeah, I do know that, Senior Deputy Marsh." I kissed her. "But I also know we have tons of food. Today will be easy. We've had these people over plenty of times before."

"Yes, but not everyone all at once." The doorbell rang, and her eyes darted to the side.

But I pulled her in for another quick kiss, just to savor the moment.

I loved her so damn much.

We'd finally completed the renovation on the ranch house, and we'd invited everybody here today to show it off. It had taken an entire year and countless weekends. Late nights when I didn't have a shift at the bar, or—during the winter—whenever I wasn't too exhausted from a day of teaching beginners how to ski or snowboard.

Keira had helped out whenever she wasn't on duty and when she didn't have a mission with the Protectors.

Honestly, I seemed to have far more free time for home improvement than my girlfriend did. She was in high demand, whether it was as a senior sheriff's deputy or as an official member of the Last Refuge Protectors.

But Keira and I had picked all the finishes and paint colors together. Every last detail. The only room that was the same as when she'd moved in last summer was our bedroom downstairs. Keira hadn't wanted to change a single thing about it.

Apparently, I'd done a great job of decorating the place. Simply because I'd done it with her in mind. Even then, I'd already known her so well.

My partner. My everything.

If anything, *I* should've been the anxious one. But Keira didn't know what I had planned for later.

I kissed her nose. "I think you're just nervous about meeting your mom's boyfriend."

Keira huffed. "Of course I'm nervous. All these years and Mom has never dated anyone until now. What if I hate him?"

"Regina wouldn't be introducing him to you and Stephie unless the guy's a saint. You know that." My kisses trailed to her neck as more footsteps thumped on the front porch. The doorbell rang again. "Besides, all the women in your family have great taste in men."

Keira snickered, pushing me away playfully. "Take that big head of yours to the front door and greet our guests."

"All right, all right."

Then she smacked my butt on my way out of the kitchen, making me laugh.

At the front door, Stephie and Colby were the first to arrive, holding six-packs of soda and beer. Stephie gave me a hug and a kiss on the cheek, while her boyfriend shook my hand.

She was close to getting her cosmetology degree, and just a few months ago, Stephie had moved in with Colby into a tiny new place of their own. The guy was still completely smitten.

The Marsh women had a way of doing that to a man.

It had taken Regina a while to warm up to Colby, considering the sneaking out situation. But now, Colby was another part of the family. If maybe not *quite* as favored as me.

Vivian and her boyfriend stood right behind them, smiling as they followed Stephie and Colby inside. And here was Regina, walking up with a casserole dish and a look of pride on her face. A tall man stood beside her with gray dreadlocks, a full beard, and a friendly grin.

"Hello, Dean." Regina handed the casserole dish to her man, then dove in to deliver one of her patented momma hugs. *Oof.* "Couldn't ask for a more beautiful day for a barbecue."

"You've got that right. And this must be…"

"Raymond. Great to finally meet you, Dean." He shook my hand. Then he held the door and stood aside for Regina to head in, the two of them exchanging a shy, lovey-dovey glance.

Oh, yeah. Regina was in love, and it sure seemed like the feeling was mutual. I was thrilled for her. Regina was the closest thing to a mom that I had, and I wanted nothing but the best for her. For all the Marsh women.

And I was especially glad they could be here with us today. Because I had a secret reason for inviting all our friends and family here. A certain piece of jewelry had been burning a hole in my pocket for weeks now.

I'd been waiting for the right moment. But I expected this one to be perfect. Sun, smiles, good food. Everyone we cared about standing there to witness it.

Assuming Keira said yes when I popped the question.

I mean...of course she would say yes. *Right*?

Owen and Genevieve showed up a few minutes later, followed quickly by Aiden, Jessi, and Zoe Shelborne. Aiden held up Ziploc bags of marinated meat. "Where's the grill?" he asked gruffly.

"Uh, out back. Keira's firing it up. Hello to you too." I laughed, giving him a fist bump and Jessi a quick hug.

Owen and Gen had brought wine, and she went off to the kitchen for a corkscrew with Owen gave me a *look* and dramatically pulled me down the hallway.

"You've got the ring, don't you?" Owen said.

"Have I ever mentioned what a loud-mouth you are, Tex? I should never have told you what I was planning."

"It would've been obvious. Look at you. You're sweating like a defendant awaiting sentencing."

"It's hot today! This house doesn't have air conditioning."

"That's got nothing to do with it."

I snorted and patted my pocket. "I've got the ring. Are you happy now?"

"Of course. I'm your bestest friend. It's my job to get excited for you." He clamped his arm around my neck, practically a headlock. "I just don't want you to stroke out before you ask the big question."

"Like you almost did before asking Genevieve?"

He laughed, letting me go with one more slap to my back. "Exactly. Now, are you going to give me a tour of this place, finally?"

I rolled my eyes. "Yeah. Let's round some people up and give them the official tour."

Keira was chatting with Raymond and Regina. And Keira seemed to like him, so that was good. Together, we took a group around the house to show off all the work we'd done. When that was finished, Keira, Regina, Jessi, and Gen gathered in the kitchen to help put finishing touches on the food, with Zoe underfoot. Raymond went outside to see what Aiden was up to at the grill.

After another hour, the backyard was hopping. We'd set up extra picnic tables to hold everyone, with a long folding table the designated spot for food. *Way* too much food.

River's wife Charlotte had arrived, and they were holding hands and sipping beers. Cole Bailey chatted with Genevieve and Trace's wife, Scarlett. Trace and Brynn were murmuring about something and laughing.

Owen sidled over and stood next to me on the deck, handing me a fresh can from Hearthstone Brewing. I thanked him and lifted the drink in cheers.

"I never thought I'd have anything like this," I said quietly to my friend.

Not just the beautiful home or the most amazing girl in the world at my side. I meant all these people too. A family who would always have each other's backs.

Owen squeezed my shoulder. "It was waiting for you here the whole time. You just had to believe you deserved it."

It was pretty amazing. Seeing all these people who cared about us and had supported us. They'd all believed in Keira and me, even when she and I hadn't figured ourselves out yet.

Over on the obstacle course, Trace and Scarlett's son Toby was scaling a rope, while Stephie's guy Colby was showing off on the climbing wall.

Hell, I hoped Colby didn't fall and break something, but he was a fit guy. And he adored Stephie too much to be reckless around her again. That had been clear to me since the moment I'd met the guy. Same night we'd spent hours together cleaning up the mess Ryan Garrett had caused.

That night had been the last time any of us had seen or heard from Garrett. Harris Medina had been true to his word. He'd settled things with Garrett in his own way. Medina had also stayed away from Keira since then, and I was glad for it.

Shocking to think it had taken Keira almost dying to knock sense into me. I'd been an idiot back then. A miserable idiot.

And now, I had everything I wanted. Well, almost.

Over a year ago, I'd asked Owen if I deserved Keira. Back then, our relationship had been fake. But my love for her had been real. His answer to the question had stuck with me.

It's about treating her right every single day.

I liked to think I'd been doing a bang-up job of that in the last year. Keira seemed to think so.

But I wanted to keep deserving her for the rest of our lives, and what better way than to declare my undying love and commitment in front of everyone we cared about?

I hadn't planned out the exact moment to propose, though. I'd figured inspiration would hit me at some point during the barbecue. So the minutes kept slipping by. We ate steaks grilled by Aiden, mac and cheese, Regina's gourmet potato salad. Laughed and talked and cracked open more beers or canned cocktails.

The ring in my pocket was constantly on my mind, but I

still didn't know the *when*. I'd been like this as a sniper too, searching out the perfect moment based on instinct. But today, my instincts were staying quiet.

Fine. I was sweating a little, and it wasn't just the late summer sun.

Then I saw Trace frowning at his phone. He got up, gesturing to Brynn, followed by Keira. They took a few steps away from the deck and started talking quietly. River glanced over, clearly interested, though he didn't leave his wife's side just yet.

But I could tell. My instincts? They were screaming now. Something was up.

Keira nodded at whatever Brynn was saying. Then she jogged up to the deck and headed inside.

I followed her, heart pounding. Keira was in the kitchen getting out a platter of cut fruit from the fridge. I put my hand on her back, sliding it around to her stomach.

"Hey, everything all right?" I asked. "Looked like you and the others were discussing something serious."

Keira glanced up at me, her expression calm as she set the platter on the island. "Everything's fine. There are some developments in a case we've been keeping an eye on lately, but nothing big."

I exhaled. "Just making sure you and the other Protectors aren't going to jet off somewhere."

"Nope, I'm not abandoning you." Keira turned around to face me, frowning as she got a better look at me. "Dean, what is it? You were really that worried?"

Keira had joined the Protectors officially about nine months ago. After Ryan Garrett had disappeared, courtesy of Medina, Keira had gone back on duty as a deputy. First on the desk, then on patrol after getting full clearance from her doctor and a therapist.

But it hadn't been long after that when Trace finally extended the invitation.

I'd gotten over my own mental block about firing a rifle. Even came to Last Refuge on occasion to work with the Protectors on their shooting range, giving them some tips for improving their accuracy and their skills in the field.

Keira had continued her training as a sniper with me as her instructor, and I was proud to see all the progress she'd made.

But I would never be one of them. I no longer wore that pendant at my neck with the rifle round, but I didn't feel any need to return to that life either. Sometimes I asked myself if I should be out there alongside her, protecting her. But Keira would never have wanted that.

It was still hard though. Every time she went out on patrol as a deputy. Every time she ran off with the Protectors. Knowing she was in danger.

But that was just life for anyone who loved a warrior. Keira was *my* warrior. And I was just a lover now, not a fighter.

Fuck, I loved her.

Keira was still staring at me with concern. "Dean?"

I pulled the box from my pocket and dropped to one knee. I was following my instincts.

"Dean, what are you..." Her hand flew to her mouth.

"My sweet Keira." My voice came out steadier than I expected. "I spent a lot of years thinking I didn't deserve someone as wonderful as you. But you loved me anyway. You *waited* for me. You don't know how thankful I am for that."

Her eyes filled with tears.

"You've given me a real home. A family. A reason to believe in second chances. I love you, and I want to spend the rest of my life proving to you that you made the right choice in loving me." I opened the box. A simple band with a single diamond that caught the afternoon light streaming through the window. "Will you marry me?"

For a moment, she just stared at me. Then tears spilled down her cheeks and she was nodding, laughing and crying at the same time. "Yes. God, yes, Dean. Of course I'll marry you. Been wondering when you'd ask me."

"I was wondering that too." I stood and slipped the ring onto her finger. She held her hand up, watching the diamond sparkle, then threw her arms around my neck and kissed me. I lifted her off her feet, holding her close, breathing in gardenias and feeling her heartbeat against my chest.

When we finally broke apart, she was grinning through her tears. She looked down at the ring again, turning her hand to catch the light. "Want to go outside and see who notices first?"

I laughed. "Your mom will spot it in about three seconds."

"I think Stephie will beat her."

"Owen already had a heads-up. He's probably watching the back door right now."

She took my hand, lacing our fingers together. The ring pressed against my palm, solid and real. "I love you, Dean."

"I love you too."

We stood there for a moment, just looking at each other. The sounds of laughter and conversation drifted in from the backyard. Our family. Our home. Our future stretching out before us, full of possibility.

I'd spent too many years running from my past, convinced I'd never escape the shadow of what I'd done. When all the while, I'd been wearing the weight of it around my neck.

But Keira had shown me that redemption wasn't about erasing who you'd been. It was about choosing who you wanted to become. And every day, I chose her. Chose us. Chose this life we were building together.

She squeezed my hand. "Ready?"

I kissed her forehead, then her lips, taking my time. "Ready."

We walked toward the back door together, her engagement ring catching the sunlight, our friends and family waiting just beyond. I didn't know exactly what would happen next, and I still loved that feeling.

But I knew who'd always be standing right beside me.

Ready for more suspense and small town feels set in Hart County, with appearances from the Protectors? Read Starcrossed Colorado, book 1 of Hart County!

A Note from Hannah

I almost didn't write this book at all.

After I finished *Iron Willed Warrior* (book 5), I knew I had to write a story for Keira and Dean. Someday. But when I tried to think of what kind of story to give them, y'all... I was out of ideas. Which is a tough place for a writer to be.

I worked on my Hart County series instead, but in the back of my mind, I kept thinking about Keira and Dean. Then the idea came to me out of the blue.

A revenge story. Where a man (with a certain set of skills, of course) has to come out of retirement to avenge a friend or loved one. Those are some of my favorite action movies, but I wanted to give the hero a happy ending too.

It's hard to say goodbye to this series, but I hope you've enjoyed these characters as much as I did! (You can see some of them in the Hart County series as well).

Thank you to everyone who's supported the Last Refuge Protectors, especially if you've been here since the beginning! I've loved sharing these stories with you, and I appreciate every one of you for reading.

Until next time—

Hannah

Also by Hannah Shield

THE LAST REFUGE PROTECTORS SERIES

Hard Knock Hero (Aiden & Jessi)

Bent Winged Angel (Trace & Scarlett)

Home Town Knight (Owen & Genevieve)

Second Chance Savior (River & Charlotte)

Iron Willed Warrior (Cole & Brynn)

One Last Shot (Dean & Keira)

———

Also check out the Hart County series, which features appearances from the Last Refuge characters!

Starcrossed Colorado - An age gap, single dad romance

Moonlit Colorado - A brother's best friend romance

Stormswept Colorado - A forced proximity romance

Sunkissed Colorado - An enemies-to-lovers romance

Homeward Colorado - A single mom romance

About the Author

Hannah Shield writes steamy, suspenseful romance with pulse-pounding action, fun & flirty banter, and tons of heart. She lives in the Colorado mountains with her family.

Visit her website at www.hannahshield.com, where you can join her newsletter for access to bonus content, info on new releases, and more!

Made in the USA
Monee, IL
07 January 2026

41172400R00198